Praise for
Beth Harbison

"Smart, funny, and unapologetically romantic."
—*Publishers Weekly* (starred review) on
Chose the Wrong Guy, Gave Him the Wrong Finger

"Harbison dazzles in her latest, a perfect blend of chick lit and women's fiction . . . Absolutely first-rate." —*Publishers Weekly* (starred review) on *When in Doubt, Add Butter*

"A lighthearted romantic romp." —*USA Today* on *Chose the Wrong Guy, Gave Him the Wrong Finger*

"Harbison continues to wow readers with her charm and genuine characters." —*Booklist* on *Hope in a Jar*

"Reader favorite Harbison infuses the story with wit and heart . . . High-school high jinks and the search for meaningful love make this novel both lighthearted and poignant."
—*Booklist* on *If I Could Turn Back Time*

Also by Beth Harbison

A Shoe Addict's Christmas

One Less Problem Without You

If I Could Turn Back Time

Driving with the Top Down

Chose the Wrong Guy, Gave Him the Wrong Finger

When in Doubt, Add Butter

Always Something There to Remind Me

Thin, Rich, Pretty

Hope in a Jar

Secrets of a Shoe Addict

Shoe Addicts Anonymous

Every Time You Go Away

Beth Harbison

St. Martin's Griffin
New York

EVERY TIME YOU GO AWAY. Copyright © 2018 by Beth Harbison. All rights reserved. Printed in the United States of America. For information, address St. Martin's Press, 175 Fifth Avenue, New York, N.Y. 10010.

www.stmartins.com

THE LIBRARY OF CONGRESS HAS CATALOGED THE HARDCOVER EDITION AS FOLLOWS:

Names: Harbison, Elizabeth M., author.
Title: Every time you go away / Beth Harbison.
Description: First edition. | New York : St. Martin's Press, 2018.
Identifiers: LCCN 2018001445 | ISBN 9781250043832 (hardcover) |
    ISBN 9781466842212 (ebook)
Subjects: LCSH: Domestic fiction.
Classification: LCC PS3558.A564 E94 2018 | DDC 813/ .54—dc23
LC record available at https://lccn.loc.gov/2018001445

ISBN 978-1-250-04387-0 (trade paperback)

Our books may be purchased in bulk for promotional, educational, or business use. Please contact your local bookseller or the Macmillan Corporate and Premium Sales Department at 1-800-221-7945, extension 5442, or by email at MacmillanSpecialMarkets@macmillan.com.

First St. Martin's Griffin Edition: June 2019

10 9 8 7 6 5 4 3 2 1

Dedicated to John F. X. Harbison,

and all the happy memories we shared.

I'll be loving you always.

Acknowledgments

Thanks to so many friends who have been there through good times and bad: Connie Jo Brown Gernhofer, Carolyn Clemens, Annelise Robey, Mary Rast, Chandler Schwede, Tris Ziegler, Devynn Grubby, Steve Troha, Isaac Babik, Lucinda Denton, Denise Whitaker, Brett Winston, Jordan Lyon, Brian Hazel, Jennifer Mai, Elizabeth Flynn, Kristin Murphy, Bill Elliott, Basia Atkins, and my dear Nicoletta Poungias. You have all meant so much to me!

Two people helped, inestimably, to give me my start: Cristine Grace and Melissa Senate. I owe you so much!

So many thanks to Jen Enderlin, for carving so many of my ideas into books, and to Holly Ingraham, for stepping in with such great humor to get my words in line!

Love and thanks to my mother, Connie Atkins; and to my sisters, Elaine Fox and Jacquelyn Vincenta.

Adam Smiarowski, you came out of nowhere and made everything so much better. I love you! (*Ja kocham ćiebie!*)

And, as always, thanks to my truly wonderful children. Paige, you are hilarious and inspire me daily. No one words things better than you do! And Jack, you are so incredibly talented—writing, singing, playing music—I can't wait to see what you do next. Both of you: your father would be so proud of you.

Every Time
You Go Away

Chapter One

Willa

I can tell you exactly when I lost my will to live.

It was three years ago. The day I found out my husband, Ben, who I'd contentedly believed was happily working on our beach house in Ocean City, Maryland, and getting ready to come home at the end of a long weekend, had actually died quietly in his sleep there.

That was when I, Willa Bennett, effectively ceased to be. That's when the Willa who could laugh easily and speak her mind confidently went quiet. That's when the Willa who enjoyed a largely anxiety-free life could no longer drape over the end of the sofa and have a conversation, and began, instead, to be a tight bundle of nerves. That's when the Willa who could accept an unanswered phone as less than alarming became the kind of person who freaked out instantly if her son didn't answer a call or text. It had already happened a few times, when Ben didn't respond because he was driving, or he'd forgotten to charge his phone, or he was busy with power tools, and I'd jumped to the conclusion each time that he was actually lying dead, alone and unattended for perhaps a whole day. Sunrise and sunset, and sunrise again.

Three years ago. That's when the Willa who believed in happily-ever-after and joy grew lonely, afraid, and hollow. That's when she lost all hope, and even a slew of medications and meditations couldn't bring her back.

That's when I became Dead Willa.

Dead Willa, who, three years after the fact—tired of knowing that damnable house was still sitting there, untouched, since Ben had died—decided it was finally time to get rid of the place. The house had become an empty tomb, a sad monument to what had once been, what had happened, and what would never be again.

I finally decided that I had to be present for my now-seventeen-year-old son before I blinked again and he was twenty-one, and so on right through all the lyrics of "Cat's in the Cradle." I had become an incomplete person the moment he lost his father, when he needed me most. It was time—well past time, actually—for me to pull myself up by the bootstraps and join life again.

The only way to do that was to face the house. To move in for the summer—easily done, as I am an English teacher at a private high school in Potomac and had the summer off—fix it up, and get the place sold.

Did I mention that the old Willa didn't believe in ghosts? Much as she might have wanted to, she just couldn't bring herself to buy in. Ghosts and spirits and psychics and tarot cards—it was all nonsense to her.

But she believes now.

Chapter Two

The boy was running along the beach, kite trailing behind him high in the air like one of the signs tugged along by a biplane later in the summer. It was as if he were the only person in the world. And he practically was, truth be told. There didn't seem to be anyone else here besides me, him, and my old golden retriever mix, Dolly, and she was busy sniffing the new environment and undoubtedly trying to find stinky new things to roll in and make herself repulsive.

We might have been the only living creatures in the world, even though it was late May in a beach town and the throngs were about to descend. But it was a cool, gray day with the kind of wind in which, my husband used to say, it "takes two men to hold one man's hair on." Anyone who had already come for vacation had probably decided to stay in and play board games or go to the movies, the boardwalk, or the nearby outlet center, which boasted junky beach food galore and no sales tax. That center probably attracted as many people as the ocean did.

The waves crashed on the shore over and over, a slow meter in the background, like in the song "Bridge over Troubled Water." It was soothing.

It was alive. It held life, I reminded myself. I was determined to be Zen during this sabbatical. So, while the ocean looked a cold battleship gray on this overcast cool day, I took a deep yoga breath in and told myself it was full of life, from the dolphins leaping along the surface to the unknown prehistoric creatures that still lived at the very bottom.

I tried to picture *Finding Dory* but the full-color vision eluded me. It takes a lot of imagination to see fireworks in this particular variety of gray. The words, though, the words stayed with me.

Just keep swimming.

Ben and I had had what felt like a million nights here together, but it had always been our tradition to come straight to the shore to say hello to the ocean before we went into the house, and I held fast to our old tradition out of pure habit.

I had a feeling there would be a lot of that.

Hello, ocean.

The answer was a gray crash and a spray of phosphorescent foam.

We'd met here, in this tourist haven, twenty years ago. Senior week at the beach. We didn't go to the same school—he was already in college—but he was a friend of a friend of a friend, and as soon as we'd laid eyes on each other, it was the same old tired story of love at first sight. Only, in our case it was true. Or I *think* it was true. It certainly turned into love. The best love I'd ever known.

At the time I'd been the kind of beach blonde with wavy curls that they showed on the Sun-In bottle, and, while I didn't feel any conceit about my looks or believe I was any great beauty, I loved the feel of the wind in my hair and the way I knew it looked. Now it was shorter, above my shoulders, and best described as dirty blond, though a merciful stylist might have seen some hope for highlights and shaping. I just hadn't bothered for years.

But once . . . once I had felt like a real beach girl here. I'd met Ben with all the confidence I could muster.

My group of friends were renting the house I now owned. It wasn't such a nice place back then—the floor saw a lot of pizza, spilled beer, and vomit. Usually, in that order. And, with a landlord who evidently didn't mind renting to a hundred raging underage alcoholics as long as they could pony up the deposit, I could only imagine it had seen a *lot* of that treatment over the summers before and after our time here, until Ben and I had finally seen it was up for sale and had bought it in what seemed like the coup of the century.

It was a money pit. But a beautiful one. Sandblasted white siding, old-fashioned shutters that actually closed, but probably wouldn't protect from a hurricane, and a tall, thin Victorian shape that would have made it the perfect candidate for a *Titanic*-era beach movie.

In fact, before we started renovating, we were literally offered two thousand dollars to let a small production company shoot a horror movie there (not quite *Titanic*), but we figured two thousand wouldn't be enough to scrub the fake blood off the walls and floors afterward, or to scrub the gory images of the movie from our minds when we were enjoying some peaceful time at our second home.

"Besides," Ben liked to say, "it's already haunted."

"You think so, huh?"

"Sure," he said easily. "Ghosts have more substance in the damp air." He said this with great authority, like he was Dan Aykroyd in *Ghostbusters* or something. "That's why England has so many hauntings. It's an island."

"I thought it was because it had hundreds more years of organized civilization. They've been telling ghost stories there since they were wearing loincloths."

He shrugged and smiled. Ran his hand through his dark, wavy hair the way he always did when he was trying to emphasize a point that he knew wasn't very strong. "Moist air."

I laughed. "Ugh, stop, you know I hate that word!"

"Moist," he said again, then came toward me like a menacing creature from one of the very stories we were talking about. "Moist, moist, moist—"

"Stop!" I put my hands to his chest, and he laughed and wrapped his arms around me. And suddenly everything from the ghosts to the dreaded word dissolved, and there was nothing in the world to worry about.

Bit by bit we'd worked on the house until *finally* the whole thing was done and pristine and beautiful. The floor was new, the walls were new, the fixtures were new, the appliances were new . . . Honestly, I'd be hard-pressed to tell you what remained of the original place except it was still basically the same shape and in the same location.

We thought we'd have it forever, that it would be a place to bring our children and, someday, our grandchildren. Ben used to talk about all the little tchotchkes he picked up at yard sales and in our travels, and how the grandchildren would remember them all their lives. "The old ship's light at Granddad's," or "the glass Pinocchio figure at Grandma's," and so on. God knows he collected a lot of funny old weird things, but I never protested. They were dust collectors, but they gave him such a kick I didn't have the heart to point out that what he was spending on them could probably have put a pool out back.

We didn't know then that Ben had a rare heart condition that was going to take him down at just thirty-six, suddenly and without mercy.

Death can be so swift, can't it? I know a slow death is agony for the sick patient. I know the old "he never knew what happened" is a great blessing to the dead, but for those left behind, the sudden death is the worst kind of torture. You grieve over and over again because it breeds so many futile, circular thoughts.

No, I'd find myself thinking. *Ben was annoyingly trim no matter what he ate. Every ounce he lost, I'd find. If I ate a Big Mac it seemed like he lost a pound and ran an extra quarter mile. He was incredibly healthy, there's no way he just dropped dead.*

Or, *I have a message from him right here on my phone from this morning. This isn't possible. I can listen to the message right now, I can hear his voice, he's got to be here still!*

The impulse to call and the certainty that he'd answer were tremendous. And, just like that, I'd have myself convinced, for just a fraction of a moment, that it hadn't happened. It couldn't have, it didn't make sense, so it hadn't.

But of course it had. And, as dumb as it is, that realization, even after just an instant of rationalizing why it couldn't be, brought it all back like a surprise. A shock. There were times, even months later—hell, even years later—that I sincerely had to stop and ask myself if he was really gone or if it had just been a bad dream.

I'm sure there's an element of genuine madness to that, but so many of us endure it that I guess it's a socially acceptable form.

But this wasn't all about me. Agonizing as it was, the loss was arguably worse for someone else. See, when he'd gone, he'd not only left me behind, but our son, Jamie, who was only fourteen at the time. Fourteen. And even that birthday was only a few weeks old. This boy who had, to that point, grown up so loved and nurtured by two parents, who had admired his father so much, was suddenly thrust into a world of grief. He'd wanted to be like his father and we thought he had a lifetime to learn. He still could, of course, but the lessons from Ben had ended before the biggest challenges of manhood had come along.

We had been a happy family. The happy, ideal little family with the nice house, the dog, the financial security—we were the Cleavers, the Petries, the Flintstones without the rocks. We even had the beach house with a nice story behind it. Our little haven held memories I'd never forget.

So it had been hard for me to even consider coming back until now. I just couldn't face it. This had been our place, our *home*, in many ways even more than the one in Potomac, where we lived most of the year. They'd taken Ben out of here to Baltimore—and I'd driven the endless hour to identify him. That was the end of the beach house for years. The neighbors closed it up for me, kept half an eye on it, and I just paid the bills as they came in. I never wanted to come back.

Which was probably another reason I was standing out here on the beach watching a boy fly a kite, instead of going inside and getting down to the business of getting the house sold.

Then I'd never come back.

Ben had been getting it ready for our summer. Shaking out the dust and making sure everything was working before we descended on it with friends and relatives and plans for parties. He'd come alone for the weekend because I was just too lazy to face the hard labor after a week of exams.

I beat myself up about the place for a long time after that. What if he'd overexerted himself and that was why he'd died? The doctors said no, but what did they really know? *I* knew that when Ben got working, he worked like a horse, and here he'd been at our vacation home, fixing it up for me. It was a luxury. "The beach house." It sounded so . . . unnecessary. Wouldn't he still be alive if he hadn't come here?

That was another one of those games my mind played with me, but still I couldn't help but wonder. I'd wonder anything if the wondering could make me feel like it was possible it hadn't happened.

My grandfather would have asked, *Why can't you just stay at a motel like everyone else?* And, indeed, many of the motels where he would have stayed in his youth were still there. It was hard to argue that the Starlight Venture smells like urine and looks like prison when he remembered the glory days when the little neon lights out front worked and the rooms inside were the height of luxury because they looked out over the ocean (well, half of them; the other half looked over the bay) and smelled of thick fresh salt air.

It must have been nice then.

It was still nice, in many ways. Ben and I had loved it.

And once Jamie had been born (to my then twenty-year-old self), he had loved the beach too. For a while. Weirdly, once he reached teenage-hood, he was less interested in coming. And obviously, once his father had died here, any thoughts he might have had of coming here for fun had disappeared like smoke in the air. He didn't even want to come help me work on the place to be finally rid of it. Instead of joining me, he'd opted to stay home. Which meant he wanted to play video games, loaf off, and hang out with his crummy girlfriend.

So I was on my own. In so many ways.

The life insurance payment was safely invested, leaving my salary to dwindle as it always had, quickly, and leaving very little at the end of the month, particularly with a child, and with the hefty mortgage payment on a vacation house I didn't need and which we never came to visit anymore.

I returned my attention to the beach. The beautiful beach. A place of peace and sunshine even when it's overcast, at least in my mind.

Breathe.

In seven and out fourteen . . .

The boy looked over his shoulder and his eyes met mine for a moment. It sent a jolt of shock through me, partly because he looked familiar suddenly. I realized it was because he looked a bit like Jamie had a few years ago. Like Jamie, the boy's coloring was like Ben's—wavy dark glossy hair, icy pale blue eyes. Central casting would have him filed under Cute Kid. Active, carefree.

Happy.

Unexpected tears filled my eyes. I envied him at that moment, that lone kid. For my son and for myself. He looked so peaceful, so focused on his one task. No painful thoughts, apparently; all he wanted was to fly that kite until, presumably, he had some other childlike thing to do. He looked to be about seven, maybe eight. It would be years before he had the troubled thoughts of adulthood.

He turned sharply, kicking a spray of sand up behind him. That got Dolly's attention. She looked up, eyed him for a moment, then took off running toward him, kicking sand up behind her.

"Dolly!" She ignored me. "*Dolly!*" She reached the boy without even glancing back at me, and he looked down at her for a moment. She seemed to delight in his attention and ran by his side, looking up at him with that big loopy dog smile, trying to jump on him but unable to catch a moving target.

He didn't seem to mind, so I stopped calling her and just watched them run together, thinking how nice it would be to travel back in time to when Jamie was that age.

Had I failed him irreversibly? I wondered. Had my devastation at Ben's death put me into such a selfish tailspin that I hadn't been there for my little boy's needs upon his own father's death? I wanted to tell myself no. I wanted to believe that my efforts to be cheerful, even when they seemed superhuman, had made a difference to Jamie, but all I could think of was the old chestnut everyone said. *Kids know.* And they do. They know when you're lying, when you're faking, when you're not interested, when you're drunk, when you've been crying. I'd committed all of those crimes at various times in my grief, and even though I'd tried to smile through every one of them, I'd failed him. Of course I had.

I needed to get him back. We needed to be the pals we used to be, back when he was the same age as this child. I needed to bring out the little boy he'd been and run *with* him on the beach, laugh with him, play with him. Make him know he wasn't alone in this world no matter that his heart was broken.

Looking at this boy now brought it all back to me in the most poignant way. I wasn't a wife anymore. I needed to be a better mother. Before it was too late.

The dog barked, bringing my attention back. The boy had stopped and was pulling the kite back in. Dolly was watching with rapt attention. So was I, come to think of it. When he was finished, he put the kite under his arm and walked toward me. I found myself straightening, as if I were about to have an important conversation, but he didn't even look at me as he approached. In fact, he seemed to look everywhere *but* at me, yet there was something in his eyes that struck me. Loneliness. The definition of *old soul* curled up in those little blue eyes.

"Hello," I said, as he passed.

It was the strangest thing. He slowed his gait, looked around, eyes never actually landing on me even though I was just a few feet away from him, then gave a tiny shake of his head and kept walking.

Of course he didn't answer. That was good sense. I was just some strange woman standing on the beach watching him fly a kite, and not only should he not talk to me, but, given all the stranger-danger stuff we try to teach our kids, he probably should have *hurried* past me.

I watched him go, with a small ache and a measure of envy for his joy, then turned back to the sea.

"Hello, King Triton." I whispered the greeting that Ben and I used to call out loud like crazy people.

Dolly stopped in front of me and panted her greeting. I knelt down and scuffled her shaggy head. "Hey, girl. Good girl! Did you have a good run?" I thought maybe I should get a kite too, good exercise and a little more interesting than just running along avoiding the horseshoe crabs that had washed up.

She jumped and hooked her front claws on my shirt, digging painfully into my stomach. "Down!" I ordered, and, chagrined, she got down and looked at me, probably wondering why I never wanted to hug. "Stay down."

She obeyed and immediately set off sniffing the sand like she was onto something big. God knows what she was picking up on. Then she stopped and her hackles rose and she barked as if someone were climbing in the window in the middle of the night. She *never* got like this. She was such a dopey girl usually that to hear her growl and bark so low and ferociously was unfamiliar to me.

"No! Calm down, Dolly. No bark." I glanced behind me for the boy, afraid he'd be frightened. "I'm sorry, she's harm—" Although he had only just passed me a moment ago, he was gone.

Vanished into thin air.

Chapter Three

Jamie

Two and a half years ago

The sun was almost down and she wasn't here yet.

Baseball practice had ended an hour ago and Jamie's mom hadn't been there with all the other parents waiting to pick up. The minutes had stretched on awkwardly, until finally—in the face of his coach's obvious concern at having to wait with him—Jamie had snuck off when the man wasn't looking, so he'd think he'd been picked up normally and had left.

Now Jamie was back by the driveway to Kingsview Ballpark, starting to feel his own apprehension about where his mom was. Maybe he shouldn't have been so quick to dodge his coach.

She'd been distracted lately, that was for sure. Well, ever since his dad had died she'd been distracted. A real mess, really. So it wasn't a huge surprise for her to be scatterbrained, but usually she was so paranoid about where Jamie was at all times that she'd never miss a pickup. In fact, she'd gotten so nervous about something happening to him that she'd bought him a cell phone, despite the fact that she'd previously vowed he didn't need one at his age.

He had one now, but unfortunately he'd let it die. Cheap flip phone barely held a charge. It was hard to believe they even still made these things. But as long as she could get ahold of him when she wanted to, and as long as she felt like he could get ahold of her if there was an emergency, it seemed to bring her some peace of mind.

He wondered what she was thinking now.

The moon was a slice of crescent in the sky. He could see it in the darkening blue with that one little star that looked like it was dangling off it. Venus? His dad had told him that. It wasn't a star at all, it just looked like one.

He'd asked, at the time, if it was bad luck to accidentally wish on a planet instead of a star.

"It's *good* luck!" his dad had assured him. "*Really* good luck! There are billions of stars out there visible to the naked eye, but not so many planets. It takes a special eye to catch the planets."

"What about the moon?" Jamie had asked. "That's bigger than all of them." That's how his little-child mind had worked. His dad had explained to him how the moon was closer, so it *looked* bigger, but that it was actually really small compared to everything else.

"You can wish on it anyway," his dad had told him. "Your crazy mom does. She loves the full moon."

Funny how that one fact about his mother had never quite left his mind. She'd never said it to him and he'd never seen her doing anything weird about the moon, but his father had told him she loved the full moon, so every time the moon was full, he wondered if his mom was happy.

The last few full moons hadn't been able to do much to lift her mood, unfortunately.

Or Jamie's, but he didn't feel like he could say anything about that.

Yeah, he'd lost his dad, but his mom had lost her husband, and she was so upset about that that it didn't feel like there was room in the house for his grief as well. That was okay, though. Maybe it kept Jamie stronger. Try not to cry for long enough, and soon you don't even feel like doing it at all.

Dusk settled around him. It felt heavy and loud. Crickets were fine outside a window, but he'd never realized how *loud* they were when you were out among them. The sound ran right through his brain.

Where *was* she?

The sun was setting quickly now, the shadows stretching as far as they could go before disappearing completely. He began to think about walking, but it was a good five miles home, maybe more. That would take forever, and if she came to pick him up in the meantime, she'd freak out that he was nowhere to be found. He didn't need the police out looking for him, or his frantic mom getting into some sort of car accident or something because she was beside herself.

He looked at his phone again, as if it might suddenly have gained power, but it hadn't. He closed it and put it into his bag and sighed.

There was no telling how much longer it was—it felt like hours, but the sun had only just made its final dip below the horizon—before his mother's white minivan came screaming around the corner and jerked to a halt in front of him.

"Why didn't you *call* me?" she cried, sounding much angrier at him than the situation could possibly warrant. But even in the increasing dark he could see her face was pale, her ever-darkening blond hair pulled back in a messy bunch. Her brows were knit up into worry, though, and her eyes looked wide and scared.

Jamie made a vague motion toward his bag. "Phone's dead."

"Why can't you keep it charged? It's not that hard, Jamie. Just plug it in every now and then so this doesn't happen!" She was a dark figure in the car; not the pale-haired Barbie doll she used to resemble—in a good way—but a tired woman who had given up and gone dark in the most literal sense.

"Jamie!" she snapped.

Okay, so whatever else she was feeling, she was definitely mad at him, and it definitely wasn't fair.

Another car rounded the corner and pulled up behind her. Coach Tom. He got out of his car, raking his hand through his hair, and walked up between Willa's window and where Jamie was now standing up to collect his stuff.

"Willa," he said in a calming voice. "I'm so glad you found him. I thought you'd picked him up or I never would have left."

Jamie felt his face grow hot. This was his fault. He shouldn't have escaped. He thought she'd be along any minute and he didn't want Coach waiting for him, both of them twiddling their thumbs, with nothing to say.

She looked totally flustered. "Thanks, Tom. I was just telling Jamie that he needs to keep his phone charged, and . . ." Her voice cracked and disappeared. Jamie noticed her swipe the back of her hand across her eyes.

"Listen, Willa," Coach said, while Jamie silently put his equipment in the backseat and went around to get in the car beside her, "I told you before, I'm glad to give Jamie a ride home after practices. It's really no inconvenience."

Jamie looked down at his feet in the interior lights of the car. Shoes that he'd had for almost a year. Shoes that had outlasted his father. Meanwhile, everything else was changing, even his feet within them—the shoes had been a little loose at first and now they were feeling tight. Soon he'd have to chuck them and he wouldn't have any more parts of the uniform he'd had when his dad was alive. Which was a stupid thought, he knew that. Who cared if his dad had seen these particular shoes or that particular jersey? They couldn't magically bring him back. He was being sentimental about stupid things, but sometimes that was the only way he could think about it without feeling like he was going to go crazy.

Still. It was hard to let go of the thoughts now.

His father never would have forgotten to get him. In fact, his dad had come to almost all the practices and helped Coach Tom out. He'd always been there to encourage Jamie and everyone. Jamie could still hear his raspy voice now, bellowing, "Steal home! Go for it!" All the kids had loved him. Jamie often wondered if everyone else noticed the difference without his dad there half as much as he did.

". . . and it would just feel good to know I'm helping you out," Coach was saying. "Please, Willa."

But she was already shaking her head. A strand of hair fell out of her rubber band and dropped by her neck. She swatted at it like it was a bug. "No, Tom, honestly, I'll get on the ball. Things have just been so busy and . . ."

Busy? She didn't seem to do anything but sit on the sofa and look off into space, or click through old family pictures on the computer and on Facebook.

Jamie said nothing. Just glanced at Coach, who didn't see his pleading look, then back down at his shoes. The interior lights had gone off now, so all he could see was the outline of the bold black-and-white stripes.

"I do appreciate the offer, though," his mom was saying.

"Okay." Coach sounded hesitant. "You just let me know if there's ever a pinch, okay? I'm glad to pick up, drive him home, whatever. You have my number."

"Yes, I do." She started to raise the electric window, a signal that the conversation was over. "Good night, Tom. Thanks again." As soon as the window was closed, she readjusted her grip on the wheel and pressed the accelerator.

"How come you don't just let him drive me?" Jamie asked. "He doesn't sound like he minds."

"Because it's our responsibility—*my* responsibility—and I don't want to put anyone else out."

I don't want to sit alone in the dark while you forget, he thought, but said nothing.

Jamie gave a shrug he knew she couldn't see. "It doesn't sound like he's that put out by it."

"Jamie." She slowed the car at a stop sign and turned to look at him, hard, then her face crumpled. "Oh, baby, I'm so sorry. I'm so sorry you had to wait there alone and you couldn't call me. I was cleaning and I just got lost in thought, and before I knew it . . . I called Tom to see if he was still here, but he'd already left, of course, so . . ." She shook her head and covered her face with her hands for a moment, sniffling gently. "I'm such a jerk."

Jamie didn't know what to say or do. He was glad none of his friends were around and able to see this. Everyone already felt sorry for them; this would just make it a million times worse. He looked around the car, hoping for maybe some interesting thing to divert the conversation, but there was nothing. So he reached out and awkwardly patted her shoulder. "You're not a jerk."

She wiped her eyes and gave a half laugh through her tears. "As compliments go, that shouldn't feel nearly as flattering as it does."

A car honked behind them and she accelerated again.

"What do you mean?" he asked her. He hadn't meant it as a *compliment* that she wasn't a jerk, he was just trying to make her feel better. He could do compliments better than that if he tried.

She shook her head. Too much. "Nothing, baby, thank you. I'm sorry. You don't need this. I know I'm not the only one who lost Dad, you're suffering too, and I'm being so selfish here." She sniffed again and took a sharp inhale, as if for strength. "Tell you what, how about if we go to the grocery store and get whatever you want to eat and then watch a movie? Anything you want. As long as it's not rated *R*," she added as an afterthought. A piece of parenting she'd forget now and then lately, which Jamie was glad of.

He wanted to say yes. He tried to picture them doing that, watching a movie together and eating his favorite junky frozen pizza, Martino's. It was hard to envision. She didn't really want to do that and he knew it. They didn't like the same sorts of movies and even if they agreed on one, half-way through she'd probably get on her computer and he'd feel like a bother and just sit there, tense, until it was over.

This wasn't the first time they'd tried to hang out together since his dad had died.

"Nah." He shook his head. "I'm pretty tired. It was a hard practice today." It wasn't. He wasn't. But he'd have to make a show of going to bed early now.

"Oh." Something in her posture deflated. "Sure, okay. I understand. Another time, then."

For a moment he thought about changing his mind. She looked genuinely disappointed. But something inside of him wouldn't let him conjure the words. So instead he just nodded, half to himself, and said, "Another time," to the window.

Chapter Four

Willa

Now

I gave a whistle to the dog and started to head toward the house. I tried to ignore the dread in my chest, and realized that's why I'd invested so much thought into where the kid had gone. Anything was better than thinking about going inside for the first time.

I tried even harder not to feel sad about it, but that was impossible, given how happy this trip used to make me. There was not one time Ben and I had come here together that I hadn't felt a little thrill at remembering the first time I'd seen it, then, shortly thereafter, the first time I'd seen him. I wished I could go back in time and tell that girl, first walking up to the door, that the boy she was about to meet was the man she'd marry.

That was one of my favorite fantasies: telling Young Me, who had a tendency toward the maudlin and melancholy even then, that great things were right around the corner and she couldn't even see them yet. That this guy was going to be her husband and together they would have a son. Young Me had spent so much time brooding over a breakup at seventeen when she should have been out living it up, preparing for the happy inevitability of Ben.

Then again, I'd have to stop the story there, wouldn't I? If Young Me knew *everything* that was going to happen, she might not have been able to muster the gumption to march on.

Current Me was having a lot of trouble with that too.

But there was no more room in my life for self-pity. I'd allowed myself that, at my therapist's urging, quite some time ago. And I had been very thorough about it too, dredging up every aspect of my pain, picturing all the horrible scenarios, regardless of how inaccurate they were or how little I could do about them now anyway.

Now it was time to face it all and move on.

And that began with the huge step of walking into the house.

"Dolly!" There was no way I was doing this alone.

She glanced at me, then at the house, then scampered away, back toward the beach, before stopping and looking back at me, a creature of her own habitual need for approval.

"Come on, Dolly!" I enthused in my most chipper Dog Voice. "Come on, girl!" I whistled again. That usually did it.

She looked at me suspiciously.

"Treat?"

Her ears perked up.

"Do you want a treat?" It was embarrassing how chirpy I was being all by myself. It was like when I asked her if she needed to go "potty." God knows why we used that stupid word instead of some less embarrassing word or phrase. She was a dog, she would have come to understand whatever we said. I had a friend who sent his dog out to *poo corner*. But not me, I had to stand at the back door for all the world to hear me calling,

"Potty! Come on, go *potty*. Dolly, potty *now!*" Strangers would have thought I was the world's meanest mother.

I clumped up the front steps and opened the door, feeling the inside wall for the light switch. I found it and yellow light filled the inside hall. "Come on! Let's get a treat!" To the neighbors who weren't used to having any activity in this house, I probably sounded like a head case.

Dolly reluctantly came up the steps, looking at me as if to ask where this supposed treat was. I dug in my purse and found a small pack of Nilla wafers I'd picked up at the gas station on the way in. I ripped it open and took one out. "Here you go!" I tossed it to her. She caught it midair and all of her misgivings about the house seemed to fade. If someone threw me a Nilla wafer, I probably would have made all efforts to catch it as well. I loved those things.

But now: the house. I heaved a sigh and turned to face the place inside. Up until that moment I had been *so busy* trying to lure the dog in that I hadn't had to concentrate on any other task. That was the way I was going to have to handle this, I realized: one single task at a time. If I allowed all the thoughts and feelings to flood my mind, I'd truly go nuts. But if I did one thing at a time and viewed everything as an accomplishment, I could make my way through the whole thing.

1. Pack up and drive to the house.
2. Observe happy child on the beach.
3. Fool the dog inside using Nilla wafers.
4. Call Jamie, try to avoid argument about whiny girlfriend.
5. Look around, assess the house, make list of what needs to be done to sell.

That was it. So far, that was the list. Now I was on item number four. I took out my phone and scrolled to my Favorites menu. Ben was still there, right above Jamie. I couldn't take him out; the action would seem so permanent.

I know, I know. Death is pretty permanent as well.

There was no answer when I called Jamie. I squelched an impulse to panic. Every time he didn't answer the phone I had a moment of thinking The Worst had happened. The fact that The Worst had already happened once didn't help matters much. I was being paranoid and I knew it.

"Jamie, you need to answer your phone," I said after the message prompt, to what I knew would be deaf ears. "I just got here and everything's fine. I really wish you'd come join me. Think about it. We could have . . . fun." He wouldn't think so. "And we could have Grotto's pizza." That was his favorite, but I was pretty sure even that couldn't get him to spend time with his drag of a mother. "Okay, so give me a call back as soon as you can and at least text me when you get this to tell me you're okay. You know how I am. 'Bye."

Call me back, I wished silently. *Let me at least relax about that.*

That done, it was time for item five on my to-do list. Actually go into the house instead of standing outside like a thief casing the joint.

I took a steadying breath and stepped over the threshold. So far, so good. Absolutely nothing happened. No drama whatsoever.

Of course. What was I expecting?

I turned left into the living room. The wide-planked dark hardwood floors were scuffed and dirty, with sand settled into the grooves. That was hard to get rid of, but I considered it evidence of a lot of happy trips. The wood was dusty and scraped. That was going to take some work to clean. I wasn't even sure if waxing would be enough, or if I'd have to have it refinished.

That's how this visit was going to be: a lot of uncomfortable questions about what I could do and what I'd have to have done by someone else . . .

and how much it would cost. And often, how to do it. My friend Kristin would call all the work around the house "a job for someone with a penis." The feminist in me wanted to defy that, but the lazy girl in me agreed wholeheartedly. *All* of this was a job for someone with a penis. I only wished I had unlimited funds to hire someone, or some*ones*, to do it.

In the midst of these thoughts I realized I was alone and turned around to see Dolly standing on the front porch looking in, but she had not followed me. Normally she was my shadow, always underfoot, but she was acting so weird today.

"Come on!" I slapped my thigh.

She didn't move.

"Come!" More firm. I imagined she thought this was my scary voice.

She still didn't move.

"What on *earth* is your problem?" I demanded, as if she could answer or would concede. "*Come!*" My scariest voice, one I never used because she was normally so agreeable.

At last she sucked it up and came in. Then, just like that, she was normal again. Wagging her tail, lapping my hand, trying to jump up for hugs. Her regular old self. But I, on the other hand, was feeling a lot of apprehension.

Nothing surprising at all, not fear exactly, only sadness, overwhelming exhaustion, and the creepy feeling of opening a vault. No one had been here since Ben had died and the paramedics and police had cleared the place. I should have come sooner, but I'd used Jamie as an excuse not to. Yes, it would have been upsetting for him, but this was life. The grittier part, but still life.

Who knew what I'd find? Mice? Rats? A hobo lying on the couch with his feet up and his little red-bandannaed stick on the floor next to him? The only certain thing was that there would be at least small remnants of Ben's last days. Evidence of . . . what? Not knowing his fate? Moving along with ordinary ease through his days? Or would I find a scribbled will, half completed on the kitchen table? A premonitory goodbye note, folded neatly and propped up by the bed?

No, of course not. No one had known this was coming. Least of all, I had been assured, Ben.

Dolly's nails clicked along as she followed me into the kitchen, a good-sized room with top-of-the-line stainless steel appliances, granite countertops, and a gorgeous old farmhouse table that I'd always loved. The fridge had fingerprints on it—the fridge *always* had fingerprints on it—and had a couple old pictures by Jamie pegged up with magnets. They were curled at the edges, looked old, but still made me smile. The stove was a little smudged with ancient remnants of some sauce, but the counters gleamed and the sink looked empty.

My chest constricted as I looked at what truly was the heart of the home.

We'd had so many happy meals here, entertaining friends, entertaining each other. I'd made barbecue sauce for the first time by myself in this kitchen. Maybe not a big deal to most, but up until then I had only thought of it as something purchased in a bottle from the grocery store. I'd made dozens of red, white, and blue sugar cookies for the Fourth of July on that counter one year, and given them to all my friends. Except for those I'd eaten myself, that is, and they had contributed to record summer weight gain for me. Still, I considered the haul an achievement and justified my time lying on the beach when I probably should have been running the cookies off instead.

I could remember a thousand meals here, if I put my mind to it. The shelves, which held all my cookbooks—my own brand of armchair travel—still had a sense of having been abandoned. It was easy to imagine picking out a book and blowing the years of dust off it like something from an old movie. *Ah, yes, my old* Southern Living *annual. I haven't seen this since aught-nine!*

I'd loved this kitchen. And every moment spent in it. I could even still smell the woodsy barbecue scent that lingered since our many meals here.

It was an effort, but I tried not to remember the more risqué moments, though there were plenty. But, I reminded myself as I straightened my back, I'd decided a long time ago that I absolutely *had* to resist remembering moments of intimacy—that was just too difficult. In fact, I had to resist glorifying Ben in death at all and fooling myself into thinking I had lost companionship and could never have it again. Not that I could replace him *exactly*, of course; I loved him and he was gone and I'd never see him again, but he wouldn't have wanted me to live the rest of my life alone, turning my soul into some sort of altar to him and only him. I didn't want that either. At first I had, but then a surge of wanting to *live* had struck me, and I had worked very hard to maintain that since. Sure, it was a bit of a challenge at the moment, but when this task was done, then maybe the energy would shift and my life would start to feel like my own again.

"It's still the same place," I said to Dolly, who was not wondering. Still, she perked her ears up as if she understood. "There's nothing to feel creepy about."

She didn't look so sure.

But she was wrong. Her hesitation was wrong. I fancied it to be some mournful respect, but really it was probably more due to the stale air, the dust, the dark of shades being down and curtains drawn, all the things that symbolized how different things were than the last time she'd been here.

Together we moved on into the family room. This was tough. I really wished Jamie would come, but in my heart I knew if I were to convince

him to I had to get the place straightened out and homey before he arrived. Hell, I had to get it straightened out and homey even if he *didn't*
come—that was the only way it could possibly sell. It was spooky going
through like this. I couldn't stay here like this for long and I sure couldn't
sell it with this gloomy light and sense of lifelessness.

This family room was the hangout room; it had been since those de-
cades ago when my crew had first rented the place. There were overstuffed
lazy sofas, La-Z-Boy recliners (two), and built-in bookshelves full of beautiful editions of classics, as well as a few popular novels I'd read and put
there and a nice stack of board games. All the colors looked beautiful
against the white of the bookshelves and walls, even though the effect
had not been intended.

This room had seen so many happy times. There were so many memories that would be in my mind forever. They were as much a part of me
as my blood type or my internal organs. To my surprise, I found myself
smiling at the memories. God, there were so many of them. Games of
Scrabble, and Cards Against Humanity, and a million other things had
been played here. Meals had been eaten here. We'd watched the Redskins
inevitably lose their bid for the playoffs here.

It was sad to look at it right now and know this was how Ben had left
it. A Michael Chabon book was lying facedown on the coffee table,
marking a place he would never return to read. I went over and sat down
on the sofa in front of it, and touched the book. Tears returned as I picked
it up and read a few words. These are the details of death that make it all
the harder to accept—the many things left undone. The unfinished book,
the dishes I was sure were in the dishwasher. Gross. I'd have to throw those
out. Maybe replace the whole thing. That hadn't occurred to me before.

Then again, what would I have done? Made a special trip three hours
just to come here and empty the dishwasher? Face all of this before I was
ready just because I didn't want to throw a few spoons out or have a piece

of spaghetti noodle stuck to the bottom of the dishwasher? No, I'd done everything I could, the best I could.

All of a sudden I was overwhelmed by everything that needed to be done. My energy zapped, I leaned back. I closed my eyes and saw stars. Low blood sugar personality withdrawal, probably. No protein all day, just Diet Pepsi and Nilla wafers. Who would feel good running on so little? It would have been smart to stop at the store and pick up some cheese and eggs, maybe some milk. More Nilla wafers. Now that would have to wait until later.

I took a deep breath like I'd learned in the yoga class I'd taken to try and combat grief. It worked. The breath, that is, not the yoga. My hamstrings had resisted yoga like Poland resisting the Soviet Union, but the breathing techniques were solid. I felt my shoulders relax fractionally and took another deep breath.

Everything was fine. I'd known this house almost all of my life. I'd been here a million times. I'd been *alone* here a million times. I'd never in that time felt anything sinister or desolate about the place. It was home. It was as much home as anything in my life could get. If anything, I should be *relaxed* in this space, not tense.

Dolly whined and looked at a spot across the room, ears forward, head tilted as if trying to comprehend what she was seeing.

"No, no," I said, pointing a finger at her. "You are *not* going to freak me out like that. You are *not* going to convince me to wig out and leave here. Absolutely not. Come here."

Nothing. She kept looking at the spot. That made me look too. Squint and try to see whatever it was she was seeing. Maybe a rodent or, god, no, a snake? I'd heard of them coming into houses for the warmth, but it wasn't that cold out.

There was nothing there, just nothing.

And then, suddenly, a shimmering column of light. So faint it could have been the sun coming in the window through the branches of a tree outside when it moved with the wind.

I stared, willing it to take some understandable form or go away, but it just stayed there, swaying slightly, before *slowly* fading like smoke in stagnant air.

Maybe it hadn't been there at all. Probably just had been the sun, but it still made me very uneasy. "*Come. Here,*" I commanded, pathetically looking to Dolly for comfort.

She paused, then ran over and jumped up on the sofa next to me. Normally we—I—discouraged her from getting on the furniture, but in this case I was pretty glad to have her here, her warm fur nudged up against me. She was panting, but she was always panting. I couldn't read any meaning into that.

"Good girl," I murmured, looking around warily, half wondering if I'd feel a wave of cold come over me or whatever they said happened when a ghost came nearby. I realized I was talking quietly because I didn't want to disturb—or awaken—anything that shouldn't be here. Which was, of course, nothing, because nothing else was here. I said it to the dog, just to be clear. "See, there's nothing here. Nothing at all. Now stop acting all creepy, because you're totally freaking me out."

It was at that moment—of *course*—that the entire atmosphere seemed to change. It's hard to describe, but it was as if the fireplace I was looking at warbled out of focus for a moment, and the room took on a stillness like I'd never felt in my life. Not just quiet but the absolute definition of silence. Noticeably, disconcertingly so.

Then I saw it. From the corner of my eye, but I swear it was clear as day, I saw a person walk right up to the side of the sofa next to me.

Ben.

Chapter Five

Jamie

Thom Yorke crooned from the record player in Jamie's room. It was loud, louder than he could have it when his mom was there. She was forever telling him to *turn it down*. It was like she hated music. It was a relief to have her at the beach house for a while, though he wasn't sure how long she'd be gone or how long she'd be okay with him staying home alone. She never participated in anything with him anymore, they never hung out in any capacity, she just seemed to hover over his life and drop walls down here and there for him to bump into.

He turned the music up again and went to his bed and to his computer. It was so tempting to fall right back asleep. He flipped over his phone. Two missed calls from his mom. "You need to answer your phone." Her siren call. She said it at the beginning of every message like most people would say *hello*. She didn't get that the more she told him that he *needed* to do something, the less inclined he felt to do it. Whatever it was.

There were also five missed calls and eight missed texts from Roxy.

"Come on." Could she never give him a rest?

He tossed the phone back on the mattress and covered his eyes with his forearm for a minute before forcing himself to pick up the computer, its metal hot from the sun and hotter from being on and running for two hours.

All right, he could do this. It's just an online summer-school English class. So easy it almost pained him. A three-page essay on the dynamic between Lennie and George in *Of Mice and Men*. He should be able to do it in his sleep.

He nodded his head and pounded on his thighs like he was getting ready to run instead of write.

He poised his fingers over the keys. The cursor blinked.

Was that relentlessly rhythmic line taunting him or encouraging him? Fuck that cursor.

Finally, after ten minutes of agonizing over how to just *start* the essay, he got going. Intro paragraph done. Only two-point-eight more pages to go.

Almost as soon as he got going, his phone started buzzing.

It was either his mom or Roxy, he knew that. And he didn't want to answer either one of them right now. But if he didn't, he'd only be prolonging the agony.

He answered without looking. It didn't even matter who it was, either way he was going to get shit. "Yeah."

"*Jamie!*"

He shut his eyes hard. Her voice was like microphone feedback shrieking through his brain. Always. No matter if she was happy or if she was pissed, she was always a sharp whine.

Right now she was pissed. In person, that usually came with the tangibility of tears or punching.

He could see her flipping her currently magenta hair in anger. Unless, of course, she'd made it blue again. Or some other color to throw him off. "Roxy."

"What the *hell* is the matter with you, huh? I've called you like a hundred times and you're ignoring me. Seriously? Like you think it's that easy to get rid of me? Seriously, we've been together for almost two years. You're really trying to act like you don't love me just like that?"

"I didn't say I don't love you—" One *millisecond* after the words came out of his mouth, he knew it was a monumental mistake.

He waited to find out which of her silences it was that followed. Was it going to be the smug laughing-at-him kind? The tricked-you kind? The rarely heard we-are-making-a-huge-mistake kind where she accepted some blame and told him how much she already missed him?

He listened hard to figure out the sound coming from the other end of the phone.

Ah. It was the sobbing kind of silence. The kind where she only let a sharp, shuddering intake of breath be heard before eventually letting out a soft whimper and whine, like a dog.

Jamie shook his head and sat up, braced. He ran his hand through his hair and waited.

"Jamie . . ." she said in a tremulous whisper. "I can't do this. I can't, I can't do it without you."

"Yes, you can, Roxy."

After a few seconds and a deep shuddering breath, she said, "I miss you. I already miss you! Give me another chance."

Jamie cracked the knuckles of his free hand. "You know how it's going to go. Same as always."

"I don't know." Her voice was a croak. She cleared her throat and said, even more quietly, "I can change."

"You shouldn't have to." He thought about all the changes she was always trying to exact from him. "Neither of us should have to."

"You don't understand. You *never* understand."

An accusation. That was another thing she always pulled out of her pocket—there was always an accusation at the ready. Some way in which he'd wronged her. "I'm sorry," she said, her voice self-consciously pathetic. "I've taken up too much of your time."

He resisted telling her it was okay. He couldn't give her any more. "You're going to be all right, Roxy. Promise."

She hesitated. "I really loved you, you know. I can't even tell you how much, you just have to feel it. Or not."

One of her lines, dramatic and ripped from the script of whatever drama she was watching most recently.

"You too."

Voice tight, she said, " 'Bye." She made sure to let him hear her sob once more before hanging up.

Overall, that went pretty well. As far as Jamie and Roxy's post-breakup conversations went, that was one of the easier ones. She hadn't given him as much shit as usual. Sometimes the conversations went around and around, circle after circle. She'd act like she got it, then get mad when she realized it was really happening, then lean on one of her many tactics to reel him back in.

It was all so transparent. He saw right through it. He knew it was psycho. His friends called her Bobbitt, as in Lorena Bobbitt, the notorious penis hacker from the nineties.

The nickname would have bothered him less if he didn't know that it was his mom who had started it.

It didn't matter, though, how much Roxy drove him up the wall. When it was good, it was fucking fantastic. Psycho girls make the best and worst girlfriends. At least his friends kind of understood why they never ended up staying broken up. When his defenses ran short, he'd just say, *Have you seen her?*

That usually got a solid, *That's true, man.*

He ignored a flash of regret and tossed his phone aside.

Essay. Essay, essay, essay. He had to finish his make-up assignment for school, so he could be finished with eleventh grade.

Forty minutes later, it was finished. It was solid B quality. If he read through it once more he could knock it up to a hundred percent, he always could, but why bother with that?

He just didn't care enough.

Chapter Six

Willa

For a moment I sat paralyzed.

Ben.

I said it. "Ben."

Oh, my god, oh, my god, it was *him*, he was there, right in front of me. What should I do? What should I feel? I'd thought of this, wished for this, so many times since he'd been gone, but now I found myself with a sickening feeling of fear battling with my joy at seeing him.

"Please talk to me." I had to try. I needed him to be real, even while I needed this all to be a dream. "Please say something, Ben. I see you. You're here. You're home." My voice caught in my throat. "Please say something. Anything."

He looked past me. At the dog? At the book I'd closed? At the window where I thought the light had come in? Maybe it hadn't been light at all, but him, trying to come into form.

"Ben, please—"

It seemed like minutes he stood there, but it was just seconds. It all happened so fast, then just like that he disappeared, as if vapor, so fast that I couldn't even define what he'd looked like before he'd gone. Was he wavery and watercolored like a sitcom dream sequence? Solid like a person? Vague like my imagination? Transparent like a ghost? Had I even seen anything at all? Or just *sensed* him—real or imagined—and extrapolated that out to some crazy image?

What was I supposed to do with this? I was sure I'd seen something, whatever the qualities, but it was impossible, and one look proved it. There was nothing there. Of *course* there was nothing there.

But I couldn't have convinced Dolly of that. She was staring intently right where I'd . . . seen it? Felt it? Sensed it?

I reached out carefully, feeling the air in the space, absolutely certain it would be ice-cold. Or that maybe I'd even bump my hand into something, some form that was there but that I couldn't see. If the guys from *Ghost Hunters* were here, they'd have all kinds of equipment to measure temperature, magnetic charges and changes, voices that couldn't be heard by the human ear, maybe even images I could no longer see but were somehow there still.

Slowly, slowly, I moved my fingers, holding my breath. I wasn't sure what I was hoping for. "Ben . . . ?" I asked.

Even if there was something there—which I was sure there was not, but if there was something there—it could very well have been someone other than Ben, but naturally my mind went directly to him and stayed there.

This was nonsense. The crazy thoughts of a woman with an empty stomach and a tired mind.

So, like a woman with an empty stomach and a tired mind, I asked, "Is someone here?" I listened intently.

My phone rang, and I screamed. Straight-up screamed. It was embarrassing, though that was stupid, because I was the only one here. I fumbled for it with shaking hands, hoping to see Jamie's name. Instead I saw it was my friend Kristin calling.

"Holy *shit*, you scared me!" was my salutation.

Pause. "I scared you?"

I took a shuddering breath and nodded, even though she couldn't see me.

"Do you want me to call back and try to ring more quietly?" she asked, and I could picture the wry twitch of her lips as she said it.

"I'd appreciate the consideration," I said, and gave a halfhearted laugh. How could I possibly explain what had just happened?

"I don't mean to seem dense, but I feel like I missed the bottom step here. What the hell is going on?"

I thought about telling her, pictured myself saying, *I just saw Ben*, but those words would not come to me. She'd have me committed—if she could—in no time flat. "Nothing. I'm just easily spooked today, for some reason."

"Are you at the beach house?"

"Yeah, I got here a little while ago."

"Why do you sound like this?"

"I don't know, it's just been . . . weird."

"Oh, no. Why?"

After too long of a hesitation, I told her about my day and what I thought I'd seen, and when I was done it all sounded like nothing. Imagination or wishful thinking combined with low blood sugar and a dash of depression. Definitely not scream-worthy, but the thing was, it was more about *feeling* than about any actual events, and, whatever had happened, I couldn't change my feelings about it.

"I know," I said before she could speak again. "I imagined I saw something and totally freaked out when my phone rang. Next thing you know,

I'm going to be afraid of toilet paper or something, screaming in the bathroom like a lunatic."

She laughed. "Hopefully it won't go that far. Look, it's normal for you to be having a tough time with this. You are so full of emotions right now that you probably almost *have* to reassign them to other things, because to hold all that in your heart would be just . . . too heavy." Her answer surprised me, as I had thought she'd think I was just plain nuts.

I wanted to cry. That's how it was these days. I was so quick to cry. And at a kindness more than anything else. I cried once at Target when the cashier didn't charge me five cents apiece for the two bags she'd used (a county surcharge). Truth was, I think she just didn't enter it on time, but I was still so touched by what I took as a small kindness that I found myself tearing up.

Now my friend's support, which I had always had and taken for granted, was hitting me in the heart.

"Thank you," I managed.

"Oh, honey, are you crying?"

I nodded again, speechless.

"You're nodding, aren't you?" Her voice was tender. She knew me so well. I could see her *I Love Lucy* red hair bouncing as she nodded back in a futile effort to try and communicate with me over the phone line.

I gave a laugh through my sniffles. "Yes," I squeaked. "I'm sorry I'm such a basket case."

"Are you kidding?" she asked with genuine incredulity. "Who on earth wouldn't be? You shouldn't be there alone. I knew that the moment you said you were going, but I just couldn't get away."

"It's not your job to babysit me. I'll be fine. I guess the initial period is just bound to be tough. And I *am* tired. That's contributing, for sure."

"Maybe." She didn't sound so sure.

"I'm *fine*, Kristin. No one ever died from feeling a little off."

"Not that we know of!"

I laughed. "Touché."

"So I thought I'd come down this weekend," she said, all business now. I'd noticed she always tried to let me off the hook for my tears. If I wanted to talk, she was there, but she always did some verbal gymnastics to let me move past it. "Is that okay? I can come sooner if you want. Maybe pick up Jamie and force his ass down there . . . ?"

Today was Monday. Kristin was a teacher at my school, so she also had the summer off, but her husband, Phillip, worked constantly and she didn't like to leave her teenage daughter, Kelsey, alone too much. Not that Kelsey wasn't a really good girl—she *was*, apart from her junk-food addiction—but Kristin wasn't comfortable leaving her on her own for too long, and Kelsey had a summer school class to finish before she could get away and hopefully come to the beach.

So what was I going to do? Say yes? *I need you to come watch* Fixer Upper *with me?* I mean, yeah, that would have been great, but Dolly and I could watch HGTV by ourselves.

"No, no," I said, my voice more insistent than I felt. "Honestly, I'm fine. You know me. This was just a glitch."

"Okay." She sounded relieved now. "But I'm going to be checking in on you regularly."

"Fine. Oh! Shit!"

"What?"

"Sorry, I just remembered I didn't turn the water on. I won't have hot water for hours. Got to run." And it was true, I *had* forgotten to turn the water on and that *did* mean it would take some time for it to heat up, but even truer was the fact that I was actually kind of panicked at the idea of hanging up the phone with her, so I had to force myself to do it before I became a whiny little baby and asked her to come early after all. That would have been shameful.

We hung up and I looked at the phone for a moment, considering calling her back. Then I reassured myself that I could call her back if I needed to at any point, so I got up, went to the utility room, turned the crank for the water, and then moved the setting on the hot-water heater from vacation to normal.

That done, I looked around the small room to see if anything else needed to be taken care of. Everything looked in order, so I went back out to the kitchen. It was time to get started, spit-spot, like Mary Poppins. There was no reason to wait or hesitate, no reason to dread the inevitable, I just had to do it.

I began by opening the dishwasher, bracing myself for what I was sure would be a bunch of Ben's used dishes staring me in the face. But there was nothing. Well, almost nothing. One lone coffee mug sat in the back of the top rack, rinsed and clean-looking. I breathed a big sigh of relief. For once Ben had emptied the dishwasher. I almost made a mental note to thank him, but then remembered, for the ten millionth time, that he was gone.

Nothing to put in, nothing to take out, so I closed the dishwasher and checked the sink. It was also clean. Not even so much as a spoon was there. The toaster was empty and crumb-free, the coffee machine was spotless, and the microwave had been broken for ages, so I knew it was empty.

It's funny, but I think I felt a little bit deflated at the impersonal sanitaryness of it all. I'd been hoping, and saying I hoped, that there would be no eerie vestiges of his life's interruption remaining, but now I wondered if I had been just contending that the way a mother says she hopes her toddler doesn't miss her when she drops him off at nursery school for the first time. It's all well and good to make the case for everything going smoothly, but there's also a case for being needed.

In some crazy way, Ben's having left the place clean felt, even more, like he didn't need me. It wasn't just that he'd managed to *die* without me, that he'd gone on to some great beyond and hadn't even bothered to say goodbye (much less wait for me), but he didn't even need me to clean his cereal bowl after he'd gone.

Silly. If he'd gone home alive and I'd come here alone and found his cereal bowl and other dishes waiting for my attention, I would have been pissed. Now I was almost unspeakably sad.

There was no pleasing me.

I went to the hall linen closet, took out some flowered Laura Ashley sheets, sniffed them to make sure they smelled clean, and went into the bedroom to make the bed.

That was where I'd found my mess. The bed was unmade, the sheets rumpled and strewn off. The pillows were in place, but the rest of it looked like a struggle had taken place. Of course, it always looked like that after Ben had slept. But the last time he'd slept *here* he'd also died here, so it was disturbing to see it and imagine the scenario. This was ridiculous. I had no patience for my meandering melancholy anymore. I went straight to the bed, ripped the sheets off, threw them on the floor, and set about putting the new ones on. I didn't allow myself the luxury of stopping or sitting on the bed and crying, trying to feel his presence or whatever essence he might have left here as his last; I just pushed forward and made the bed.

Then I picked up those dirty sheets and marched right back into the utility room and opened the washer. There was a pair of his underpants in there, a couple of T-shirts, and some shorts. I hesitated, braced my hand against the washer, and had a little war with myself over whether or not I should take the things out and examine them.

I felt some weird reverence, as if they were holy things, having been near him when he died. But it wasn't like I'd found the Shroud of Turin; he hadn't been *wearing* these things, for heaven's sake! I actually knew what he'd been wearing because, as I learned, that's one of the first lines of an autopsy report: what the subject was wearing. Apparently it helps define mood or intention. All it did for me was make me feel even sadder, because I could picture him so completely.

"No," I said firmly to myself, right out loud. "You don't need to do this. There is no benefit. Only sadness. Don't. Do. It." I threw the sheets in on top of the clothes and went to toss some Tide pods in and start it, but I stopped.

I wasn't ready for that quite yet. I could walk out of the room, but I couldn't commit to washing all the stardust and scent away.

Not yet.

I flipped the light switch off and went back out, feeling accomplished. This was a little bit of progress. No, it hadn't been complete resistance, but at least I'd moved on and didn't get totally hung up on the sadness of it all.

For the rest of the afternoon and evening, I emptied out the rest of the things from the car, made a grocery list, put linens in the closet, and put my suitcase in the bedroom I never thought I'd be able to face again . . . Dolly half followed me, but she did seem disturbed. Then again, it was ocean air, and she wasn't used to that. She'd run some on the beach. Back in the old days when Ben used to take her on his morning runs, she'd often limp for a few days afterward because the sandy terrain was different for her, she wasn't used to it. Maybe her behavior now was just a variation of that.

I decided not to put too much thought into it. This was the new me: I was going to stop overthinking, worrying, fretting, and wringing my hands over every little thing. Particularly since, as life had shown me, I had virtually no control over anything anyway. What a waste of energy it was to try.

So I finished straightening the house and went to the bedroom to go to bed. It was a little daunting, I'll admit. But, again, this was something I'd done thousands of times. It was not a big deal.

At least not until I saw him again. When he walked right through the damn room in front of me.

Chapter Seven

Jamie

After fulfilling the duties of mollifying Roxy and finishing his essay, Jamie went downstairs to demolish the rest of the rotisserie chicken in the fridge and sneak a beer or two from the basement fridge. He could throw on some mindless TV and pass out on the couch instead of his bed. Last night he'd been up until it was bright out dealing with Roxy's shit. Tonight he could just do *nothing*.

He left his phone in his room, just in case Roxy decided to call again. He knew he could only ignore a few calls before giving in, if only to stop the incessant ringing. The texts were easier to not respond to; he could gauge her Crazy Levels, but they were harder to resist reading.

The fridge was always stocked with wine and beer, always had been. His parents always socialized, and his mom still did now that his dad was gone. Less. She did it less. But she was always prepared in case someone stopped by. She had a lot of friends and they always seemed to talk over drinks.

He felt sure she knew he siphoned off a couple of bottles here and there.

He had this feeling because beers were always in there and stocked, and they were always IPAs, which he tried to like, but which he still kind of hated. Seemed sort of on purpose to him. *Sure, you can take some beers, but you're not going to like them.* She always seemed tired, and this was one of the biggest manifestations of it: she didn't argue about him stealing beers, didn't correct him or punish him, just tried, in this small passive-aggressive way, to make it unpleasant for him.

That was her "handling things" these days.

He *kind of* missed the days when she'd ground him or yell or in some other way look alive. It was almost as if, when his father died, he'd lost his mother too.

He cracked open a Flying Dog Raging Bitch. It was hoppy, strong, and bitter. But it would work.

It's Always Sunny in Philadelphia was on marathon, so he watched a few episodes and stripped the bird down to the bone, eating like Henry VIII himself. At some point he fell asleep. Content, slightly buzzed, and happily deluding himself that the Roxy drama was actually over.

If he were in a band, *The Roxy Drama* could be the name of an entire album—he had enough material. Just like Adele's breakup breakout songs. All he was missing was the band, the musical talent, and interest in making an album.

The moment he fell asleep, it seemed, he awoke to the jarring cacophony of a relentlessly ringing doorbell.

Over and over it went. The bell didn't even make its way from ding to dong once before being rung maybe fifteen times.

Jamie shot up and bolted to the door.

"Jesus *Christ*," he said, whipping open the door to find her there. Of course it was her. "What the hell, Roxy?"

"I called you." Black tears ran down her face and her chest rose and fell like she'd run a mile at Olympic speed. Her hair, at this moment, was a dirty green streak. He knew it would be different in a couple of days . . . it always was. "I called you about *a thousand freaking times* and you *ignored me!*"

He touched her arm and tried to make his voice soothing. "Lower your voice, Roxy, seriously—"

She had that look in her eyes like she wasn't sure yet if she was hopeful at his patient tone or going to pretend to be angry that he'd touched her like that. She could turn that into jail time if she got mad enough.

He stepped outside into the darkness, essentially moving her and the conversation out of his realm, and shut the door behind him quietly.

"You can't pull this shit again," he said in a harsh whisper. "This is total bullshit and you know it."

She glared at him. "Fine. I won't come to you when I need you. God, you are *such* a selfish pig. Of course, you're the best I can do. If I wasn't so fucking miserable right now, I could probably get a real boyfriend."

"Is that supposed to make me, what, jealous? Insecure?"

She thought for a second and then her chin started to quiver. "I wish I didn't love you so damn much." She ran a hand through her long hair. He knew it smelled like cigarettes and her perfume. He used to hate that combination, but now it just smelled like Roxy.

He got her to sit down. He said the same things he always did. She cried. She apologized. She acted real, like the person he always considered was the Real Roxy. He saw what a product of her circumstances she was. He wished she was strong enough to grow beyond them. He listened to the voice that told him he could help make her stronger.

They went inside. She kissed him, her cheeks damp from tears still, her kiss desperate, her grip hard on his arm. They fell asleep in his room, her before him. Her breaths went steady and calm with her unconsciousness. Right before he fell asleep with her, he remembered he never sent the essay in for his online class.

Too tired to move, and not wanting to wake her and experience more wrath, he rationalized that he'd take the late grade instead. He could afford the C.

The dichotomy between Roxy and his mom was probably no coincidence. A psychologist would have a field day with it. His mother had grown detached, let him do basically what he wanted, and his girlfriend was a helicopter, watching his every move.

He couldn't win, between them.

Finally, he slept and stayed that way.

Chapter Eight

Willa

I stood still. I couldn't even run after him and talk to him, I was just rooted to the spot. This was impossible. I mean, of *course* it was impossible.

The mistake I made was in blinking. Because that's how long it took for him to disappear. If he'd ever been there at all, that is. Which of course he could not have been. Most of me knew that, but it sure looked like he'd been standing there.

It *felt* like he'd been standing there. As in, it felt like his energy had been there. Not like I'd *wished* him there, or remembered him there, or anything like that. It's hard to describe, but it left me with a certainty that he was still around.

This, I thought, must be what crazy felt like. Or maybe it was just longing. At one point does someone's longing get so intense, so overwhelming, that they actually lose their sanity? Was that what was happening to me now?

Of course I knew it sounded crazy and that it would have sounded crazy to anyone. And who would that *anyone* be? The police? What could they do? What could anyone do?

Who do you call when you're being haunted?

On top of which, I was *not* being haunted. I'd only seen him for a moment. Admittedly the moment seemed to stretch on and on as he walked right out the bedroom door and turned the corner. This was imagination, the thing I'd expected to see, on some level, and so I did.

So who do you call when you're going crazy?

I remembered that old song we used to laugh about as kids, *They're coming to take me away . . . to the funny farm . . .* It didn't seem so funny now.

Well, then, I simply wasn't going to let this make me crazy.

Apparently life was going to take over and give me some solid practical stuff to worry about. I went to the family room and picked up my laptop to contact the Realtor. She'd suggested we do an assessment of the place when I first got here, but it was past nine-thirty and my mother had always told me not to phone anyone past nine-thirty P.M. Old habits die hard, so I bypassed the phone and emailed the Realtor, letting her know I was in town and eager to get moving on the sale.

To my surprise, she answered right away, offering to come first thing in the morning. That worked for me, and I told her so. We arranged for her to come at eight-thirty A.M.

Only a few hours, I told myself, though it was longer than just a "few," technically. But it was going to be hard to stay in the house alone, so I needed to keep looking forward. Keep ticking off the boxes, getting things done, until it was all finished and I could move on.

I went to bed uneasily, spending most of the time awake, staring out the window, which I'd left open because somehow it felt easier to escape if the house felt open.

Escape. That wasn't a feeling I'd anticipated having.

Finally I must have fallen asleep, although when my phone alarm went off at eight in the morning I didn't feel any more rested than when I'd gotten into bed.

I was cleaning up the kitchen when there was a knock at the front door. I glanced at the clock—she was right on time.

My heart deflated. Somehow I guess I'd hoped she'd be late, or wouldn't show at all. Something to give me an excuse to put off this meeting. It was going to be the single hardest thing I'd ever done.

With no choice but to soldier on, I went to the door.

She was older, somewhat heavy, with her brunette hair styled into a 'do she'd probably had since high school in the eighties. Still, I liked the kindness in her eyes and invited her in.

"I'm Sue Branford," she said, her voice the entire brass section of a small band. She extended her hand. "Thank you for putting your trust in me, I hope we can get this place sold quickly and for a profit beyond your wildest dreams."

It sounded like a line. I guess she introduced herself to everyone like that. I imagined her at a Christmas party. *I'm Sue Branford. Thank you for resting your gaze on me. I hope we can get out of here quickly and after having more fun than we'd imagined in our wildest dreams.*

"Come on in, Sue." I led her to the sofa.

She followed, sat where I indicated, then took a clipboard out of her distressed leather messenger bag. "Now. Tell me about the place. How many bedrooms?"

And for the next half hour she asked questions about the layout, the history, and my projected sale price. When I told her that, she smiled like she had a secret.

"Oh, I think we can do much better than that." She pressed her lips together, her cheeks growing merry and red and her eyes alight. "*Much* better."

Her words should have thrilled me, but instead I felt dread course through my chest. Why? This was good news.

"Great," I forced myself to say, and tried to force myself to believe. "That's just great."

"Now, can I take a look around?" she asked.

"Of course!" I gave a sweep of my arm. "Right this way." We started to walk toward the kitchen, and that's when I saw it.

She saw it too. "Oh, dear."

"What is that?" I went over to the corner and looked up at a large stain on the ceiling and running down the wall. "That wasn't here last night."

"Pipes are leaking," she said, and made a quick note on her clipboard before adding, "You'd better turn off the water main quickly."

Shit! Shit shit shit shit shit!

"Did you just turn the water on for the first time in a while?" Sue asked me.

I nodded. "Last night."

She gave a shrug. "It happens. I've got a guy who can come out and take a look at it, if you'd like me to give him a call?"

"Yes, that would be wonderful," I said gratefully, and this time I meant it wholeheartedly.

She did a few clicks on her phone and then explained the situation to the person on the other end of the line. "Terrific, Dave. Thanks a million!" She clicked off and looked at me, satisfied. "He's working on a job now, but he'll come by afterward, maybe forty-five minutes?"

It wasn't like I had any pressing plans. "Perfect." I glanced back at the water stain and wondered if it was my imagination that it looked kind of like the outline of a man. The thought made me shudder.

"Shall we finish the tour?" Sue asked.

The leak was so upsetting to me that I couldn't imagine how she could look at the rest of the house objectively, but if she was ready to, far be it from me to object.

Fortunately there were no more catastrophes awaiting in the other rooms—a fact for which I thankfully knocked wood—and then we returned to the front room to discuss her to-do list.

It was extensive.

"You're going to need to paint the whole thing, of course."

Of course? I'd thought it looked good. "Are there rooms in particular you think need it?"

"Yes. All of them. People *love* the smell of fresh paint! It's like that new-car smell they put in used cars. Makes the buyer feel like they're getting a deal."

I wondered if there was some sort of Lysol Fresh Paint Scent I could spray around, but I could already tell it wouldn't fool Sue.

"Plus it needs to be lightened up. These sage greens and gold beiges might be fine for *living* in, but for selling they're just too *specific*."

"Oh."

"No offense, of course," she said, only then introducing the idea that maybe I *should* be offended. "People want to imagine their *own* lives in a new place, not yours."

Who could blame them? "Well, that's fine, I'm not that eager for people to imagine my life." Talk about *specific*. "That reminds me of something, though."

Sue looked up from making notes and raised her eyebrow. "Do we need to go back to the disclosures?" She started riffling through her papers.

"No, no," I said, and she stopped. "At least, I don't *think* so."

She started again.

"My question is this. My husband . . . well, unfortunately, my husband passed away here. Three years ago. He was . . ." This was all coming out so clumsily. "Well, he was the last one here before I got here yesterday. Is that the kind of thing that needs to be disclosed?"

"I am sorry for your loss," Sue said, returning her stack of papers to rights. "But no, that's not a material factor in selling. At least not in Maryland."

"Oh, okay." I let out a breath I hadn't realized I was holding. "Good." But not good for the reasons she would have thought—not good in the way she undoubtedly thought. I wasn't relieved that I didn't have to deliver such "ugly" news to each and every prospective buyer; it was more that I wanted to keep it private and let Ben's end be its own thing and not just some weird fact that freaked strangers out.

"Now, if you had a ghost . . ."

I stiffened. "Then what?"

She looked startled, and I realized my question must have been sharper than I'd realized. "Do you have a ghost?" she asked, her voice taking on the lilt of one about to disclose excellent gossip.

But she wasn't going to disclose anything; she wanted *me* to, she wanted a good story, and all I could give her was pretty convincing evidence that I was a crazy person, so I decided not to say anything. "No ghost," I said, spreading my arms wide and forcing a little laugh. "Just everything you see."

She looked slightly disappointed but returned right back to work. "Which brings us to the furniture."

"What about it?"

"There's too much of it."

"Too much *furniture?*" I looked around. It looked like a normal sitting room to me.

"Not for daily life," she hastened to correct. "Just for showing. The place would seem much bigger with less in it."

"I see."

"That piece, for example." She pointed to a weird little cabinet by the front door. We'd never known what to call it, so Ben and I had taken to referring to it as *Burt*. As in, *"Where are the playing cards?" "In Burt, behind the tapers."* "You don't need that here," she went on. "It interrupts the energy flow."

"Okay." I wondered how much a storage unit would cost.

"And the love seat. No need for that *and* the sofa. The sofa gives sufficient seating."

"Anything else?"

"Oh, my, yes, I'm afraid you'll have to weed out every room if you want to give the place an open, spacious feel." She eyed me. "And you *do*, believe me. A big place like this right on the beach could go for quite a pretty penny."

And a pretty penny would be nice, I had to concede. I made enough to support us, and had a decent amount invested from the insurance, but with a kid about to go off to college, it would certainly be nice to have a big cushion to pay for incidentals.

There were *always* incidentals.

Sue went on with her list of things that needed to be done. Windows cleaned ("and then we'll see if we need to replace them"), whole house power washed ("it's almost cheaper to buy a power washer than to hire someone to do it for you"), floors waxed ("though sanded and refinished would be better"), garden spruced up ("you cannot underestimate the value of curb appeal, both front *and* back"), and a list of about twenty other things, both large and small, that needed to be done before we could put it on the market.

She was confident about it selling, which begged the question of why not just put it on the market "as is" and let the buyers battle it out, but Sue seemed to think that the difference in price would be significant if I just "put a little elbow grease into it."

And, truth be told, I could use some hard physical labor and a feeling of accomplishment at the end of the day. I wasn't fooling myself that this would be fun, exactly, but I did think it would be rewarding.

But one thing I knew for sure: I was going to need help.

Chapter Nine

Willa

The plumber showed up about half an hour after Sue left.

He looked just like I expected: medium height, medium-brown hair, middle-aged, with skin that showed he probably didn't believe in sunscreen. I couldn't tell what color his eyes were because he was wearing those adjustable sunglasses I hate and they were a 1970s yellow on him as he stepped through the doorway.

"I'm Dave. Where's the leak?" he asked briskly.

"I think it might be in the upstairs sink pipe," I said, a bit proud of myself for having done the math on this and figured it out.

"What room?" he asked.

"Oh." He didn't care what my assessment was. "Over here." I led him to the corner of the living room from the direction of the kitchen. "See? It's spread even since this morning when we called."

"You need mitigation, after I've found and fixed the leak," he announced.

Mitigation? Wasn't that a legal term? I wasn't in some sort of trouble, was I? "What do you mean, *mitigation?*"

"Got to pull down the drywall and put a fan in to dry it out before we can repair it."

"Take out the drywall?" Suddenly this sounded way more expensive than anything I'd anticipated. "Won't it just dry?"

He shook his head. "Ruined." He took out a telescopic metal stick and poked it at the ceiling. I saw dents behind where he'd touched it. "We'll probably need to replace the whole ceiling," he said, and I think we both heard the *cha-ching* of cash registers in our heads.

"There's no way to patch it?"

He shrugged. "I'll check it out. Where are the stairs?'"

"This way." I led him around the corner to the steps and started up. "Like I said, I think it started in the bathroom, because that's directly over that part of the living room. I think."

"Mm-hmm." He clunked along up the stairs behind me.

I turned the corner and stepped back, indicating the bathroom. "So. There."

"Okay." He went in and started tinkering with the pipes behind the sink. After a moment, he looked at me. "You don't need to wait here."

"Oh! Oh, I'm sorry. Right. I'll just go downstairs and . . . work. On some things. Work on some things. You can give a shout if you need anything. My name's Willa." I was yammering helplessly. "Do you want a water or coffee or beer or something?" Oh, sure, the guy was going to ask for a beer while he was on the job. It was probably insulting even to offer.

But for the first time he actually gave a hint of a smile. It made him look nicer, and my shoulders relaxed fractionally. "I'll be fine here," he said. "You don't need to offer me anything. Lady, you're like a cat on a hot tin roof. No need to be so nervous."

"I'm sorry." Why was I apologizing to this guy? Because that's the kind of person I am. If you tell me I apologize too much, I will apologize for apologizing too much. It's a vicious cycle. "You just go ahead and let me know if you need . . . me to see anything or sign or whatever."

He gave a nod and turned his attention back to the sink.

I was ridiculous. Honestly, sometimes it was terribly embarrassing being me.

Going down the stairs, I tried an old self-hypnosis trick of feeling more confident and relaxed with every step down. It kind of worked too, until I heard a bang and an expletive coming from upstairs. "Everything all right?" I asked automatically.

"Fine."

Dubiously I returned to the kitchen, where all of my supplies were. Where to start? I guessed I should begin by cleaning up. Everything needed a clean surface before beginning, didn't it? Even life needed a clean slate to start again. I'd look at this exercise as beginning my life over.

It turned out it was less of a philosophical meditation and more of a painkiller commercial. The sink, counter, stovetop, all of that was easy to do, but it was a lot harder to get inside the cabinets and under the stove, and so on. I bonked my elbows, knees, and my head half a dozen times. Yet it felt strangely good to be putting elbow grease into a job, to work hard and see results.

I heard Dave the Plumber walking around up and down the stairs, in and out of the house, into the laundry room where the water main was, but I squelched the urge to ask if I could help. He'd made it clear he didn't need my help, and what could I do anyway? Besides, I didn't *want* to help. I was pretty tied up myself.

It was when I had my head under the kitchen sink, hitting the reset button on the disposal, that I heard the voice.

"I think we're going to need a new dishwasher. This one's about a hundred years old."

"What?" I asked, trying to back out gracefully but pulling off more of a Winnie-the-Pooh-stuck-in-the-tree sort of move. "How can I need a new dishwasher? I haven't even run this one yet!"

There was no one there.

"Hello?"

No answer. I got up and walked around the wall and into the hallway with the laundry room, where I ran smack into Dave the Plumber. "There you are. Why do I need a new dishwasher?"

He ran his hand across his forehead and through his hair before looking at me wearily. "Is this a quiz?"

"What do you mean? You just said I needed a new dishwasher."

"Lady, I haven't even *seen* you for half an hour, I definitely haven't been chatting with you about your appliances. Are you saying it's broken and you need me to take a look?"

"No, it's *not* broken, that's exactly my point."

"You're telling me that your dishwasher is not broken?"

"That's right." I could hear it myself, I was starting to sound like a mental patient.

He shook his head. "Is there anything else you'd like to tell me about before I get back to work?"

Panic gripped my chest. *Was* I losing my mind? "Sorry, no. It's just . . . I thought I heard a voice when I was working in the kitchen. Saying—"

"That you need to get a new dishwasher."

I sighed. "Yes."

"You'd better look into that, then."

I looked at him. "It was a really long night."

He smiled, barely. He may be an ornery guy, a curmudgeon even, but he was nothing if not grounded, and that was what I needed around right now.

"Maybe get yourself a glass of water. Or something stronger. Unless . . . ?"

"No, I haven't been drinking this morning," I said in answer to his unasked question.

He shrugged. "No sin in it. Just might make you hear things."

I can do that all by myself. "I'll get back to work now."

"Me too."

He clomped off back upstairs, and I stood there for a moment glued to the spot, trying to figure out what the hell had happened and what the hell I was going to do about it. When I heard him clanking on pipes, I found the sound reassuring. It was nice to have a man around the house, even if it was a hired crabby plumber.

I found myself thinking that should be the name of his business. *The Crabby Plumber.* Described him and yet had a lovely ring of beachy whimsy. I chuckled to myself at the thought and returned to the kitchen.

The dishwasher sat there, gleaming stainless steal, conspicuously begging attention. I opened it, as I had earlier, and everything *looked* normal. I closed it back up. I'd run it when the water was back on.

It was probably fifteen or twenty minutes later that it hit me. The new dishwasher. We'd gotten it when we first bought the place. We'd been pretty cash poor then and had hoped to make do with most of the appliances and plumbing as they were, planning to replace them one by one as money allowed. But the dishwasher had leaked the minute we'd started it.

All these years later it was hard to remember exactly *what* Ben had said, but I know he said we needed a new dishwasher. I was Mary Sunshine, trying to make everything seem better than it was so he wouldn't change his mind and think we'd made a mistake in buying this place I'd so desperately wanted.

It was just like him to say we needed a new one because this one was a hundred years old. In fact . . . I tried to rewind the morning . . . had that been Ben's voice I'd heard saying it? In this wildly inconsistent nonsense world I'd found myself in, that would make more sense than the plumber walking through and saying random things like that, then hiding and denying he'd said anything.

One thing was sure: I knew I'd heard it.

Dave worked until early afternoon, cutting out the ceiling, taking a huge fan off of his truck and directing it toward the dampness, and making noise about *water mitigation*, which was apparently the process of fixing the damage caused by a flood.

He said there had been several leaks in the pipes upstairs and that it looked like they had frozen at some point during some winter because no one had emptied the faucets when winterizing the house. That was true, it hadn't even occurred to me. When Ben had died, I knew to make sure the house was locked and secured and that everything was turned off, but the whole process of draining the pipes had eluded me. There would probably be an unpleasant surprise when I went to turn on the hose bibs outside as well. I remembered Ben being fastidious about that.

"I'm going to have to run out and do another job I committed to," Dave said. "Plus get a few parts, but I can come back tomorrow, if that's okay with you."

"Yes! Absolutely! Anything to get the water back on." Tomorrow suddenly seemed very far away.

He gave a salute and turned to leave.

"Mr. Macmillan?"

He stopped and turned around.

"About earlier, the whole dishwasher thing?" What was I going to say? How was I going to follow up with this? Why on earth had I even brought it up?

He looked at me expectantly. "What about it?"

I floundered. "Well, it looks like the dishwasher is working fine, so I won't need you to look at it after all." Lame lame lame. I had tried to *mitigate* my seeming insanity by increasing it.

He gave a slow nod. "Good." Then, without further examination of me or the conversation, he turned and left.

"Good," I echoed in his wake. "I've made a hell of an impression. I'm probably going to be charged extra for having an unsound mind and subjecting the poor man to it." I realized I was speaking out loud, but I didn't care. "Damn it, Ben, why did you have to do this to me?"

It would have been easy to just collapse into a self-pitying heap of grievances, but I'd done enough of that since I'd gotten here. That wasn't why I'd come. I'd come to do a job and that's what I was going to do.

But I couldn't do it alone. I called Jamie's number, and this time he answered.

And I was relieved to hear his voice, I really was. Part of me felt so tender toward him, so happy that he was safe, and so eager to see him and try—again—to have a fun time together, to heal our relationship and make it what it had once been and what it undoubtedly still would have been if Ben hadn't died.

The tenderness wasn't what came out, though. Instead, I felt a hot stream of angry air fill me and I let him have it, leaving no clue whatsoever of the love I felt for him or the need I had to be with him and have his help and support.

Instead I was just a screaming meemie, and I absolutely hated myself for it.

"Jamie, good god, how many times are you capable of ignoring your own mother?"

Chapter Ten

Jamie

Roxy was gone when he woke up. Probably off to the mall to talk to her friends. She'd sip an Orange Julius and recall her meltdown in a totally different way than it went down. The way her friends glared at him after nights like this, the way she did too when she was around them, always told him that somehow he'd come out as the bad guy, regardless of the truth.

Let's see, how would she recall the night before through her own little magic filter?

All she'd need to say was that he tried to break up with her while she was *going through all this*. Whatever *all this* was at the time. She was always going through something, and a lot of it *was* really bad. But some of it was just bullshit. Exaggerations, just like she made about him. Sometimes he wondered if the whole thing was fabrication.

He'd met her dad—he was friendly and kind of quiet. Not in a brooding way, more in a shy way. Jamie had to give her story the benefit of the doubt, though, he got that he couldn't truly know, and he'd feel like a real

jerk if he said, *He seems like a perfectly nice guy!* and then she turned up
with a black eye from him someday.

He rolled over and finally sent in his essay. Within half an hour he'd
gotten a disappointed email back from his teacher. She told him to ask
himself why he made his own life harder by not doing the easy things—
the essay was easy for him and she knew that; pressing send on time was
also easy.

He didn't answer, and he had a feeling she'd be a little harsher with
the grading of this one out of sheer principle.

He got his room together and then headed downstairs.

His phone rang.

Again. His phone rang again. It had been alive with the buzz of his
mom's calls and Roxy's on and off all morning. He should have just put it
on silent, but instead he'd thrown it into a pile of dirty laundry so he could
sleep a little longer.

Roxy would eventually just show up, but for now she probably believed
he was still sleeping, so he could still wait a bit on that. His mom, though,
was just going to keep calling.

He pulled turkey, cheese, mayonnaise (his mom had gotten him the
chipotle-seasoned kind—he hadn't even told her he liked it, she just noticed he ate more sandwiches when that's what she picked up), and Wick-
les Pickles from the fridge. The bread was almost gone. He'd have to grab
some from the store.

The phone buzzed again. Mom.

He shut his eyes and put his head back before returning to making his
sandwich and ignoring her again.

It felt shitty ignoring her like this, especially after what had happened
to his dad. He could picture her alone in the beach house right this second, trying to call her son, probably knowing it would go to voice mail

again. She was pissed or she was sad. There was no chance she was calling because it was so much *fun* going through the house.

But he also knew she was calling because she wanted him to come help.
The second he pictured doing that he shut down. He was a pretty calm,
level person. But certain things sent his anxiety crunching right up and
down his spine. Pretty much anything to do with his dad or spending a
lot of time alone with his mom was cringe-inducing.

If he answered, she'd ask him to come, he'd say no, and she'd either
rally and say she understood or she would give him crap for it. Either way,
he'd hear it in her voice—that need, that desperation. He'd feel guilty
either way. Unless he actually said okay and went.

He couldn't even picture the house as it must look now. Empty and
quiet, dusty, and half packed. Memories hanging in the air like spiderwebs,
sticky, frustrating, complicated, and dying to wrap themselves around his
skull.

He could feel the thin strings on him right now.

Plus his mom was bound to start crying at some point. He wasn't an
unfeeling jerk—his whole life he'd been able to pat her on the back and
say the right things to make her feel better when something struck her
this way. He wasn't fooled by her smiles after his dad died. There was an
unbearable heaviness to her sadness and he couldn't always take it. He
wanted to escape it and pretend it didn't exist. But most of the time he'd
straighten up and do his best, knowing it was what his dad would have
wanted. And knowing, frankly, that it was what he was *supposed* to do.

But he couldn't do it with this. He felt like a prick, but he couldn't be
strong for her this time about his dad's death. Not this directly, with the
beach house. He couldn't muster the comfort she needed. He wasn't any
good at it in this case. Or maybe just not anymore. He didn't know yet.

If he answered, she'd also ask him if he'd just woken up, and then say,

Lord, really? and then she'd ask what he was doing. He'd say he was making a turkey sandwich, and she'd say, *For what is basically your breakfast? That's so gross. Scramble an egg for it, at least.* And then he'd ask if that was all, and the conversation would wind down, and—

Buzzzz . . .

All right, fine, he just played it out in his head. He may as well answer.

"Hey," he said.

"Jamie, good god, how many times are you capable of ignoring your own mother?"

"It looks like about ten."

She sighed. "Very amusing. Are you just waking up?"

Check. "No."

"Yes, you are."

"Maybe."

"I've been up since eight."

He wanted to say, *I wouldn't be able to sleep there either*, but he didn't want to introduce more weirdness to the situation.

Besides, she took over on her own. "This is really . . . just strange being here . . ." Her voice trailed off, and the pang of guilt started to play in his chest.

"I'm sure."

"Please . . . listen, I know we talked about me coming and doing this myself, but it turns out it's more work than I anticipated."

Here it came.

"I need you to help me," she finished. The words were strange, almost. She never admitted she couldn't handle things, even though it was patently obvious at times.

And if it was anything but that house, he'd make himself do it. "I can't. I've got schoolwork and . . . stuff."

"You're taking that class online and it's almost finished."

"Yeah." True. "But I'm doing other things too."

"What are you so busy doing right this second?"

He paused. Any point in lying? In embellishing? What could he even say that was important? "Eating a turkey sandwich."

"But you just woke up?"

"Yes."

She made a sound of distaste. "That's not breakfast."

Check.

She used to say that about his dad eating salad for breakfast too. But in that case he had to agree. Salad was never exactly great, but for breakfast? It was pretty disgusting.

"Is that all?" he asked. "You called to complain about how late I slept and my breakfast choices?"

Tension swooped into her voice. "I called because you ought to come help your mother." A beat. "And I'm complaining about your *lunch* choices, considering nothing about a turkey sandwich is breakfast."

"It's a perfectly healthy choice no matter which one it is. Beats having Skittles for breakfast *or* lunch, right?"

Another sigh. "True."

She remembered, as he did, his Skittles binge. There had been some Jolly Ranchers thrown in too, but he'd gone through a pretty long period of eating mostly candy, in between forcing down the vegetables his mom made him eat.

But he wasn't going to give her that now.

"I gotta go," he said. "Roxy is calling."

"Roxy is always calling."

He gave a half shrug that she couldn't see. "True."

"I bet she called more than I did today and she's *not* packing an entire house by herself." There was a hint of anger to her voice. "This isn't how life is supposed to be," she went on, softening. "Sleeping all day, having lunch for breakfast, and probably nothing for dinner. I . . . I haven't been on top of things enough."

He was about to try to reassure her that she had been, but that wasn't true. She hadn't. They both knew it.

In the background he heard the doorbell. It was an old one, an actual bell that you had to turn instead of press. He'd completely forgotten about that sound.

"Who's at the door?" he asked, suddenly, uncharacteristically, worried about her being alone there.

"Oh, that's just the Grotto pizza I ordered for lunch. No big deal. Why don't you get some Grotto tonight?" She hesitated, purposely, knowing it was his favorite. "Oh, wait, you *can't* because they only have that here at the beach."

She very nearly got him with that one. " 'Bye, Mom."

"Roll your eyes at Roxy for me."

"Will do."

She hung up before he did. He looked at his sandwich. Grotto really did sound good.

Why was it that all they had around here was crappy chain restaurants, but only a couple of hours away they had all that good, beachy food?

He could almost smell it now. The greasy, salty Thrasher's french fries, covered in so much malt vinegar that the tang almost hurt. The ice-cream cones from Kohr Brothers. He could distinctly remember the creamy vanilla-orange swirl dripping down his fingers, melting in the hot sun, all over his face and even sometimes dripping down his bare chest if he was "horsing around" with his friends enough. That was his dad's expression, which must have come from *his* dad, because it was unlike him to use such antiquated terms.

His hand and chest sticky. His sandy feet bare on the shady part of the boardwalk wood, his mom worried he'd get a splinter (which he often did). His hair so filled with salt that it stuck up at all ends. His mom always lamenting how much lighter his dark hair got in the summer, saying life would be cheaper for her if hers did the same. His skin got dark brown, just like his dad's, never burning, but they were always being chased down by his mom and a spray bottle of SPF 50 anyway. He was the kid who could actually look cool on a skim board (an inherently uncool thing, really, but girls always came up and wanted to try it).

That's what summers were always like at the beach. Salty. Greasy. Sticky. Hot. Damp.

Sometimes his parents' friends came too, and some of them had kids the same age as Jamie. They'd play cards in the shade, girls would work on their tans unless they wanted to flirt, and then they'd play too.

A memory came back to him now. One of the times when Kristin and Phillip, his parents' best friends, and their kid Kelsey came. She was always his favorite of the Parents' Friends' Kids, but he always claimed it was this kid Tyler. It felt weird to say he was excited to see Kelsey, especially because his mom teased him the one time he said so.

He liked her best because she wasn't like other girls. She didn't complain or whine about anything. When he and other kids on the beach got a game of Frisbee going, she would keep up. She was tall—almost taller than him, the last time he saw her—and skinny. When they raced, he had to really go all-out to keep her from beating him. Sometimes she still did. He always said he let her win. But he really didn't.

She was funny too. She bothered the parents sometimes, had a loud voice, and was prone to sugar-highs, but it was one of the things he found so hilarious back then. Plus she could eat just as many hot dogs as he could—he only barely beat her in the one-on-one hot-dog-eating contest they once put on. Then they got caught by Kristin, who said they were going to choke to death if they did that, and that if she caught them doing it again, she'd strangle them.

The irony of this had sent Kelsey into a sugar-hyper giggle fit, her face still covered in ketchup.

Considering the way she ate back then, she was probably six hundred pounds by now. And toothless, if she'd kept on with her candy addiction.

But the memory that came specifically to him now was the last time he saw her. The last time he'd even gone to the beach. It was the last night of vacation, school only a week away. Late-summer winds already ruining perfectly good card games.

They'd spent the entire day on the beach. It was a long August dog day. Phillip had the wraparound sunglasses tan he always had by the last day. Kristin's voice was raspy from laughing and telling stories for a week straight. (Kelsey got her boisterousness from her mother.) His dad was wearing one of his Hawaiian shirts for the last time of the season, the blue one. His mom was in this long gray dress Jamie knew was her favorite. He knew she only wore it when she felt really good about herself. He remembered feeling glad that she was feeling confident instead of being insecure, like she was at other times of the year. Surrounded by the people she liked best, everyone sun-painted and heat-crazy, she was happy. The blue Hawaiian shirt was also her favorite of his dad's ugly shirts.

Kelsey and Jamie were in the living room, the parents out on the porch drinking beer and playing a game. Trivial Pursuit or something. He couldn't imagine how much playing they were fitting in with all the shouting and laughing.

Kelsey and Jamie were listening to the Smiths, which Jamie was years away from realizing were an extremely depressing band, and which he was playing for her because they were one of his favorites. They were really only one of his favorite bands because his dad loved them. They were eating popcorn that they had made in their special way, covered in a gross amount of butter, salt, and melted cheese. They were playing Outburst, some ratty edition from a million years ago, so they had to skip half the rounds because they made topical references they didn't get at all.

It didn't matter, it was still fun. Mostly because even when they screwed up or she was losing, Kelsey would crack up, which always made him crack up.

It was almost midnight, and they were sent to bed in adjacent rooms

After they brushed their teeth and shut out the lights, Jamie heard Kelsey sniffling. It echoed lightly into the hall.

"Kels, are you crying?"

"No, shut up!" She took in a deep shuddering breath.

"Since when are you such a girl?"

"Now you *really* shut up!"

He did shut up.

"I'm just sad the summer's over, that's all," she went on.

"You've never cried before when it was over."

"No, I haven't!" She sniffed. "Well, maybe when I was little, once we were in the car."

It made sense a little, now that he thought of it. She was dramatic. But it was usually in funny or at least amusing ways. Her overreactions seemed almost fake—she would act like she was slapped just because the orange juice was gone.

"I don't know, this year I'm crying, that's all, stop asking me."

"Okay, fine."

"Okay, fine."

He heard her roll over in her bed and could picture her, frowning.

"I'm just . . ." Her voice was as quiet as a mouse's skittering. "I don't want this to end."

"I'm gonna miss you too, stupid," he said, the words coming from his mouth without his decision or permission.

"When did you become such a girl?" He heard the smile in her voice.

But it was never like that again.

Life was never like that again. Because that was the last time they were all there. The last time his dad wore the blue Hawaiian shirt.

And definitely the last time his mom wore that gray dress.

Chapter Eleven

Willa

I don't know how long I'd been asleep, it felt like just a few minutes, but I woke to a noise. A vaguely familiar noise that reached far back into the reserves of my memory.

Tick.

Tick.

Tick.

What *was* that?

And why did it tap into my subconscious and excite me the way it did?

Then, into the fog, the memory came. I knew what the sound was. Pebbles being thrown at my window.

Ben had done that when we'd first met and he wanted to wake me up in the middle of the night to go out and meet him. He could have walked right in the front door and come to my room, of course, but he liked the old-fashioned romance of the pebbles. Said it was like something from an old movie.

Tick.

Who would be doing it now?

What used to be a thrill was now a bit scary and I got out of bed carefully and put a loose sweatshirt over my nightshirt. Then I crept over to the window and looked out, painfully aware of what a target I must look like, moving like a parade float into the window frame for anyone out there to see.

At first I didn't see anyone. That spurred my nervousness even more than actually seeing someone. I could *not* take this vague, ethereal sort of "haunting." I was a strong, reasonable woman. Okay, maybe not always all that strong but certainly reasonable. I had good sense. I wasn't prone to imaginings.

I looked again and was relieved to see movement.

There was a kid out there. His stance reminded me of Jamie's, so I put him in his late teens. He wore jeans and some logo'd T-shirt I couldn't read.

Tick.

A pebble hit the window right in front of me. I started and stepped back reflexively. Then, slowly, I moved back to look outside. He was still there, whoever he was.

His face was shrouded in darkness. I could only see a vague outline and some small movement. I wondered if I should call the police or just put my big-girl pants on and go confront him. He was obviously a kid, not someone I should be afraid of. And the fact that he was throwing pebbles at the window kind of indicated that maybe he had the wrong house.

I settled on that explanation and was about to open the window and tell him to go away, when he bent over to pick up another stone and stepped into the light.

And when I saw his face, it took my breath away.

This time I didn't sit there in disbelief, wondering if I was losing my mind. I was feeling pretty done with that game. Instead, I got dressed quickly and ran down the stairs to the outside, certain he'd be gone, but hoping—logic be damned—that he would be there.

And he was.

"Ben!"

"Hey." He smiled. But he was looking right past me. Still, I heard his voice. He was right there.

And he was as he'd been when I had met him as a teen: wiry, muscular but thin, blue eyes bright in his tanned face. His hair looked darker than its usual deep amber, but the lights were low and distant.

"What are you doing here?" I breathed, immediately thinking it was a stupid question, but I was unable to come up with a better one. There is nothing *clever* to say when the teenage ghost of your late husband shows up. "*How* are you here?"

The ocean was the only answer, rolling and groaning in its dark place out of sight.

What was going on here?

He smiled at something beyond me. God, that smile. I'd loved it when he got older, the lines got a little deeper, the crow's-feet a little more pronounced, but it was heart-stopping when he was young. He would have aged wonderfully; he had already been on his way to George Clooney aging, but what an amazing thing to have a close-up vision again of how it had been when he was young and beautiful.

"Oh, Ben." I said it on a sigh. Damn the logic, or lack of it, it was so good to see him.

He didn't respond but seemed to be watching someone approach from behind me. When I turned to look I saw nothing.

I sensed nothing.

"I just wanted to make sure you're okay," he said, to someone else. "That wave really knocked you for a loop. We were worried about you. I still am."

I reached back into the far cavern of my memory. Yes. I remembered. That had happened a long time ago. The week I'd first met him. I'd always been nervous swimming in the ocean, so when a huge wave rose before me, it just didn't make any sense to my incorrect brain to dive into it, so I'd stood there, paralyzed with fear, as it descended directly on me, whirling me in sandy, shell-filled water like a sock in a washing machine. It even whipped the top of my bikini off, though that was the least of my concerns at the time. The entire event had been terrifying, and though I'd tried to hide it, I'd been disoriented for some time afterward.

That was something solid I could get a grip on.

His brow relaxed and I thought I heard him sigh. Breath. Voice. This was all so incredible. "I'm relieved. I just wanted to check on you. You need to rest, but I'm going to the boardwalk for something to eat. Can I bring you something?"

Yes, he could take me with him. He—or I—could wake up from this dream and we could be together.

Whatever this was, dream or imagination, I wanted to stay with him as long as possible.

"Okay," he said. "Call me if you change your mind. Rest, baby. I'll see you tomorrow."

Maybe he would see me in his tomorrow, but I was going to stay with him as long as possible now. It was hard to believe, now, that I had ever given up one moment of time that I could have spent with him. Of course, that's how life is, you can't spend every moment with someone, both of you would go mad. But now that I knew how ultimately short our time together would be, I shook a mental fist at the me who was apparently just turning and going back to bed while Ben walked the beach alone.

Only this time he wasn't alone. This time I followed him.

We walked across the sand, down toward the shore, where the water broke and made it easier to walk. I could feel the spongy texture give under my weight, the water trickle over my shoes. There was no one else around us, though, several blocks in the distance, the boardwalk was alight and more alive with activity than it should have been this time of year. Usually the big crowds didn't start until the end of June, when the ocean was more apt to be warm. A lot of things were open by this time of year but there weren't usually so many people.

Ben, thinking he was alone, sang lightly to himself. A Smiths song. He'd loved that old alt-rock so much. Even passed this love on to Jamie. I'd never realized the subtlety of voice changes in the twenty years from teenage to thirties, but I recognized the voice as young him. If this was a dream, my subconscious was *very* thorough.

I wished so much I could talk to him, this Ben who was so close to his age at our initial meeting. I'd always asked him, *What did you think when you first saw me?* Silly, romantic girl. I think I'd always wanted a romantic answer about knowing I was The One, but I'd never gotten that. He always said he didn't really remember but that he'd married me, so what else did I need?

But now I'd seen in his eyes something I hadn't recognized at the time. He'd looked at me—the me I couldn't see—with familiarity. Like he knew me so well already, even though I know now we'd been operating primarily on hormones.

When I first saw Ben I was struck by how damn cute he was, how my heart pounded when I saw him. That gleaming dark hair, light eyes with the dark fringe of lashes, a smile that lit his face up from very serious to joyful in a split second. I had reacted to him viscerally, but my feeling had been more that I *would* know him all my life, not that I already had. I felt certain that I would know that face forever.

And I would. That was true. Even when I saw pictures of him now, it wasn't like when my father had died and details of his appearance began to fade from my memory. When I saw pictures of Ben, I knew every single detail of him and I knew that I always would. Even in our early days I just *knew* he'd be in my mind for the rest of my life.

It never occurred to me that those details wouldn't keep changing with age. It never occurred to me that there might come a time when that face was gone and it was never going to see another birthday again.

A feeling of loss overwhelmed me and I chastised myself for wasting this extra time that way.

We went along a couple of minutes, with me catching up to him and trying to figure out if this was real and how it possibly could be.

There was no figuring that out. I had to just go with it. We moved closer and closer to the lights of the boardwalk.

Suddenly I could smell all the junk food in the air: buttery popcorn; Thrasher's french fries with malt vinegar; greasy funnel cakes; pizza; Boog Powell's barbecued meats; and the aroma of all the fudge and candies from Candy Kitchen drifting out on the breeze. It was a sweet, salty, savory tapestry of scents that could only have been, had always been, Ocean City.

He started to run. He'd always been a jogger; it was far easier for him to exercise than for me to. I'd gotten out of shape over the years; I hurried to catch up with him, a little breathless. The sand shushed under my steps.

But not under his.

Whatever *this* was, he was totally unaware of it.

The beach was wide by the pier, maybe twice as wide as it was anywhere else. This was the widest point, right by the end (or the beginning, rather, depending which way you're going) of the boardwalk, and we walked slowly. I relished every moment, every sensation. If he noticed that I kept looking at him, gaping at him, really, he didn't acknowledge it.

Lights were blaring, the arcade was clanking and whistling and shrieking, and it was, for all the world, like midsummer in full swing.

As I walked side by side with him up to the boards, the people ignored us completely. I didn't know what I was expecting, but I guess when you're walking with a ghost you get kind of self-conscious. But no one seemed to think a thing of us. In fact, a couple of times I had to dodge people because otherwise they would have walked right into me.

We—rather, I—clomped along the boards. Tony's Pizza was to the right, next to Love's Lemonade and near a Candy Kitchen. But he went for his favorite.

Thrasher's french fries.

We went and got in line, still side by side, though it was strangely troubling to me that he didn't seem to sense me at all. If our love was true, shouldn't it have spanned our realities?

We moved forward in line.

The wind lifted and the smell of grease and potatoes touched my nose.

I reached out and touched his face. It was a strange sensation; more solid and real than expected yet not quite warm. If this was a dream, why wasn't he warm? And if it wasn't a dream . . . well, it had to be. There was no other possibility. I could almost believe in a haunting, but not one that involved time travel as well. It was like those were two different movie genres that couldn't be mixed.

We got to the front of the line and the guy looked at me. "What can I get for you?"

I looked at Ben. He didn't say a word.

I turned back to the Thrasher's guy and thought he was looking at Ben oddly, then he turned back to me. I couldn't tell which one of us he could see—which time we were more present in—but I took a chance on it being me.

"Two," I said at first. Then quickly corrected, "I mean one." I looked at Ben again, but he didn't seem to be paying attention. He was just looking off in the distance at the sea.

"One," Ben said suddenly. "Thanks."

Of course. He couldn't see me, he couldn't see this clerk, he was or-dering for himself. But if this was not really happening, if I was following Ben into his past reality, why was the guy addressing me and not Ben?

He handed over the fries and I suddenly panicked. "Good lord, I don't have any money!" I'd jumped out of bed, pulled on some shorts with my nightshirt and run down. It was just lucky I'd managed to pull on my shoes on the way out the door.

"Uh," the Thrasher's guy said, shifting his eyes between us, and I won-dered what exactly he could see. Any sense of Ben? But there was no way to ask without sounding like a lunatic. "You can just go ahead and take them."

"Really?"

"Just—yeah, just go." It was unmistakably rude the way he said it, like he was trying to get rid of us—me—but there was a long line.

"Thank you so much."

"Yeah, yeah." His answer was clipped, and as soon as he issued it, he looked to the next person and asked, "What can I get for you?" He looked at her, then at me, then back at her like I was crazy.

I took the fries and we walked away. After a few minutes we came upon an empty bench and Ben sat down. Unsure what else to do, I set the fries down next to him. He looked off into the black that was the ocean, sud-denly very still, like an animatronic doll after giving its performance.

"This is the best night of my life," I said, shaking some vinegar from a pouch onto my fries.

He didn't answer. Of course.

"I love you," I said, and people walking past gave me odd looks. But I couldn't stop myself. I had to say it, just in case any part of him could hear me, could register it.

For a long time we sat there in strange silence, looking out over the ocean. I could feel his presence, but nothing about him indicated he could feel mine.

What really struck me was how *alone* he seemed. I was struck by that impression, but I wasn't sure why. He was a kid, I knew he was—at that time—staying in a house full of people, and he had a new girlfriend, although she hadn't felt like going out for food with him that night. He wasn't lonely.

So why was that idea worming its way around my brain so disturbingly?

Then I realized it. With shame, I realized it. I wasn't just seeing Ben. Whether this . . . this *vision* was real or my imagination or a dream, it had a purpose, and that wasn't just to torture me with a past I couldn't reconcile, it was to show me a present I wasn't paying enough attention to.

It was showing me *Jamie.*

Jamie, who had lost his beloved father so suddenly—a loss as great as mine, albeit different—and whose mother had then indulged in a career as a basket case. I—we— had brought this child into the world and we were everything he had. Now that Ben was gone, I was all Jamie had, and I had been letting him down repeatedly.

Hell, I'd even left him home alone during this really important time when we needed to work together to move forward and leave the past behind us. I knew it would be painful for him to be at the beach house again, it was painful for me as well, but it was necessary.

I had to get him here.

After a while, Ben stood up and started to walk.

I looked at my fries and realized I'd been chomping on them reflexively and I was full. This was how I tended to handle my angst—I ate it. A walk would do me good, and, let's face it, it wasn't like I was capable of *not* following him.

I dumped the remaining fries into the trash can and we turned back onto the beach, making our way to the inky blackness that was the sea. A thread of phosphorescence wound up the coast, guiding us back to the block where our house was.

We approached it and he stopped. I watched him look at the window that had been mine, then ours.

"I love you, Ben," I said to him, wishing to god it would somehow register, that he would acknowledge me at last.

But he didn't.

Instead, his color went first, then his form, leaving only a blotch of mist that could as easily have been the last remnant of a nighttime mist that had shrouded the shoreline.

"Come back, Ben." I started to cry, pointlessly. "Please don't go. Don't go again. Come back, I'll do anything if you could just come back for even one more minute." My crying grew harder.

"Willa." His voice came, far away now.

But he was gone.

I went inside and moved through the dark living room and kitchen to sit down on the sofa in the family room. The comforting family room. A soft light glowed by the fireplace, warming the room and making it feel cozy. I simply sat for a long time, staring at the dormant fireplace, not even thinking, just coming down off of the strange experience.

What had just happened?

I was crazy, that was it. I was crazy. Losing my mind. The grief had made me snap somewhere along the way and I hadn't even realized it. In fact, I would have thought I'd made the whole thing up, but I could still smell the boardwalk scents, and taste the fries and vinegar in my mouth. There was no doubt that I'd gone there, but had I gone alone or with Ben? And if it *was* with Ben, *how*?

My phone sat on the coffee table before me. Should I call Kristin? I looked at the clock. No, it was after midnight. It would be completely obnoxious to call her and tell her I was going crazy. There was nothing she could do about it tonight. There was nothing she could do about it at all.

There was nothing anyone could do.

Maybe I needed another therapist. Or church. Or a psychic. Or, I don't know, *something* bigger than myself to cling to, like driftwood, in all this rushing water of emotion. Because, as much as I hated to admit my own weakness, this was more than I could handle.

I got up and went to the kitchen counter where my purse was, then dug around through the miscellaneous coins, receipts, an old packet of tissues that had been in there forever, until finally my hand touched the pill bottle I was seeking. Xanax. My doctor had first prescribed it for me for anxiety after Ben had died, and I rarely took it—I rarely took anything—but if there was ever a time I needed it, it was now.

Once upon a time, we had all been at Disney World, in line for the Tower of Terror ride. I was not a ride person, so I was extremely apprehensive about going on a thriller, but Ben and Jamie—little at the time, maybe ten or so—had convinced me to do it. Bullied me into it, more like. And as I stood there in the endless line, telling them I didn't want to go, that I'd meet them in the gift shop at the end, and so on, the woman in front of me suggested I take a Xanax and put it under my tongue so it got into my system faster.

I didn't have it at the time and I wouldn't have taken it if I had. No use in making myself exhausted for the rest of the day just because I was afraid of two minutes of standing in a claustrophobic hydraulic elevator. So I sucked it up and went, hating every single moment of it. But I never forgot what the woman had said, and when I later got the prescription, that was how I took it.

The bottle was hard to open—I always had trouble getting around the childproof lids. Once I did, though, I took a whole pill instead of the half

I usually took and put it under my tongue. It was bitter. Most people would have hated it, but I associated it with the taste of relief.

I put the bottle back in my purse and returned to the family room to sit down and wait for it to work. The bedroom was out of the question before that. What if I heard the tapping again? What if I saw him again? What if that was my new thing, seeing dead people? How old had Theresa Caputo and Tyler Henry been when they began to bleed into the spirit world for, sorry, spirited conversations with the dead?

Was I becoming a medium?

The thought made me laugh despite my anxiety. If anything proved I was losing it, it was me imagining I was going to be psychic in some way. Half the time I couldn't understand what people were *saying*, much less what they were thinking.

I got up and flipped on the fire. The gas was off, so nothing happened. Disappointed, I looked for a candle instead and found one in the cabinet beneath the built-ins. There was a stick lighter there too and that, at least, still worked. I lit the candle and put it on the coffee table, then sat down to meditate on the flame.

Before long, I felt the drowsy pull of sleep tugging at the corners of my thoughts. Everything was going to be okay. I was going to get some sleep and wake up refreshed and sane in the morning.

That would be really great.

But first I blew out the candle, then went into the bathroom to brush my teeth, something I was fastidious about. I put the toothpaste on the brush and counted to sixty while I brushed my teeth, just like my mother had taught me, then turned the faucet handle to rinse.

Nothing happened. The water was still off. I'd totally forgotten.

There I was, mouth full of toothpaste and nothing to do with it. So I went into the kitchen, took a diet soda out of the fridge. (I always had them there but wondered if it was still okay after three years.) It fizzed when I opened it, so I guessed it was okay, and I used that to swish the toothpaste out and spit it into the kitchen sink. It tasted god-awful. Almost as bad as orange juice after brushing your teeth. But it was better than nothing, and I used the rest of the soda to rinse the bubbly mess down the drain.

Hopefully *that* was still working.

Foggy-headed, I went back to the family room and lay down on the sofa. Just for a few minutes, I told myself. Until the tranquilizer took its full grip on me and I could go to my room without dreams of young Ben waiting for me in the dark.

I slept.

Chapter Twelve

Jamie

Roxy had come over in the afternoon, just as he'd suspected and feared she would: bolstered by her friends' support, feeling like maybe he was more of an asshole than she realized.

Her hair, this time, was mahogany. Really almost purple. It was like she was a magical creature, able to express her changing mood through her changing look.

She'd acted annoyed with him for the first hour she was there, then seemed to lose interest in it when she seemed to realize that her passive-aggression wasn't catching the same flies it usually did. He was distant and disinterested in her BS. So she changed tack, and instead jumped on the counter in front of him and suggested that they watch something he wanted to tonight—anything he wanted.

He'd picked an old Bond movie. His dad and he used to watch them, though he didn't tell her this. She was bound to ruin it either way if he let her. Plus he never *let her in*, something she was always correctly accusing him of.

She'd hung all over him trying to make out the whole time they were watching, since she was evidently bored by the movie. He eventually gave in and figured he'd watch the rest another time. She slept in his room that night, but just when he started to fall asleep, she started talking.

What will we do when we graduate?

Should we move in together?

I'll follow you wherever you get in!

He didn't draw the comparison of this line to the famous one from *Wedding Crashers*—the one where the redhead girl says (threatens?), "I'll find you!"

Instead he'd tried not to say anything that bothered her and avoided promising her anything.

Somehow it was just striking him that Roxy could become a long-term problem. Beyond anything he'd ever even thought of before. She'd already been this way for such a long time, but somewhere in his head he'd sort of been subconsciously thinking that it would sort itself out after graduation. Like the slate would be clean and he could . . . what, use it as an excuse? Move away?

No. If he didn't break up with her she was going to stick with him like glitter.

He *hated* glitter.

His phone buzzed and he leapt up, taking the opportunity to get away from Roxy's questioning.

"Sorry, it's my mom, I've gotta go answer her."

"But—"

"Shh." He held a finger to his lips and then ducked out of the room.

He didn't answer his mom's call on time, and went downstairs to the kitchen. It was dark except for the stove light. He leaned against the counter, considering the realization he'd just had.

If I don't make Roxy go away, Roxy will never go away.

And even then she might not, said some depressing voice in a corner of his mind.

He rubbed his face.

His phone did one quick buzz, indication of a voice mail. It was, of course, from his mom. It was only three seconds long. He almost didn't listen. Usually voice mails that short are just an indication of not hanging up on time. But he'd do almost anything not to go upstairs yet.

The message wasn't an accident.

"Jamie, I need you to come to the house and help out," she said, then added the kicker that got him: "I'll expect you tomorrow. *I mean it.*" She sounded serious. Almost angry. That wasn't like her. He'd listened a second time, half expecting there to be more, maybe a *please*. But there wasn't.

She didn't sound right. Not at all.

Even when she was mad, there was usually a lift of lightness to her voice. Something that said, *If you just say you're sorry, we can laugh about this in ten seconds.* Not always, not when he really screwed up (then she'd get sad and retreat), but usually.

This was different.

She sounded upset.

What could be upsetting her enough to call him this late, and without information like that? He was always up late (unless he was trying to pretend to sleep to make Roxy cease her monologues), but his mom liked not to call or bother him.

A wash of guilt went over him, this one bigger than the usual ones he felt nowadays. Of course his mom was upset. It suddenly seemed ridiculous that he'd let her go do this by herself. It was one thing to want to avoid the scene of . . . what, the crime? But to let his mom go do weeks' worth of heavy lifting, that was just shitty-son behavior. He should have separated his own . . . whatever, and just gone and helped her.

He ignored the other voice in his head that said, *Yeah, but come on, you also kind of want an excuse to ditch Roxy.*

True. But even when he wasn't lying to himself about that, he felt like a dick for not being there for his mom if something was really messing her up this bad.

He should have remembered that she didn't complain until long after most people would.

That's when he decided he would go. He had to. As much as he wanted to leave Roxy, though, he still didn't want to go to that house, but he had to.

For his mom. He owed her that.

He went back upstairs. Roxy had all the lights on, and all her clothes off.

"God, Roxy," he'd said, and not in the flattering way. "Look, I've got to go to sleep. I've gotta go to the beach in the morning."

She made the decision to figure out why, instead of deciding to feel insulted. She covered herself with a sheet. "The beach? What? *Why?*"

The way she'd asked it implied that he was going for some fun trip with the guys or something. Leave it to her to turn it into something that could hurt her feelings, rather than put together the fact that his dad died there and his mom was out of town dealing with that.

"I have to help my mom. Obviously." He realized with shame that it should have been obvious to *him* much sooner.

"Oh . . ." She made a face like she was trying to remember exactly what it was that his mom was doing, and if she was supposed to know.

"Yeah, I'll probably be gone for a bit. Like, weeks."

"Well, do you want me to come? Does your mom need a girl?" She said this part with pity. "Girl time can help almost anything."

He couldn't even articulate how much his mom would hate having "girl time" with Roxy. He also couldn't find the words to tell her that girl time didn't solve problems involving dead dads and packing old houses.

As far as he knew.

"No. Roxy. No, I just need to go help. So I gotta get some sleep."

He rolled over, and felt her not move. He knew she was sitting there, straight up, naked and barely covered, feeling offended and ignored, unprioritized.

Good, he thought, *maybe she'll get fed up.*

A minute later she lay down, making a point of not touching him.

"Where's your beach house again?"

"Fenwick," he lied. It was Ocean City.

"Ah. Okay, just wondering."

He didn't know what sort of surprise visit she was considering—*plotting* was a better word for it—but giving her the wrong beach would throw her off. If she called him on it, he'd just say something about it being on the line between the two beaches and . . . blah blah blah, BS.

Or, he thought with a deep, deep breath, he could just finally dump her.

But that's when he realized that he'd done this for too long. He'd played this game, and lost at it, for way too long. He told himself he'd *handle it later* so that he didn't have to handle it now, and so it never got handled.

When had he begun this pattern? Was it lifelong? No, surely not; he could remember so many times as a kid when he was waiting for his parents to get ready to go somewhere or do something, and he'd been dressed for it and waiting for hours.

He'd been like that right up to the time his dad died.

Maybe *that* was what had changed things.

Oh, boy.

Obviously that was when things had changed. If he was a sitcom character, he'd have slapped himself in the forehead. The minute he'd heard about his dad, he'd turned his mind away from it, pretended—as best he could under difficult circumstances—that it wasn't true. Thinking about it was painful, incredibly painful, so every time he did, he thought about something else. The release of a new video game he'd been anticipating,

or the return of *Doctor Who*, or whatever else he could come up with to
turn his brain from channel three to channel four.

His mom had done it too. That's why she hadn't been to the beach
house in three years. Going there, cleaning it up, *selling it*, made it real.
And he knew, from every not-so-subtle clue her life had given him, that
she could not bear for it to be real.

But they had both skidded along that same road, barely talking about
his dad or What Had Happened, sniping at each other here and there, living on the surface, and handling everything from dinner to baseball
practice to school and work in the most minimal way possible.

So going to the beach, going to *face it*, had been a huge step for his
mom. Of course she needed his support. They hadn't exactly been the best
of friends these past few years, but there was no question that he was the
only one fully in that boat with her. Obviously it was his responsibility to
see this through with her.

And now that she'd made such a bold step on her own, he was going
to take the cue and make a much less bold one himself.

"I think you'd better go," he said to Roxy.

"What?" she asked, purposely making her voice sound foggy and sleep
heavy, even though she obviously wasn't asleep or anywhere close to it.

"I'm sorry," he said, because he was. It was pretty ungentlemanly of him
to just kick her ass out in the middle of the night, but that's exactly what
he was doing.

Forever.

"You've got to go. This just isn't working. It's not good for you." Normally he would have left it there and she would have snaked in on that
point and "assured" him that he wasn't bad for her. So this time he added,
"Or me. This isn't good for me."

That riled her. She sat up in bed and frowned at him. He could see it clearly in the muted glow of all the electronics in his room. "Oh, I'm not good for you, huh?"

He shook his head. "No."

"Where would you *be* without me?"

"We'll see."

Her face registered shock. "You've got to be kidding."

He stood up and rummaged around for his clothes. "Actually, Rox, I'm not kidding. We should have done this a long time ago."

Her mouth dropped open.

His shorts on, he went to her pile of clothes on the other side of the bed and tossed them next to her. "There you go. Get dressed, I'm taking you home."

She looked at the clothes, then back at him. "Are you *serious*?"

He nodded. "Yeah, Rox. As a heart attack."

"Fuck"—she picked up the clothes—"you." She frantically scrambled into them, steam practically pumping out of her ears as she did. "You are a *huge fucking asshole*."

"I know." And he did. In more ways than even she could ever count.

"Don't expect me to take you back when you come crawling!"

"Roxy," he said, his voice low and serious, "I'm not coming back."

Despite her bold words, her face registered shock and devastation. She'd wanted, clearly, for him to panic at the idea of things being Actually Over. She didn't expect him to really walk away, she'd *never* expected him to really walk away. They'd long ago set a firm precedent of her whining, him capitulating, and them limping on. Not *forward*, precisely, but at least marching in place, as opposed to turning left or right and moving forward.

Now he was turning left or right, he didn't care which, to move forward.

"Jamie!" She was suddenly flooded with tears. The bold threats of three

moments ago were gone and they were on to begging. "Please think about
this!"

He shook his head resolutely. Kind of like a three-year-old who refused
to eat broccoli. "Don't make this harder than it needs to be."

"But . . ." She didn't have a follow-up.

Neither did he. It was obvious that so much was wrong that nothing
could ever be right.

"You need to go," he said. "I have to leave early and I need my sleep."

"So that's it? You're just . . . done?" She was building up a steam of anger again.

"That's it," he confirmed.

She took three steps toward the door then turned back to him. "If I
leave this house, I'm never, ever coming back."

He nodded. "That's right."

Her face crumpled again, but this time he could see it was anger, not
heartache. She was pretending to cry, but there were no tears.

"Goodbye, then, Jamie," she announced. "It was . . . fun."

He gave a single nod this time—an insult, he knew. "Goodbye."

And she turned and left. He stayed absolutely still until, just a few seconds later, he heard the front door slam downstairs and then heard her
car start outside. He'd forgotten she'd driven here, or he wouldn't have
offered to drive her home. That would have been a nightmare in and of
itself, especially behind the wheel of a car.

When a couple of minutes had passed after she left, he finally moved.
And, to his surprise, he felt a genuine freedom. He'd let go of a huge stress.
There was no regret or second-guessing whatsoever. Just relief.

Nothing but relief.

It wasn't much, he realized. He should have done it a long time ago, so
he couldn't claim this as any grand accomplishment that people should
laud him for, but nevertheless, it was done. And he couldn't see a circum-

stance under which Roxy would be willing to swallow her pride so much that she'd come back begging. All the times in the past, she had held the cards, usually because of emotional or circumstantial ransom, but now . . . nope.

He was done.

And it felt good.

Not great. Great was hopefully still in his future. He had a lot more things to do—and a lot more things to undo—but this was a start.

And he'd take it.

Chapter Thirteen

Willa

I woke with the sun in the morning and got dressed. It was a bitch without water, but I managed to be at least presentable. Enough to go to the big-box stores anyway. And McDonald's.

I love McDonald's breakfast. The sausage, egg, and cheese McGriddles are manna from heaven as far as I'm concerned. Ditto the greasy, crispy, un-diet-y hash browns. And the coffee is better than any I've ever made, which isn't really saying much, since I am particularly ungifted at making coffee. At any rate, after using their bathroom, I got my usual, a large coffee with four creams. The hell with being skinny, I needed to stop being hungry. I was half convinced now that everything that had happened yesterday was the result of hunger. Plus McDonald's always smells like vacation to me, so I considered it aromatherapy.

That was the closest I was going to get to therapy this week.

Home Depot was the first stop after that. There was something comforting about its big feel, the familiarity of the layout, and the smell. How is it that all Home Depots smell the same? I guess it's the wood, paint, and steel. I like it, and I particularly liked it today after the night I'd had.

Today I felt sane. Or somewhat sane.

I picked up some neutral paints, moving boxes, and switch plates to replace a few that I'd noticed were cracked. What else did I need? Light bulbs were always going out, so I picked up some of those too, as well as some plants to spruce up the outside.

The idea of gardening made me groan. Maybe if Jamie came I could persuade him to do it. I hated working outside with the heat beating down on me. I could lie on the beach layered in oil and sweat my ass off in the middle of August with no problem, but working outside was a drag.

I dragged the heavy wagon of goods out to my car and loaded it all into the trunk. Next stop: Walmart. This was a task I never felt like doing, thanks to the crowds and long lines, but it was a necessary evil. I pulled into the parking lot and looked at the wading pools and sandboxes out front. A pang of melancholy pierced my heart. It hadn't been so long ago I was picking those up for Jamie. One time we'd gotten a kiddie pool and it hadn't fit in the car, so we'd put it on the car's roof and both kept one hand out the window, holding on to it. That was a much harder task than we'd anticipated, even going an obnoxious thirty miles per hour in a fifty zone. Fortunately, it was only a few miles.

Those days were long gone now.

I took a bracing breath. There was no room for those thoughts, I reminded myself for the hundredth time. Besides, working would keep me busy, and that would keep my mind off of everything that had happened. Or that hadn't happened. Hard to say at this point.

The store was crowded, as usual. I went straight to the pharmacy area and picked out toothbrushes, toothpaste, soap (which I'd totally forgotten), drinking water, and ibuprofen. Then on to the cleaning aisle, where I got an armload of different products for everything from cleaning the sinks and toilets to refurbishing the leather sofa. I'd been told by the Re-altor that it was better to leave some furniture in the house so people could picture a life there, but to remove anything bulky and all personal items.

The question was, what was I going to do with all the personal items? I wasn't sure I wanted them at home with me. Everything had a memory attached, and when you're trying to move on, memories are not very help-ful. Hence the moving boxes. I would box everything up, maybe keep *one* for things I wanted to save, and have Purple Heart pick up the rest.

Goodbye past, hello future.

Right.

I rolled my eyes at myself, knowing how damn successful I'd been at abandoning the past so far, but pressed on and went to the area that had trash bags. I'd need a lot of those. Thinking that should do it for now, I headed for the registers but a big square stand of beach souvenirs stopped me. Magnets with crabs, sandy beaches, lighthouses (there were no light-houses in Ocean City), and quippy sayings like *Son of a Beach* and *Sandy-man at Work* crowded the display. There were also candles with plastic seagulls glued to the sides and plaques with the footprints-in-the-sand story. It seemed to me that maybe it would be a good idea to make the house a little more beachy and a little less homey. The way it was now, it could have been the house in Potomac, or any suburb of D.C. That wasn't the market for a beach house.

So I grabbed some candles, a few magnets, including one that had a road sign for Route 50 (the main way in from Potomac), and a hand soap bottle with 1950s "bathing beauties" on it for the downstairs bathroom.

Loaded with supplies that would last me awhile, I went slowly through the checkout, and back to my car. By the time I was finished putting every-thing in, the trunk was packed full and my energy was flagging. It had been a pain to shop, but now I had to go back and unpack all this stuff, take it into the house, and then *use* it.

I drove back at a leisurely pace, enjoying sitting down in the plush car seat as opposed to doing hard labor. But clouds were building in the distance and creeping slowly over the shore. It looked like rain. Time to face the music and get everything inside before the downpour.

I hauled everything in to the kitchen. Then stood back to assess. Where to start? Perhaps by hiring people to do everything for me? If only. A handyman and a maid would have come in very handy right now, but my budget didn't allow for that, so I was on my own.

I had just unwrapped a sponge and picked up the all-purpose cleaner when my phone rang.

Thank God.

It was Kristin. "How's it going today?"

What a relief it was to hear her voice. "If I told you," I said, "you'd think I was crazy."

"Girl, I already think you're crazy." She gave a good-natured laugh. "You're not going to be changing my mind about that anytime soon."

"What a relief."

"Come on, tell me: What gives?"

"Okay." I sat down at the kitchen table, surrounded by all my purchases. There was a lot of work to do, but it was worth taking a break for a moment and talking to my best friend. "I've just had . . . the strangest feeling in here sometimes."

"That seems normal. I mean, given the circumstances."

"No, I mean . . . beyond normal. I don't just mean the occasional dark or sad thought. I get plenty of those too, but"—in for a penny, in for a pound—"I swear sometimes I feel like Ben's here."

"Well, of course!"

"No, I mean *here*."

There was a long pause while I knew she calculated what I'd said, and while I calculated the wisdom of having admitted such a thing to a concerned friend who inevitably would worry about me and feel too far away to help. So I decided to negate it. "Wait, I don't want to sound too wacky, I think it's just because there is so much stuff of *ours* here, and so much of *his* that it feels very present. I guess it *is* very present."

"Yes." She sounded relieved. "Naturally. Nothing crazy about that! Boy, for a minute I thought you were suggesting it was something like— oh, forget it, I think I'm the one who's crazy."

Something like a ghost, she'd been about to say. But she stopped herself because she didn't want to upset me with the idea of my house being haunted when my husband had died here, and because it sounded nuts.

I sighed. There was no way I could tell her the rest. She was so damn practical that she probably would find a way to have me sent away for a nice "rest" in order to recuperate.

"Do you have Dolly with you?"

"Always."

"What about her? Did she . . . sense anything?"

I thought about Dolly's strange behavior since we'd arrived. Had she sensed anything? It seemed like she'd done nothing but sense things. But that was something Kristin would have to see for herself. Me saying it would only seem like I was trying to back up my own story. "She's been a little wonky too. But she's mostly herself. Good old guard dog." Though what could a dog—or anyone—do about a ghost?

"That's good. She would totally react if something were off."

"Right."

It was a strange thing not to be able to tell my best friend what was really going on with me, but it would have been more upsetting for her to hear everything and worry about me from afar. And of course she'd worry. A week or more ago, if she'd said something to me about seeing dead people, I'd have been totally alarmed.

"I've got to run," I lied. "The plumber's here."

"Call me later," she said. "This afternoon."

"Okay."

"Promise."

She was looking for a reason to not worry. "I promise. Look, don't worry about me, everything's fine here."

"Be that as it may, I'm going to try to come down there this weekend. I'm staying with you, chicken, I got it all figured out."

"That would be great." I tried to temper my voice so she wouldn't hear how desperate I was for the company. "I'll put you straight to work."

"Hey, I'm ready!"

"I've got to go," I repeated, sadly. "Talk to you in a bit."

Chapter Fourteen

Willa

After heaving a heavy sigh, I went to the Walmart/Home Depot haul and decided to put things where they belonged. Cleaning supplies under the sink, toiletries in the bathroom, magnets on the refrigerator (where, alone, they looked kind of pitiful, a sad attempt at cheer). It was when I took the paint into the family room that I saw him yet again.

No sense in drawing out the suspense: it was Ben. But still not the Ben I had last known. This time he looked to be in his late twenties. He was wearing a sweater I'd given him for Christmas. A rag wool sweater that I think he hated but I loved it and he wore it because I had given it to him. But, listen, if I didn't give him warm clothes, he was the kind of guy who'd go out and shovel snow in shorts, so even though he didn't love the sweater, I didn't feel too bad about keeping him warm.

Dolly bristled and began to growl at him.

"Come here, buddy," he was saying, seemingly without any awareness of the dog, and I knew right away that he was talking to Jamie. He'd always called him that, *my buddy*.

I could have sworn I heard the faintest echo of a child's laugh, but I didn't see anything except Ben, walking purposefully through the room with his eyes on something in front of him.

"Whoa, slow down, there, pardner." He reached down and picked up what could have been a child—his motion was that of picking up a child, but there was nothing there. Nothing in his arms but air. And yet I knew, just from that, the size, the weight, like a bag of rice from Costco. The way it set on your hip, and the little hands, usually sticky, reaching for your face.

"You can't run off like that," he went on to the child that wasn't there. "You know how your mom worries about everything." He gave an affectionate tap to a nose that wasn't there.

I knew the gesture; I'd seen him do it a thousand times. But still it gave me shivers.

Dolly was on full alert, ears perked, eyes fastened on the same thing I was seeing, and her hackles up. She didn't move forward or away, just waited and watched with what looked like the same caution and skepticism I was feeling.

"Yeah?" Ben called suddenly, looking over his shoulder to the threshold between the family room and the kitchen. "Hell, yes, it smells amazing. You're a culinary magician. The fryer is ready; I just need to get a bunch of peanut oil. Jamie and I can run out. Need anything?"

Thanksgiving, then. He was talking about Thanksgiving. He always liked to fry the turkey. It was the thing the men did, stood around a vat of molten oil, risking their lives and our house, in the name of having a big fried bird, which, if you ask me, wasn't quite as good as a roasted one.

But they enjoyed it so much, I never said anything. It was no skin off my nose, as they say. As long as little Jamie didn't get too close to the danger, it was good for him to see his dad's bonding time with his pals.

And to learn that men cooked.

"Sure," Ben went on, his voice softening somewhat, and I realized that whomever he was talking to had moved closer.

I also realized he was talking to me. Old me. Or, rather, young me. It was confusing. A version of me that was apparently standing three yards away and I couldn't see her. Not only could I now see dead people, but apparently I could *only* see dead people.

That would make for a very inconvenient superpower, constantly following the dead around, and knocking into the living. *Sorry, I didn't see you there, I was talking to my great-great-great-grandmother* . . .

"Ben?" I said, wondering if there was some magic by which I could make him hear me now.

He laughed and looked very fondly at the kitchen entry. "You're a pisser, you know that?" One of his favorite sayings.

I walked over to "me." There was nothing there, of course, no change in temperature or pressure, *but* I did smell a whiff of the Lauren perfume I used to wear. They didn't make it anymore, so there was no reasonable explanation for smelling it now, but I did.

Other than that, there was absolutely no sense of anyone there.

I kept my eyes on Ben and slowly made my way over toward him as he continued to talk to phantom me. It was an echo, I thought. A visual echo of a scene from long ago, but if that was what was happening, why couldn't I see all of us? Why didn't we all echo instead of only the one who was gone?

Dolly joined me, walking at my heels. I don't know what she would have done if there had been any sudden movement or acknowledgment, but I suspected it would involve urine and a floor cleanup.

From both of us.

The closer I got to him, the more out of focus he became. It happened quickly, and by the time I got to him he was a watercolored hologram of color without features. I reached out to feel the air and, indeed, it was cold. In fact, it was dramatically cold compared to the rest of the room. If the whole room was that temperature I'd be shivering in a down coat.

"Ben," I said again, and I could have sworn there was a shift in the entity. Toward me? Maybe away, I couldn't tell. But it was a *reaction*.

"Willa," I heard, but it was as faint and far away as the wind at the shore. It could have been the water or the air-conditioning kicking in.

But I was sure it wasn't, I was sure it was my name.

"Ben, please. Answer me. Tell me where you are. Come back and just talk to me for a minute." I felt a bit like I was pleading with a criminal. "I won't tell a soul, no one needs to know, just come talk to me. I don't care if it's breaking some rule or other, I need you!"

Then, as fast as it had gotten cold, the air warmed up and the vision disappeared. I didn't know if it was because I had approached it and spooked it away (imagine—spooking a ghost), or if the vision had simply run its course. They all seemed to, didn't they?

I remembered the boy on the beach with the kite. Had that been another vision or a real boy? I couldn't recall if the air temperature around him had been different, because the wind was so strong.

But he'd looked so much like Jamie, and therefore like Ben. On top of that, I hadn't seen the kid since, even though I walked Dolly along the shore a couple of times a day. It had only been a couple of days, of course, but a windy couple of days; wouldn't he have come back with his kite?

Now I was being too fanciful. It was madness to start wondering if people I was actually seeing were real or not. I mean, that had to be the definition of madness, didn't it? There were probably textbook cases.

The solution was obvious. I needed to not be here alone. I needed someone else to confirm or deny what I was seeing or hearing (although I'd be subtle, I'd have to be—no point in letting anyone else know I was losing my mind).

I thought again of Jamie. Of how these visions seemed to be telling me something about him. About us. I hoped they weren't a warning, but suddenly I was worried about how I couldn't get ahold of him or get an answer from him.

It was probably just a symptom of our estrangement, as I had long thought, but once I had the idea in my head that something was wrong, I couldn't quite shake it. I tried his phone. No answer.

So I called Kristin. She answered on the first ring.

"Have you seen Jamie?" I asked her. She lived three doors down from us, though the truth was I never even noticed the neighbors who were three doors up, so if she hadn't seen him, that alone was nothing to be alarmed about.

"Actually, yes," she said. "I was going to tell you. Believe it or not, he was out mowing the lawn earlier!"

Relief flooded me. "Of his own accord? That's impossible."

"Exactly what I said. I thought I was seeing things, so I asked the kids if they saw it too, and they did."

That was a familiar story.

"Well, that's good news. It's damn near impossible to get him to call me back."

"Kids."

"Right? But it's worrisome."

"Want me to go check on him?"

"Oh, would you?"

"Sure! Give me five and I'll call you back."

Relief flooded through me. She'd call back and everything would be fine and I'd have nothing more to worry about. Except, that is, for everything that was happening to me in the house. But that was nothing compared to worrying about a child.

It was about five minutes later that she called back. "No answer at the door and his car isn't here."

The relief I'd expected ran out of my veins, chased by a shaking agitation. "You're sure?"

"I'm sure, but I'm also sure there's nothing wrong." She gave a laugh and it sounded sincere. "When I think about how many times I was just gone, and with no cell phone for my mother to pester me with, well, I just know karma is going to come back with these kids and bite me straight in the ass."

It was true. I'd done the same thing to my mom. There was always a seemingly good reason to stay out longer, to not bother finding a phone or trying to reassure anyone. I always went back and never understood what the big deal was. I was not only a teenager, I was immortal, and I was sure that's how Jamie felt.

"Are you okay?" Kristin asked, when I waited too long to respond to her.

"Yes. Yes, I'm fine, I'm sure you're right. He's just off being a selfish teenager like it's his job."

"It is."

"I miss that job."

Another dry chuckle. "Tell me about it. So listen, I thought I'd come late Friday night, will that be okay?"

"Okay? That would be *awesome*. Seriously, I will be so glad to see you."

She clearly heard the desperation in my voice and asked, "Do you need me to get out sooner?"

It was already Wednesday, it would be selfish for me to ask her to get away any faster. "No, I'll be fine." And I would. I might be scared, but I would be fine. "I'm warning you, the Realtor gave me a pretty ugly list of things that need to be done."

"Well, we'll whip it right on into shape, then," she said, and we hung up, promising to talk in the meantime.

She was picking up on the tension in my voice. Even I could hear it, and I was the one who was trying to keep it under control. But what could I do? If I told her over the phone what was happening, it would be nothing short of alarming. Better to get her here and see if she saw anything herself. Dolly did, so why not another person? On *Ghost Hunters*, they frequently all saw or heard the same thing. Maybe that was the nature of ghosts, who knows?

Maybe I should call them in, I thought.

Before I could pursue the idea, I heard a rattling at the front door. My first instinct was to hide. *Hide!* This was getting ridiculous. I wasn't going to be this timid person! I was going to face whatever came my way head-on. Enough with the bullshitting around.

I went to the door and threw it open, then stood in shock.

That dark hair, those blue eyes, the slightly muscular build twisted into that slightly defiant stance I'd seen a million times.

I just couldn't believe my eyes.

Jamie was here.

Chapter Fifteen

Willa

The relief of having Jamie here was unexplainable. It wasn't like I thought he would *protect* me from anything, or, indeed, that I *needed* protection from anything. I had come to believe, and somewhat accept, that what was happening to me was in fact supernatural in some way.

Not that I was super-comfortable with that, but it wasn't like Jamie could do anything about it any more than I could.

I did wonder if he'd see Ben as well, and, if he did, if that would be bad for him or good for him. I still wasn't sure which it was for me, so there was no telling what it would do to a kid.

All I knew was that poor Jamie had lost his father at a hell of a bad time—at fourteen! Is there a worse age than fourteen?—and he missed him in ways I couldn't begin to comprehend. Of course, I missed him in ways Jamie wouldn't understand, it was just the nature of relationships, but maybe what he needed from his dad he needed so badly that even this pale echo would at least partially fit the bill.

He came in and looked around. His expression was one of . . . distaste?

Fear? Whatever it was, it wasn't nostalgia or anything pleasant. My heart clenched at the idea that this might only be painful for him. I had honestly hoped, and I think even believed, that when he got here some pieces would fall into place and he'd feel *better* about his loss. Like a puzzle piece was missing, and it was a major one—maybe Mona Lisa's smile—but the rest of the picture was still fully intact and recognizable.

Then again, if you lose one piece, how hard is it to conceive of losing another? Particularly since I was selling the house. The mouth was already gone. What if the house was an eye? Eventually the dog would go, as she was already getting up in years—a piece of the hair or the folded hands? And his grandmother—jeez, this could go on and on. Even landing on me at some point—at *any* point, we had learned—leaving Jamie with none of the people he was supposed to be able to take completely for granted as pillars of his life.

Sure, he'd get new pieces; he'd have girlfriends, a wife someday, children almost certainly. New dogs, old dogs, houses near or far away, but they'd never be part of this original puzzle. They'd never fit into the work of art that was, so far, our life together.

As much as that made my heart ache, I realized it was also true for me. Pieces were missing from *my* puzzle too. In fact, I was going to lose most of the same pieces Jamie was too. If it had just been background or even hair, then, sure, I could inch along without them. I could rationalize that I'd had the great gift of my life but that I'd lost it early on.

But didn't I want a whole puzzle—a whole *life*—myself? If I didn't live fully I wasn't only doing myself a disservice, but Jamie too. Having seen how tenuous life was, I needed to get back on track with him, and fast. I needed to be sure that I was a piece of his puzzle that really *mattered*.

Why was it so hard? He was my son, for god's sake! Why couldn't I just step it up? Why did I feel this strange pull-back from him? I had to push past it.

"I know it's a peculiar feeling, being in here after all this time," I said to him carefully. I definitely didn't want him to turn and run back to Potomac.

"It sucks."

"Jamie!"

He turned to face me. "I'm sorry. It's just weird here. It feels weird. Like, Dad *died* here, this was the last stuff he saw."

The idea gave me shivers, as it did every time. It's so easy to do that, isn't it? To imagine the last impressions and thoughts of the dead? Did she see the car swerve in front of her or was she just humming along with the radio, looking at the blue sky, and thinking about dinner?

Had he felt funny that day in some way? Had he paused on his rounds in the house, sitting down to rest now and then and not knowing why his chest felt tight? Had he had any inkling he was about to go, that there would be no tomorrow for him?

I was tired of all these maudlin thoughts. It was more than enough; now was time to just be happy my son was here and to take joy in that.

"Was Roxy upset that you left?" I asked him, opening a door that may or may not reveal something important.

He raised an eyebrow at me. "Are you worried we might break up or something?"

I smiled. Poor Roxy had become our one "joke" together, although not a funny one. "I certainly don't want *you* upset," I said honestly.

He waved the notion away. "I'm not upset. Nothing to worry about here. I'm actually kind of glad to get away."

"Really."

He waited. "Not going to ask why?"

"I'd hate to be one of those butting-in mothers," I lied. "It's none of my business."

"I guess you're right," he agreed, nodding thoughtfully.

A moment passed.

"Why?" I asked, hoping I sounded playful and not demanding. "You know I'm a butting-in mother. Why are you glad to get away?"

He laughed. It sounded genuine. "I *knew* the curiosity would get to you."

"Well, of *course* it has!"

He sobered quickly. We didn't have many of these moments of hilarity between us and I wanted to hold on to it as long as possible. "She was just starting to drive me a little crazy."

"All that whining?" I immediately regretted saying this because, although I assumed he agreed, I wasn't *sure*, and I didn't want to introduce something new for him to be self-conscious of her for.

Fortunately he didn't seem to notice my slip. "She's really pushy," he said. "She always needs me to do this or that or *something*, and if I don't want to she's, like, suicidal. I just want to be away from all that."

Interesting that his relationship was characterized by distance. Would he say that characterized *our* relationship as well?

"Honey"—I put my hand on his shoulder—"that is the *last* thing you need at this point in your life. You should be having fun, enjoying life, playing the field, not anchored to someone who ransoms your affection. Or, rather, your sense of duty."

"I guess."

I gave his shoulder a squeeze, then let go. "Well, now that you're here, I hope you'll let go and have some fun. Maybe you'll meet another girl here."

He looked doubtful. "She's kind of still my girlfriend. I couldn't cheat."

The words made me want to scream even while I was proud of him for his loyalty. It's just that that girl didn't deserve it and this *was* a perfect opportunity for him to be away and meet someone totally new. That's what I wanted for him. And I suspected that, deep down, that's what he wanted for himself as well.

"Maybe you need to talk to Roxy and make sure you're both on the same page, then," I suggested. "Whatever that page is."

Chapter Sixteen

Jamie

She'd looked shocked to see him. He should probably feel like a jerk, that it surprised her so much that he'd come to do what she needed. Instead he managed to feel insulted, which was really asinine, since he nearly hadn't come anyway.

It was bizarre being back.

"It sucks," he said when she'd called it merely peculiar. The words had spat out of him before he even really realized how true they were.

You could put whatever fancy spin on it that you wanted. Unsettling, strange, sad, tragic, heart-wrenching coming back . . . but the simplest fact was that it just sucked. It blew. He wasn't shaking and sobbing in a corner, he was more together than all that, but it just . . . *sucked*.

He and his mom had one of their usual back-and-forths. They were talking, leaning on their dynamic, both silently admitting to each other, confiding to each other, that they weren't okay. Maybe that was progress in their relationship. Maybe, just maybe, she'd crack and become her old self. How long had it been?

It seemed like for years now all they did was throw diversions at each other every time the going got tough. He remembered a time he'd fallen off his bike and gotten a huge gash in his knee. They'd gone to the ER, and while he was getting stitches she talked to him about dinner. That was a small, literal example of what they did all the time now.

Something would happen, and they'd distract each other. They were good at it. It was okay when it was a skinned knee or she'd gotten into an argument with a friend or had had words with a student's parents or something. But ever since his dad had died, the need to distract each other and avoid the reality was just too real and too frequent. It was becoming all they had.

It was who they were.

He wondered how aware of this she was. Maybe she wasn't at all. Maybe her vision of him had become rose-colored, and it was more comfortable that way.

On the one hand, he could see that perhaps they needed to be more real. On the other, there was no part of him that wanted to sit down and look into earnest eyes imploring him to articulate all the ways that life had taken a real Bullshit Turn in the last couple years.

He could handle it if this was how it was for now. But looking at his mother now, her eyes the size of pool balls, her posture so meek, he wasn't sure she was okay. He kind of had thought they were individually handling their . . . whatever. But what if she actually wasn't okay? What if she was on a decline and he hadn't even noticed?

Even after she knew it was him at the door, she looked all bugged out like she . . . what, like she doubted it was really him?

"So where should I . . ." He'd held up his bag.

"Oh . . . well, wherever you like. I'm up there in the guest room. There's your old room, or . . . or the master, but if you want it . . ."

It hung between them like spit. She didn't want to sleep in the Room Where He Died.

He didn't blame her. Hell if he was sleeping there.

He wasn't sure where to sleep. His old room seemed a little weird to revisit. He'd never slept in the other guest room. He'd probably just sleep on the couch, really.

A small, juvenile pang hit him, and he felt like he might sort of rather sleep in the same room as his mom. Camaraderie in their unconsciousness. The compulsion humiliated him, even in the privacy of his own head.

He tossed his bag down on the floor. He'd figure it out later.

The doorbell rang. It was so loud.

It also reminded him of pizza.

Grotto pizza that they were one hundred percent having later. His stomach gave a gurgle of anticipation.

"Oh, that'll be the plumber," said his mom, going off to the door. "Probably," she added. "God willing, he's going to finish up today."

He furrowed his brows at her. Huh.

Dolly was in the archway between the two rooms, he noticed now. The dog had never *not* come hurtling toward him, all paws-on-roller-skates and happy whimpers. Instead, now, she had crept so quietly into the room that he hadn't even noticed. And even though Jamie was here now, and he hadn't been, Dolly's eyes, whiskers, and hackles were directed only at the front door. She hadn't even acknowledged him.

"Dolly. Hey, Dolly girl." He crouched down. She panted in his direction for a split second but then went back to looking at the door.

When his mom opened it, Dolly's head dropped lower. She looked so much more canine now than she ever had.

"What is it, what's your deal?"

"Hi, yeah, come on in," his mom was saying. "Wha—oh, yeah the dish-washer's *fine*, thank you. Yeah, sure, go right ahead."

The man she let in was middle-aged and looked a bit like a cartoon. Jamie could tell from the width of his torso and build of his arms that he'd probably been a weight lifter or at least been *jacked* when he was younger. Once upon a time, a million years ago. Now he looked sort of creaky, but Jamie was willing to bet he was older than he looked.

In the depressing, extremist way that he had been lately, he immedi-ately imagined the guy dying. He'd only caught a glimpse of him, but al-ready felt like that would be a shame.

Jesus. If he started picking up not-even-acquaintances to grieve over their un-deaths, he'd really be not okay.

"Why is there a plumber here?" Jamie asked.

His mom put her hands in her back pockets and walked over. "The water isn't working. Well, it's off. It was leaking. I saw this big water stain on the ceiling. Figured it was coming from the, um, the . . ." She gestured upstairs with a finger. "Bathroom sink."

Usually, when his mom made guesses about things like this, he would exchange a silent look with his dad. "Pipes froze?" he asked.

"Yeah, it seems like it—how did you know that?"

He shrugged, like it was no big deal. Really, though, he'd asked his dad a thousand questions about everything like this. Lame as it was, he loved being in a club with his dad. The club where they were the men who knew stuff like this, and his mom was the obtuse but adorable (his dad always said) one, who didn't quite understand the things they did.

"Anyway, the plumber's going to have to replace the drywall, which is one of about a million things that need to be done . . ."

They were both imitating his dad. She could say *replace it*, but she prob-ably couldn't quite envision what that would entail.

Really, Jamie was in a club with his mom too: neither one of them really knew how to be *that* kind of adult, and his dad did.

"All right, no water. So what do we need to do?"

What do we need to do to get this over with? he thought. The place reeked of conflicting memories and imaginings.

No surprise, she had a laundry list of things for him to do. Putting gloves on and moving big piles of wet pine needles and leaves into bags. Windexing the outside and inside of all the windows, which at first sounded extremely anal, but then he realized every window had a buildup of about an inch of pollen and dust. She had him vacuum every corner of the carpet and of the ceiling, which, again, sounded like not a real thing, but he was surprised they were so dusty and cobwebbed.

She had an entire other list she was forming of things that had to be done with water. Bathtubs, sinks, etc.

She worked on the oven, on the pantry, on packing their dishes into boxes marked KITCHEN.

Once he'd finished the tasks she'd doled out, he went upstairs. He wasn't really sure why. He wanted to see what the plumber was doing. He'd always watched his dad do this stuff, but that made sense. That was his dad.

Jamie decided not to think about that, or about his dad, and went up to the upstairs bathroom with as much casualness as he could.

The guy must have heard him, because he stopped cranking his wrench and then looked at Jamie.

" 'S goin' on, kiddo?" he asked, looking a little irritated to be interrupted, but—Jamie suspected—looking a little relieved that it wasn't Jamie's mom.

"Not much. Just seeing how it's going up here."

The guy glanced at him, then kept working.

"You all selling the place?"

Jamie nodded, and then realized he wasn't looking at him. "Right. Yeah."

"Bet she's got all kinds of stuff for you to do."

He couldn't tell if he was telling him to go do any of those things, or if he was just talking.

Talkin', as this guy was more likely to say.

"Yeah, she does. Taking a quick break, I guess. I already did the whole front yard, the windows, all that stuff."

Why was he going on about this? Was he looking for praise? Had he merely been silent for too long during the day, and now he needed to word-puke onto someone, anyone? Literally, anyone?

The guy gave a whistle. "That yard looked like no easy task. I saw it yesterday, boy, I'll tell you. Wasn't envying the guy who'd get hired to do that. Looks like she had you built-in, though, huh?"

There was humor in his voice, so Jamie said, "You know it."

You know it? All right, he had to stop. Go elsewhere. Be weird on his own.

"You helping your mom out here all summer or are you gonna be working?"

"Uh." He looked around, then heard the whir of a Dirt Devil start up downstairs. "Not sure."

"Well," he said, wrenching the pipe tightly, "if you wind up looking for a job, my sister's got a place, might be looking to hire somebody."

"Oh, yeah?"

"Yep. One of those seasonal restaurants on the boardwalk. Beer and wines and"—he moved something with a clunk—"crap like that. I know she hired a couple of kids who ended up flaking out on her. No idea if she's replaced them yet. If you decide you don't wanna hang around this house all summer, let me know, I'll put you two in touch."

"Cool. That'd be pretty cool, actually."

He hadn't given serious thought to how long he'd stay. The house was tough, but there was something about the salty sea smell of the air outside that made him feel at home. Almost happy. Spending the entire summer out here sounded a lot more freeing, and a lot less shitty, than he would have guessed. He pushed from his mind all the worries about the house itself and the phantoms it might possess.

"How will I get in touch with you if I want to do that?"

The guy gave a laugh. "Kid, your mom's got my number and she'll probably need to use it more than she thinks, though I hope not, for her sake." He sat up, hands on both his shins. "She hired the oldest working guy in town. Means I go to bed early, but I know what the hell I'm doing."

Jamie laughed. "I bet."

The guy looked at him for just another second, and then stood and started packing up. It seemed their conversation was over.

"Thanks," said Jamie.

He went downstairs again, feeling a lot younger than he had in a while.

His mom was standing in the living room in baggy gray shorts already splattered with old paint, a sports bra, and baggy tank top. The tank top wasn't covered in paint like the pants, but it was an ugly orange, so he was glad she'd decided it was a trash shirt. Her hair was back in a bandanna. He had a sudden flashback of her, what, ten years ago? When they'd painted his room at home. He wanted it to be gray, instead of baby blue. He'd seen a character on a TV show with a gray room and had decided the blue of his room was too infantile.

Once it was done, though, he'd sort of wished they'd made him keep it that way. The gray was so depressing. The blue, in retrospect, made him feel better.

"Did you bring any painting clothes?" she asked when she saw him. She smiled a little when she saw his face—dreading the task ahead.

"I didn't. But . . . I don't really care about these clothes."

He'd said it to be accommodating, but realized now that she'd bought them for him. She'd bought him almost everything he had; he couldn't have gestured at any of his own clothes and said this.

He watched her resist the urge to point this out, and instead said with a flourish of her hand at him, "Welcome to your new painting outfit!"

She extended a roller to him. "You're on, Jackson Pollock, get your paint on."

"That's an awful joke. If I were to do it like Jackson—"

"Okay, but if I'd said Yves Klein, you wouldn't have gotten the joke, would you? He painted solid colors, and yet—"

"Music?" he said to his mother, the art history major, the woman who could have gone on about this for hours.

"Your choice. For now. If it's the Beatles."

"I brought my speaker, I'll just go get it."

"If you drive off, so help me!" she called after him.

He turned back to her, walking away with his keys, and gave a mischievous look like that might be just what he was about to do.

He would never, though. Not after he saw how his mom was. She was herself, but she was off. She was sadder than she'd been since the news. She was jumpy.

This only proved to be more true throughout the night. They painted for two hours, took a break, ate pizza, chatted, then painted until almost midnight. All the while, though, she seemed off.

She kept looking at the walls, her eyes out of focus, or turning fast at the sound of a twig on the porch out back. She leapt whenever the dog moved. Even Dolly was weird, though. Was this one of those horror-movie-type things where whoever came into the house after a tragedy becomes possessed?

His imagination took that and ran with it for a second, imagining his father here, possessed. Or possessing.

No. That was dumb. His mom was just acting weird. It wasn't a whole thing.

It made perfect sense that she was so off. He couldn't imagine being in her position. The same could be argued for his position, but he was different from his mom. He was more compartmentalized than she was; she was always trying to put out ten fires at once.

He told her about the job prospect, just to distract her. She'd been delighted to hear of the possibility, presumably glad he might stick around, but, despite her attempts to act otherwise, she still seemed a little zoned out.

He hoped to god this wasn't her now. *Please*, he thought, *don't let her change*.

Don't let him lose both parents.

Chapter Seventeen

Willa

Jamie spent his first night at the beach house being surprisingly coopera-tive. We ordered Grotto's pizza, and patched the walls in the family room completely and even got one of them painted. The smell of fresh paint was like aromatherapy to me and the look of a nice, clean, pristine wall, in a new color (warm buttery yellow) helped me realign my purpose in being here.

The plumber had come and nearly finished the job *and* offered Jamie work at his sister's restaurant on the boardwalk. I wasn't sure how long we'd be staying at the house, but I felt strongly that Jamie getting out and meet-ing kids his own age who weren't the video-gaming losers he was used to at home would be good for him. And therefore good for me. Good for *us*.

The next day was pleasantly filled with more painting for me while Dave finished the job.

"You're about set," he said, coming into the family room. "It just needs to totally vent out up there and you can slap a coat of ceiling paint on and call it a day. Come on, take a look."

I followed him through the kitchen and into the living room, where the corner had, just a couple of days ago, been it's own little black rain cloud, complete with rain. Now it was a mismatched patch of solid drywall. He'd even sanded it in so the joints were smooth.

"It looks great," I said wholeheartedly. "How much do I owe you?"

When he cited the price, I thought I had misheard. "That's for the *whole* job?"

His face colored slightly. "You'd prefer to pay more?"

"No, no, it's just—" I shook my head. "Nothing at home is ever the least bit affordable. That's a very fair price, I'm just . . . relieved, actually. Thank you."

He nodded. "It's my job."

"You know," I said, trying to let go of my instinct to always try to do everything myself, "I was thinking about replacing the fixtures in the downstairs bathroom. If I ordered them, could you put them in?"

"Of course."

"Let me tell you what I want." We went to the room. "This sink has always driven me crazy. I need storage underneath. Do you think you could transform a bedside table into one of those sinks that looks like a bowl?"

"As long as it fits in here. I'd have to do some measurements."

"Well, it's right here." The old master bedroom was right between the bathroom and the kitchen. I rather liked the idea of replacing everything in it with something new and either getting rid of or repurposing whatever remained. I didn't need those reminders.

Dave went out and retrieved a tape measure and took some measurements of the table, and of the space in the powder room. "That'll fit," he pronounced. "And it's a pretty good height too. You just need to make sure the sink is no more than about fifteen inches in diameter and six inches high. Standard one-and-three-quarter-inch drain."

"Wait, wait." I went and opened the junk drawer in the kitchen and pulled out a pad of paper and a pen. "Let me just write that down."

He waited and repeated the information. "It's pretty standard," he said. "You shouldn't have any trouble finding it."

I pictured a gleaming new powder room. "Great!"

"Just let me know when it comes in, I'll pick it up."

When he had gone, I finally allowed myself to feel some optimism about the job ahead. Maybe it wouldn't be so bad. After all, I'd already gotten one wall painted, the leak was fixed, and the downstairs bathroom would be modernized. At his prices, maybe I'd do them all. And put a new faucet in the kitchen. That was about all it would take to update the place, since the bedrooms were standard squares that would look fresh with a new coat of paint.

If only I could stop seeing my dead husband, everything would be great.

It was not to be. I had no sooner brushed my teeth and put on my night-shirt than I walked into the bedroom and saw him there, sitting on the bed.

"You again," I said, to myself, of course, since he couldn't hear me. This illusion, or hallucination or whatever it was, was starting to get old. "I know I am imagining this; I am not going to let it put me in a nuthouse. This is just a trick of the mind. And eye."

"That's some greeting," he said.

I froze.

His voice! That voice, that voice, I knew that voice. I didn't even *remember* how well I knew that voice. This was coming out of the deep recesses of my broken mind. I was really crackers!

I shook my head. Vehemently. Too vehemently. Denial at its finest. "I don't believe this. You're not talking to me. I've finally lost it." Then, incongruously, "Say something else."

"Like what? I'm . . ." He splayed his arms. "Here."

"You're dead."

There was a moment's pause that seemed to last forever. "Yes," he said at last. "I figured that out."

"That's it." I started pacing. "I'm really going crazy. This is the end. I've finally lost it."

"Baby, you were *always* crazy."

And he always said that. But that was no proof of anything. *I* knew what he always said, what he did, how he looked, his gestures, even his stance. There was nothing surprising about any of this.

This was all me.

"This isn't you," he said, at exactly the right moment.

"There—that's proof!" I was talking at "him" but I knew I was talking to myself. "You're reading my mind. That proves you're in there. That this is my imagination."

"I can see why you'd think that, but I wasn't reading your mind. It's just a logical thought in an illogical situation. And this . . ." He smiled. "This is an illogical situation. We both know that."

Oh, that smile.

That was the thing that had gotten me first, and it was the thing I missed the most about him.

I missed seeing that heart-wrenching smile.

Knowing this was sheer madness, I went along with it. After all, it wasn't as if I could just walk away, go to bed, and pretend I hadn't seen anything. "If you're here, prove it."

"I . . . I'm here."

"Or you're my imagination."

He gave a concessionary nod of the head. "Hmm. I guess you seeing me walk through the room the other day didn't prove it either."

"Nope, I saw it." Was I talking to myself? Or was he really there? I was arguing against a situation I truly hoped was real. "Still in my head."

He appeared to think about it. "Do you know what I was reading at the time of my unfortunate death?"

I nodded. "I cleaned it all up."

He looked surprised. "Really? That doesn't sound like you. I would have thought you'd keep the whole thing intact like a mausoleum."

"That *was* my inclination," I admitted, and remembered how damn hard it had been to close that book and put it back on the shelf. I'd looked to see what page he was on—251—and felt sad setting it aside. "But that would be ridiculous. I can't sell the place with a dead man's last scene like a diorama in the middle."

"No, I'm glad you didn't. Sorry I didn't make the bed, but I was busy, you know, passing away."

"I made it."

"Good, good."

There was a moment of silence, during which I just gaped at him. I wanted to go touch him, but I knew from experience that he'd disappear, and, whatever was happening, I didn't want him to disappear.

"Do you know what's in the freezer?" he asked suddenly.

I thought about it. I had checked the fridge to see if it was clean, but I hadn't checked the freezer. That was weird, why hadn't I?

"No," I said. "I don't."

"Aha! I do. There are two Martino's pizzas—"

"Ben, honestly, that is such crap food. Why do you do that? They're so bad for you. Full of hydrogenated oils and cholesterol, they'll give you a—"

He sighed. Exaggerated. "A heart attack?"

"I was going to say . . ." My face grew warm. "Yes, I was going to say that. Wow. I'm sorry, that was insensitive." I was apologizing to a specter.

"But true. Except it wasn't the pizzas, it was just my time. I know how that works now, it was my time, and that was that." He reached out a hand. "Come on, let's go look in the freezer."

I hesitated, then reached for his hand.

It's hard to describe what I felt. It was *kind of* there, but, like the other night on the boardwalk, it felt more like phantom pain, in a way. I could feel his hand, but it felt like a memory. It wasn't solid.

I was afraid to go anywhere, even with him, for fear he would evaporate into nothingness. I didn't know how this ghost stuff worked, if this was indeed ghost stuff at all, but it seemed to me that ghosts couldn't stray too far afield. Like they were tethered to a single place at a time.

Then again, I couldn't refuse his hand or resist looking to see if he was right about the freezer. That was definitely something I didn't know, unless he had said it was just ice cube trays in there as usual. But he'd mentioned the pizzas.

I would never have dreamed that proof of my husband's ghost—I couldn't believe I was even thinking that way—would rest on the presence or absence of those awful pizzas. But I hated them, I would never have bought them.

"There's another thing," he said casually, as we rounded the corner of the counter. "You're going to be so pissed off at me."

"I couldn't be," I said, wondering if somehow this actually *was* real. *Could* it be? I didn't dare to hope.

It couldn't be. It wasn't even a matter of hope, it was just reality. This was not reality.

"You know how you always told me not to stick my Cokes in the freezer to cool them off faster?"

I did. "Oh, no . . ."

"I'm afraid so. I didn't get a chance to clean it up before . . ." He pantomimed slicing his throat. "You know."

I frowned at him and opened the freezer. Sure enough, there were two Martino's death disks in there, as well as a winter wonderland of iced brown Coke and the broken glass shards of a bottle.

"It had to be in a bottle," I said.

He looked embarrassed. "You know I like the Mexican ones best. Real cane sugar. Why don't they use cane sugar here? Everyone prefers those."

"I don't know." I closed the freezer door and turned to him. "If you're here, if you're *truly* here, how did this happen? How are you here now?"

He went to lean on the counter. I followed and hefted myself up on it, like I always used to when we were talking in the kitchen. And we did it a lot, believe it or not. Some of our best heart-to-hearts had taken place here. If that happened then, then why not now?

"You needed me."

Tears pricked at my eyes and I took a wavering breath. "I need you to not be dead."

He looked resigned. "But I am."

"Do you hate that as much as I do?" I was so scared of his answer. If he hated it, I would lose all faith, all belief in everything I had always believed and hoped to be true about the afterlife.

"No," he said with a smile. "I don't. What I hate, if I can even use that word, is that you're suffering. I never, ever wanted that."

My chest ached. Pulled and pushed and made every objection it could. I was in full crying mode now. "Then why did you go?"

He shook his head ruefully. "I didn't have any choice. This is not the kind of thing you have control over in life. Those decisions were made long ago." He paused. "Long ago, in your time. Once you're here, it's the blink of an eye."

I couldn't comprehend this. He was saying what philosophers had said for centuries, but I didn't know how to conceive of time in any way other than the way I always had. "What is *there* like?"

"Good," he said. "Really good."

"Details, please."

"Sorry." He shook his head. "Not allowed to give those out. I'm barely allowed to be here now. I had to get special dispensation."

"Special dispensation to see your grieving wife?" That seemed cruel to me. If this was possible—and I still wasn't sure what was going on—then it didn't make sense to me why people couldn't always come and comfort their loved ones in such a time of grief.

"You weren't moving on and you have great things to do. It's important that you focus on your work and on living a happy life. You need to move on without me. There's no choice."

"How can I be happy without you"—a sob caught in my throat—"when you are gone and I know you can come back but, what, you won't?"

"I'm only here temporarily."

"Exactly."

"It's how it has to be."

"And it's really you?"

He nodded and looked at me so tenderly. "I'm really here. But only for now."

"How long?"

"I actually don't know. Until you get it, I guess."

"Then I'll *never* get it!"

He laughed. "Stubborn and bucking the system, as always. I don't get to stay for you always, Willa. This is a limited-time gig." He frowned and looked up. "And I need to go."

"Go? Wait, what? You can't go! You just got here!"

He shook his head and looked at his hands, which were disappearing. "I have no choice." He looked at me. "I love you, Willa. I always have and I always will. Someday we'll be together again, don't worry. But it's different. It will be okay, I promise you that."

And with that, he was gone altogether.

Chapter Eighteen

Jamie

Maybe it was the paint fumes, the excessive carbs, or finally facing the looming threat that the beach house had been for so long. Whatever it was, that night, Jamie slept.

It drifted softly into his mind like a vapor and wrapped silkily around his cranium and made him heavy until he fell.

He slept on the narrow bed in the guest room in an old sleeping bag, which was still sandy from years ago on Assateague Island—the small beach off the main shore, where ponies ambled wild, and where Jamie and his dad had made s'mores and listened to the Beatles and Bob Dylan on the crackling old boom box that had accompanied so many of their father-son adventures.

Maybe that's what he was thinking about when he fell asleep, or maybe that's what he dreamed of. Maybe it was the same thing. Details had rushed back to him either way. He remembered the way it was kind of too cold out, but his dad was in a T-shirt, so he didn't reach for his own sweatshirt.

Now he knew he was about ninety pounds back then, and had a lot less meat on him than his dad did—he really had been a lot colder, not just enduring it poorly.

He also remembered the way the outside of the hot dogs, toasted over a fire, had crunched and how much better they tasted than when they were microwaved at home. (Of course, he knew, this was not at all surprising.)

His feet had been buried in the sand, and he'd noticed that he was unconsciously imitating his dad.

They'd talked about his dad's childhood. They talked about his friends at school.

His dad had explained the intricacies of a couple mainstream sports that Jamie really felt like he should have known by then. ("What does offsides mean?")

Not once did his dad laugh at him or look embarrassed to have a boy who didn't know better. He did get that look, though, that Jamie now understood. The involuntary smile hidden in a concentrated look and complementary action—e.g., stoking the fire with a furrowed brow.

Jamie had asked that night if his dad and mom ever intended to have another kid.

"How would you feel about that?" he'd asked back.

Jamie had shrugged. "I don't know."

"Don't feel strongly about it?"

"I guess not. More wondering."

This wasn't completely true. But by nine, as he was in this memory, he had started growing out of the idea of badly wanting a sibling. Now he sort of liked being the object of both his parents' attention. Sometimes it was too much, but were a baby to come around, it would probably wind up being more of a pain than anything else.

"I don't think your mom and I were meant to have any other kids," he'd said. "I think we got it right with you. No other kid could have been so right."

In his years since that conversation, he understood a lot more. Overheard a little here and there, caught a few implications, seen a sad look or two between his parents. Heard his mom on the phone with Kristin, saying, after his father died, "at least it was already too late," and then watching his own mind allocate that to a specific context.

His parents probably couldn't have more kids. He didn't know why, probably didn't want to. But regardless of what he'd picked up on or gleaned, the fact that his dad said what he said—"No other kid could have been so right"—had so completely ruled out the possibility of a sibling, and his dad was too conscientious to make a statement like that unless he knew.

This blissful, anesthesia-like sleep felt healing. Restorative. Like a video-game character going back to a home base and recharging. He could almost feel himself going from the red into the green.

Plunging his restoration back into red, like the mercury sinking below zero in a thermometer, he awoke from his sleep to the jarring bell of his phone ringing.

Roxy. Always Roxy.

He muted it without looking. Even if he was going to answer, he needed to mute it. His mom hadn't stirred; she was still a small bundle in the center of the bed, one leg kicked out of the sheets. Ha, he thought. He did that too. Both legs under too hot, both legs out too cold, one leg out was per—

Buzz. The phone was still on vibrate even though the ringer was off.

He pushed the power button and then jumped up with a deep breath through his nostrils. He went out in the hall, careful that the mirror on the back of the door didn't clap against the hollow door.

He ignored the call and then saw the *Iliad* and *Odyssey* of texts.

He didn't even—he couldn't even start at the beginning. Instead he picked up in the middle.

OMFG REALLY THOUGH
Youve gotta be kidding me seriously
Your really just not gonna answer

He cringed at the your/you're mistake. He'd explained it so many times. There were memes about it. How could you really not understand the difference by now?

JAMIE
I swear to god i feel like your literally not getting it. Im literally on my way to your beach house right now. And yeah i have the right address, its on a magnet at youre house, thanks for lying you fucking psycho seriously what like you cant tell me where your beachhouse is honestly you're making me into a bitch. i am not a bitch, i never ever EVER have been this is all you. and I'm fucking miserable because of you. Hope that feels good, seriously

Was it cruel that as he read through, he was not only privately correcting all her spelling and grammar, but taking note where autocorrect had clearly taken over?

im literally on may way
my*
you think I'm fucknig going
joking* jesus

Somewhere mixed in there, she'd called a couple times.

Literally getting in my car right now

Okay, so before she hadn't been "literally" on her way . . . that was the last text and that was about half an hour ago.

This had to stop. It had to really stop.

Funny enough, it was being in this house that made him truly sure. This house that he'd dreaded seeing again, this place that he thought he could never face again because of the sadness. In actuality, it was a place of happy memories much more than sad.

And it was a place where he'd learned what relationships should be. Family relationships, parental relationships. And from his parents he'd seen what a good partnership should look like. What a *marriage* should look like.

It didn't look anything like what he had with Roxy. Not that they were married, thank god, but this was not a relationship he'd look back on in ten years with fond tenderness. It was a nightmare now and he'd always think of it that way. Something he'd taken too long to get out of, maybe, but something he was lucky enough to have quit before it got really bad.

He didn't know what he'd do from here, but he did know that the hundred and fifty miles between them were important. If she was really planning on trying to come to the beach, he had to stop her.

He called her number. She answered on the first ring.

"I'm on my way—"

"Roxy." He cut her off. Sighed. "Roxy, I don't want you to come," he said, his tone sounding more masculine and Ben-like than it ever had. "This has to stop. We're not right for each other. I'm going to be up here the rest of the summer anyway helping my mom. I'm sorry I didn't end it better, but I just can't keep doing this. I'm really sorry."

"Wha—Jamie . . ."

He clearly had been on speakerphone, he heard the switch in the white noise. Obviously she had a friend with her and wasn't expecting this conversation.

"I'm sorry, Roxy, but I mean it."

She said nothing. She breathed into the phone for a few seconds, maybe a full minute, but then hung up. He'd chosen the right moment to sound like a grown man—she'd actually believed him, for once. He really didn't think she'd take that as an invitation to show up now.

He bit his bottom lip, fighting off all the compulsions to undo what he'd just done, to go back to having a girlfriend who fed him all the ego food he could ever need.

A chill coursed through him. What the hell? His mom was too cheap to put the air-conditioning on until, like, the end of July or August, but he wasn't expecting it to get so cold.

Was it his own nerves telling him something?

Did I do the right thing? he asked himself as he put his hands to his face and rubbed hard, leaving, he knew, red marks.

In his peripheral vision he could see the light in the kitchen downstairs was on. In fact, it was the harsh glare in his eye that caught his attention.

"I should turn that off," he said to himself, blinking hard again, trying to shake away the conversation with Roxy.

When he turned around, the lights in the kitchen were off. Nothing was on.

Why had he thought they were?

Chapter Nineteen

Willa

"So I see what you mean," Kristin said. Her red hair was uncharacteristically smoothed back into a sleek ponytail and she was wearing no makeup. The expression on her face was serious. "Obviously I haven't been here since Ben died either, but I can absolutely feel his presence!"

She had arrived at nine on Friday night. Ben had not been back since he had actually talked and responded to me, and I was returning to the position that I was losing my mind.

Except the pizza and the Coke in the freezer—which I hadn't cleaned up yet—*that* I couldn't explain. And wouldn't, because it all seemed too crazy. *Yeah, my dead husband told me this stuff was in the freezer, and there it was!*

I knew it had been true, *I* knew there was no other explanation for it, but no one else could reasonably buy in to that because it was like me saying, *Look! There are jeans in my closet! Ben told me that! How else could I know?*

"I think even the smell of the sea air reminds me of him."

"I can see that. The house has a distinct smell, like all houses do, so naturally you'd associate it with your times here." Kristin raised her wineglass, and pinot grigio sloshed up the side. "I do too."

I nodded, and there was a moment of silence before she said, "I'm starving, what do you have to eat?"

"This and that." I started to get up. "I'll put something together."

"No, you stay put! I can handle it." She got off the sofa and went into the dim kitchen. "We do need to get some Grotto pizza."

"Oh, absolutely," I agreed. There were times in my life when the promise of good pizza was the only thing I looked forward to.

Or, if not the *only* thing, certainly the *best* thing.

There was some bumping around in the kitchen, then eventually Kristin said, "Aha!"

I sat up. "What? Did you find something?" Strange and embarrassing as it was, my first thought was that maybe she'd seen Ben too.

"Yes." She came out of the kitchen holding a bottle. "Champagne."

"It's not new."

She was pulling off the foil wrapper. "Good. It's supposed to be aged."

This was it. We were dwindling down to small talk while the enormity of what I'd been going through grew inside of me. "Kristin."

"Mmm?"

"There is something I have to tell you."

"Oh, lord, don't tell me you're in love with me!"

"Very funny."

"Okay, what?"

"I'm pretty sure I saw Ben."

She stopped in the middle of twisting the wire hood off. "You think you saw Ben." It wasn't a question, it was a statement. A question would have allowed too much room for belief and she clearly wasn't ready to believe anything like this.

"Yes," I said quietly. This was a risk to say. Right now it was my secret, so whether it was true or not, I was the only one in control of the knowledge. If I let it out, who knew what would happen with it? But I just couldn't keep it all inside anymore. It was too insane.

Suddenly the cork popped out of the bottle, scaring the shit out of both of us. Kristin dropped the bottle.

Both of us scrambled to pick it up, like it was a baby fallen overboard on a ship.

"Get it! Get it!" I called. "It's spilling everywhere. What a terrible waste!"

"There won't be any left!" She reached down, but the bottle rolled away from her hand. "*Shit!*"

Finally I grabbed it and we both breathed a sigh of relief.

"Is there any left?" Kristin asked, hurrying into the kitchen for cleanup materials.

I took a swig. "Yup. We're kind of heroes."

She came out with a handful of paper towels. "Well, *you* are. Did you see how that thing rolled away from me? I was all thumbs!" She swabbed up the floor, while Dolly came over and tried to join in the cleanup process. The dog loved champagne, I don't know why, but I'd spilled enough in my lifetime to know that when she heard it, or smelled it, she came running.

"I'm telling you, it was Ben. That's just the sort of thing he'd do. Proving himself by inexplicable things. Next he'll be playing the piano."

"You don't have a piano."

"Thank god." I handed her the bottle and she took a long gulp from it before passing it back.

"So." She took a breath and put her hands in her lap, her best paying-attention stance. "Why don't you start over? Tell me what's going on."

She was willing to listen. That was a start. But I wasn't sure I should overwhelm her with the whole story. After all, that was a lot to swallow; more than just one bottle of champagne—elusive or consumed—could allow.

"There've just been a few odd incidents," I said. "I thought I saw him walk through the room once. And I swear I wasn't thinking about him at that moment, or remembering the past, or anything that would make me imagine him in particular at that moment."

"Did it scare you?"

"Kind of, yeah. But then I was sitting here on the couch and he came right over and stood next to me."

"Was it cold? They always say it's cold when a ghost is around." Was she humoring me or just looking for a good story?

"Not *particularly*. But I was so alarmed that I wasn't really thinking in terms of the science around it."

She nodded. "I can understand that." She looked at me. "Has there been anything else?" Her gaze was penetrating. It felt like she was on to me.

I took another glug of the champagne. It was taking the edge off, loosening my reserve. I sighed heavily and closed my eyes for a moment. "Okay, yes, there are a couple more things."

She reached wordlessly for the champagne.

I handed it over.

"Tell me," she said.

"It sounds nuts."

"You think the rest of this doesn't?"

I had to laugh. Of course it did. I was, as they say, in for a penny, so I might as well go in for a pound. "Actually, yes, I think all of it does. But you know I'm a sane person, I'm not given to wild imaginings."

"True."

"And I'm grieving, obviously, I know that, but not to the point of losing my grip on reality."

"All right . . ."

"Seriously!"

"Okay!"

"So the thing is, when I first got here, there was this kid running on the beach with a kite. He looked just like Jamie did when he was young. That is, *almost* exactly like Jamie did when he was young. When he passed me, he didn't even acknowledge me. Like, he didn't even notice me. I think it was Ben. Sort of an *echo* of Ben from a long time ago."

Her face screwed into an expression of extreme skepticism. "All this based on the fact that he looks kind of like a young Jamie or Ben and ignored you when he passed? No offense, but why would he stop and chat with some weird old lady who was watching him? I'd teach my kids to keep walking from a stranger too."

I gave a laugh. "Actually, that's exactly what I thought at the time. So that was when I first got here, but when I tried to get Dolly to go into the house, she was . . . resistant."

"It probably smelled funny." She heard what she'd just said and back-pedaled quickly. "Not because of . . . you know . . . but because it's been closed up for years. It was probably musty and dark and unappealing to her. A dog would probably much rather run on the beach."

"She comes with me wherever I go. She didn't want to even cross the threshold and come in. I even mentioned *T-R-E-A-T-S*."

From the floor, Dolly raised her head. I avoided eye contact so she'd think she'd imagined the word. I think it was the *E* sound that got her attention.

Kristin tipped the bottle to her mouth, then drew it away. "Bad news. We're out of champagne. I need more wine for this conversation."

"Not to worry." I got up and went into the kitchen. There was a jug of red in the cabinet. I'd bought it for cooking, but it wasn't bad for drinking either (I followed the old rule of thumb not to cook with anything you wouldn't drink), so I brought it back out with a couple of coffee mugs. "We're going classy. White, champagne, now red, from mugs. Can't say I don't know how to entertain."

"*That* is for *damn* sure." She watched as I glugged the wine into the mugs and set the bottle aside.

"Cheers." I handed her a mug.

She took it and tapped mine. "Cheers. Now. You were saying that Dolly wouldn't come inside with you. Which I don't think is necessarily all that great as evidence goes."

"Right, right, but she's been acting weird in general."

"She's a dog in a strange place. She probably doesn't even remember it here."

"I don't buy that." I took a sip and set the wine down. "So are you ready for a really weird one?"

"Always." She moved forward on her seat.

I told her about the pebbles on the window and teenage Ben being out there to meet phantom me, then the walk to the boardwalk. "I know this all sounds like something from *Back to the Future*, and I don't get it, but it's true," I concluded. "Everything was like an echo of the past, almost like watching a movie. I could see the details, but I couldn't touch anything or feel anything."

"Huh." She drained her mug. "Other than that, Mrs. Lincoln, how was the play?"

I shook my head. I shouldn't have brought any of this up, it just made me sound crazy. Good thing I hadn't gotten to the part where he talked to me. "Nothing else going on besides the flood and the ornery plumber. Oh, and Jamie's staying, which I'm *thrilled* about. He's at the boardwalk now, but he should be back soon."

"Get him to spend some time away from the harlot?" No one was a fan of Roxy's. Everyone saw how she manipulated Jamie, although at a certain point he had to take responsibility for that himself. In fact, that time had probably already come and gone.

Still, I had to admit I was glad he'd be away from her.

Kristin yawned broadly. "I am bushed. What's on the agenda for tomorrow, chickie?"

"Painting. And painting. And maybe some painting."

"Should we paint as well?"

I mocked surprise. "I think that's a great idea!"

"Let's do it." She glanced at the clock. "After midnight! We've been sitting here forever! I've got to scram." She started to pick up the various glasses we'd used throughout the night.

I put a hand on hers. "No, no, I'll take care of this. You just go to bed. You need to rest up so I can work you to death."

She tapped her temple with her index finger. "Good thinking."

I nodded with a smile.

"Where should I sleep?"

"You've got two choices, Jamie's in his room now so you can have either the small guest room, or"—I hesitated—"the master bedroom. I made the beds in both."

"The master bedroom where Ben . . ."

"That's the one."

She took a short breath. "That sounds fine by me. I don't believe in anything sinister. And if he wants to come talk to me, he can!"

I knew she was taking the room to normalize the idea of it for me. And, truth be told, it kind of did. Ben would no longer be the last one who'd slept in there.

Plus, given my last interaction with him—which I couldn't imagine admitting to Kristin or to anyone—I was feeling a lot less afraid and a lot more curious. Eager, even, for a revisit.

If only I knew how to summon him. All I'd been doing before—each time I'd seen him—was sitting and minding my own business. Feeling kind of sad about him, admittedly, but not sobbing to the world and making deals with God to return him to me.

Just minding my own business. So I guessed I'd do that again.

Chapter Twenty

Willa

Nothing happened.

The next morning, I woke up to bright sunshine streaming in and the smell of coffee and bacon drifting upstairs. Kristin was up.

I contemplated the shower, then decided there was no point since I'd be working, so I pulled my hair back into a straight ponytail and wedged myself into some paint-splattered jeans I'd left in the closet from the last time I'd had a painting urge, about ten years and fifteen pounds ago. I didn't have a clean painting shirt, however, so I went downstairs to get one from the master bedroom closet.

"Hey, sexy," Kristin said, catching a glimpse of me as she closed the fridge door. "You didn't have to get all dressed up for me!"

"Don't get excited, I'm just looking for painting clothes."

"Tease."

"Hey, man, if you want to paint naked, you're entirely welcome to."

She took a cookie sheet of bacon out of the oven. "It would probably be easier to clean up."

"Oh, yeah, the clothes have to be throwaways. I was going to grab one of Ben's old shirts, I'll get you one too."

"Thank you, dahlink." She gave a half bow. "Then come on in; breakfast is getting cold."

It wasn't so easy picking which of Ben's shirts I was willing to ruin permanently. Once I started looking at them, I could remember so many occasions involving each—the Ralph Lauren blue button-down I'd gotten him for Christmas, the white Halston he could never keep clean, the white JCPenney backups for the Halston. Things he'd worn on holidays, ordinary days, whatever. The things that were here weren't his first-tier choices; those were still at home. But he had a decent selection, considering that he rarely had to dress in anything other than shorts and a polo or Hawaiian shirt around here. And I wasn't about to ruin any of those Hawaiian shirts. Maybe Jamie would want them one day. If not, well, I'd deal with it then.

I could always throw things out later, but I could never retrieve them once they were gone.

"Now, *that* is gonna look hot on you."

I knew the voice before I even turned and looked.

Ben was leaning on the bedpost, arms casually crossed in front of him. A body language expert would have said he was closing himself off. Was he closing himself off from me now? In death?

As if on cue, he uncrossed his arms and ambled toward me, looking me up and down. "Go ahead, put it on."

"You're being creepy," I whispered, secretly delighted that he was here and being exactly that way. It was more flirtatious than creepy, but it had always been fun to give him shit.

"I know it." He gave a low whistle. "I like you just like this, but you really should put the shirt on, the plumber is coming to prep the table."

"How do you know?" I put the shirt on and buttoned it up. One of the Penney's ones. I'd gotten one out for Kristin too.

"Come on, I've got a few advantages in this state."

"Willa!" Kristin called. "Come *on*! What's taking so long?"

"I just—I can't decide which ones to get rid of," I improvised. I looked at Ben, exasperated. "I'm sorry, just give me a minute."

She came to the doorway. "No, I'm sorry. I didn't mean to be insensitive. Take all the time you need. I'm just worried that the popovers will get cold, but everything else is fine."

"Popovers?" I loved popovers, though at the moment I wasn't sure if I was up to eating much at all.

"I know they're your favorite."

I moved carefully, casually, over next to Ben to see if she would notice anything, since she had clearly not seen him like I did.

He watched me, amused. Honestly, he was like Cary Grant in one of those old screwball comedies.

"She's not going to see me," he said, but it was like a secret, from the side of his mouth and half under his breath.

"Then why are you whispering?" I asked through my teeth.

"What?" Kristin looked puzzled.

"I said I'll be right in. I'd hate to miss out on popovers."

"And bacon and, if the grocery store is to be believed, real Café du Monde coffee with chicory."

It *did* smell good. "Sounds great! I'll be right there."

She turned and went back into the kitchen, but it was still only a few yards away.

"Why can't she see you?" I whispered harshly.

He shrugged. "Because I'm here for you."

"Will Jamie be able to see you if you're here when he is?"

Sadness crossed Ben's expression and broke my heart. God, it was awful to think that even in the afterlife there could be longing and missing
and sadness. "He cannot," he said. "Honestly, I don't know what it takes
or what makes me visible to you and no one else, I only know that's how
it is."

"Maybe it's because I am the only one stupid enough to keep on trying to undo what's done." I was careful to keep my voice down, and glad
when I heard Kristin turn on the radio in the kitchen. NPR drowned me
out, I was sure. "I didn't come here expecting to see you, but on some level
I think I was more glad than surprised at it. Like on some level I *wanted*
to. Knew it."

He smiled. "I've been around you the whole time."

"You have? Ever since you . . ." Damn it, I hated saying it. I hated saying he'd died. Even three years later it was so hard to believe that it sounded,
it *felt*, like a lie to me

"Yeah, but not quite how you think. I wasn't watching your every
move, like Santa Claus, tallying up what I thought was right or wrong or
good or bad. And I'm not watching you in the bathroom or"—he looked
at me significantly—"the bedroom."

"Good lord, nothing is happening there, I swear it." I was so eager to
reassure him that I overcompensated. "There has been no one since you,
absolutely no one. I can't even imagine it."

He tilted his head and looked penetratingly into my eyes. "But that's
not what I want, Willa."

"I . . . I don't . . . What do you mean?"

"I don't want you to give up on love and life and sex and all the good
stuff just because I'm gone."

It's hard to explain the feeling of abandonment those words gave me.
If his words were meant to reassure me—and on the surface I could see
how they were—they only served to make me feel more alone. Less cared

for. Unclaimed and unwanted by all, including the man I had been mourning for three years. "Thanks," was all I could say, and it came out more bitter than I would have liked.

"Sweetheart." He dipped low and spoke right into my ear. "I want you to be happy. Wouldn't you want the same for me if our roles were reversed?"

"No!" I said, too loud. "Absolutely not! I would be furious and I would use whatever life force I could to break you and your new girlfriend up, I wouldn't just be showing old movies to freak you out."

"Old movies?"

I ignored his question. How else could I describe the visions he'd been in? It didn't even matter. "The fact that you can so casually suggest that I should be banging some other guy shows me that you don't care about me nearly as much as I care about you. What, was there someone here you were hoping to get your mitts on if something happened to me?" I gasped. "Or is there someone else now? Is that something you can do . . . on the other side? Is it Brigitte Bardot? You always thought she was so hot."

"Brigitte Bardot is still alive."

"She is?" *Was* she? Somewhere in the deep recesses of my mind I could remember a mean article online talking about celebrities who'd aged badly and she was on the list. Maybe that was why I'd come up with her name: because I didn't want to give him a thirty-six-year-old Marilyn Monroe ghost, or Princess Diana. "Well, whatever, you're dodging the point."

"And you're being silly." He seemed totally unfazed by my outburst. "Go into the kitchen before Kristin starts to wonder what you're doing in here with my clothes."

"I don't want to. I want to stay with you."

He chuckled. I remembered that chuckle so well. "Then come on." He held out his hand and I reached for it, though I felt virtually nothing. We went into the kitchen, and Kristin turned from the counter, where she was chopping fruit.

"There you are!" She reached over and turned the radio down. Fortunately, she didn't appear to have heard us. Me. She hadn't heard me. She'd never hear him. "You know, that local grocery store has outrageous produce. Look at this stuff! Even the pineapple seems like someone just picked it off the tree." She turned and leaned against the counter. "They come off of trees, right? Huh, I never thought about it."

"They grow underground like potatoes," Ben said, showing the telltale dimple he always got when he told a lie.

"No, they don't!"

Kristin looked at me. "Then, what? A bush? Obviously they aren't root fruits, growing down like potatoes or garlic."

"Obviously not." I flashed Ben a look. "I think they're just, like, plants, you know? Like a pineapple plant. It would look like a tropical growth of some sort in Florida, you know?"

"Hmm." She appeared to consider this, then shrugged. "Well, absent pineapple *growths* around here, these things are amazingly fresh. Go take a seat, let me serve you, milady."

"Such service!" I cried. "Ben never did anything like this!"

"I brought you McDonald's in bed every Mother's Day!" he objected. "Jamie and I."

"I guess I'm a better husband than Ben," Kristin said lightly, then looked immediately ashamed. "Oh, god, I'm sorry."

"No, no, it's fine. I think you are."

"Horse hockey," he said next to me.

Kristin brought a plate over to me—fresh fruit salad, a popover with butter and preserves, bacon, and a cup of coffee, already with cream, just how I liked it. She set it down, then stopped and ran her hands over her arms. "Jeez, there is a draft in here, do you feel that?" She looked around, presumably for a duct or ceiling fan running, but there was nothing to be seen.

"Windows," I said quickly. "They're a bit drafty." They weren't. They were double-paned. Ben had made sure of that because of the winds at the beach.

"Good one," Ben said on a sigh. "I'm a draft now."

I flashed him a look. "You *are*."

"I'm what?" Kristin asked, looking up with surprise at my hissy tone.

"Right in the draft." I raised a hand in the path between the window and Kristin. "I can feel it now."

"There." She nodded, her lips in a thin line. "I'm not crazy. We have to put that on the list of things to do. I guess we'll have to call a guy."

"Call a guy? Just any guy?"

"You know certain jobs require a guy. I'd say just about anything around the house qualifies."

"Okay, well, I think we can make it by with a little draft. We have bigger fish to fry first. Like painting."

"I'm on it!" She stood up and took her dishes to the sink. "Actually, Will, I have to say, the place is really looking lovely. It's sad seeing all these packed boxes around, but it's time to move on. We had loads of fun here over the years, though, didn't we?"

My eyes filled with tears. They did this regularly now; I was constantly a faucet, ready to leak at the slightest provocation. If only Dave Macmillan could fix *me*. "We really did. Do you think . . . do you think it's a mistake to get rid of all that stuff?"

"No," she said, rinsing her plate and opening the dishwasher with a clang. "I really don't."

There was motion in my peripheral vision and Ben moved behind her. He shook his head.

"What does that mean?" I asked him accidentally. "You don't think I should sell?"

I shifted my gaze quickly back to Kristin.

Fortunately, she didn't think it was such a dumb question. "No, I meant I agree with you—it's time to sell and move on. We'll all have fun in new places, with new people. This place has too many memories for you to move forward in it. Can you even imagine having another man here?"

"Of course not!"

"Well, someday you're going to have to think about that, and it'll be that much harder to do when Ben is so present."

Ben nodded and pointed to her. *What she said*, he mouthed.

"But I *want* him present."

"You want him alive. We all do. But, honey, it's not going to happen. So you need to leave it in the past."

"I can't stay like this forever," Ben added. "You know that."

I took a shaky breath. "Yeah, I guess I know that's right."

"It is," they both said.

"Man, it is *cold* in this draft," Kristin said, visibly shivering. "I think we should call some window guys."

"Let's just get painting," I suggested. "I'll do the dishes and worry about the window later."

Chapter Twenty-one

Jamie

When Jamie woke up in the morning, he was sore in a good way. Like his body had melted and, upon his renewing consciousness, he'd re-formed it from a pile of slime into the body of a teenage male.

From flat on his stomach, he curled up into a sitting position.

The room was so bright, he couldn't believe he'd slept this late. His own room at home was darkened like he'd turn to ash if his flesh met a sun ray. How was it that here, with windows completely uncurtained, he'd managed not only to sleep well, but to awake feeling revived?

Was this how normal people felt?

No. He was pretty sure everyone sort of hated waking up.

Something crashed downstairs. The sound of metal, wood, a small splash, and then his mother's yell made him think maybe it was a paint can falling off of a step stool.

He wouldn't ordinarily be able to so literally envision his mother's catastrophes, but he'd watched the woman teeter her full Behr cans on various precarious surfaces so many times recently.

He'd better rush down and bear witness before she pretended it had never happened.

His shorts were hanging a little lower on his hips than usual. He'd lost weight. And muscle. That whole "V" thing Roxy had so obsessed over wasn't gone, but it was more from emaciation than muscle.

Roxy.

She'd probably called or texted a hundred times.

He picked up his phone. The screen was completely clear. It actually made his eyebrows shoot up. Had he ever even awoken with this being the case? At least not since he'd been with Roxy, no. Before that, he just didn't really remember. He'd approached the morning phone scan with such dread for so long, and yet here his screen lay. On, but empty. No airplane mode, no nothing.

His first fully formed thought was . . . *Had she always been that easy to shake?*

In the slapstick delivery of a long-ago comic, his internal response was, *I shoulda ditched the broad lwwwong ago!*

He threw a T-shirt on and almost brought his phone with him, then stepped back in the room and tossed it back on the mattress.

The stairs were carpeted. A thick, plush carpet he'd forgotten about until he felt it now under his bare feet. He snuck a bit down them, feeling surprisingly mischievous about sneaking up on his mom and the inevitable paint disaster.

Sure enough, he found his mom in almost exactly the scene he would have anticipated.

Hair back in that old green bandanna. Sports bra that read VICTORIA, and made him feel weird because the girls he knew bought from there too.

Jean shorts hacked off at mid-thigh, shorts that he knew had been his dad's at one point, but which had much longer been his mother's.

More than all that, though, was the way she shuffled around the table and tried to redirect him once she saw him.

"Good morning, Jamie!"

"Uh. Morning, freak show."

"May I direct you to the fridge, which Aunt Kristin has piled high with leftover popovers, fruit, and orange juice, and coffee—do you drink coffee yet? I say 'yet' like it's a necessity of adulthood, when really it's—"

"Did you spill a can of paint?"

She swallowed her face.

He never really understood that expression. When she'd catch him in a lie during his childhood, she'd either glare or laugh at him, saying he'd *swallowed his face*. But now he saw her do it—her temples sank back above her ears, her hairline receded by a centimeter, her color vanished, her eyebrows went straight, her eyes went blank, and her chin receded hilariously, reptilian-like, into her neck.

He could literally not *not* laugh.

"Wha—no!" she turned to the obvious scene of the crime, where Dolly was quietly venturing. "Dolly, stop, no! Don't . . . ruin my new artwork!"

He moved his mom aside and looked at the enormous spill of vanilla-colored latex paint.

He looked back at her.

"I—okay, well, it wasn't *totally* my fault. Do you think you could, um. Maybe help me . . ."

He looked down at the creamy mess.

"Would you rather me help clean that up or go get a job?"

Her face lit up. "A job? Here? Really?"

He shrugged. "Thinking about it."

"Oh, I got this. You go do that!" She grinned, then surveyed him. "I mean, change. Because you look like a punk. But yeah, go!"

He got to the restaurant and was directed onward into the parking lot by a guy wearing an orange Hawaiian shirt and a frown. This took him to a full parking lot and a valet stand, where another guy in a Hawaiian shirt—this one grinning to the point of overwhelming—leaned down to Jamie's open window.

"Hey, there, Señor Tequila, we'd be happy to park your raft for you, only ten dollars—gratuities appreciated!"

The dude looked straight out of a canceled sixties sitcom. His red shiny face was at least a foot from Jamie's, and yet he felt as though they were forehead to forehead.

"I'm actually here to see if you all are hiring—fill out an application. Someone told me to come by."

The guy nodded blankly, as though he weren't programmed to answer such an inane question. "Right, right!"

Jamie looked at him for another second, expecting the full-grown adult man to kick in somewhere along the way. When he didn't spring to life, Jamie went on.

"Okay, can you tell me where self-parking is?"

"You're gonna have to head right out of paradise." He adjusted his footing noisily in the sandy drive. "Hook a right by Java Joe up there in the orange shirt, head straight down until you see the real world!" He laughed. "There ought to be a public parking lot over there. At least I hope there is for your sake! Wouldn't want you drownin' out there in open water!"

Good lord, thought Jamie. He didn't like to be the Scrooge who hated all the festivity, but this was just irritating.

"O . . . kay. All right, thank you."

He followed the insane directions until he saw a parking lot sign.

Parking was twelve dollars.

He sighed, resigned, and headed back around the loop. Once again the guy stooped to the window and started his spiel. When he recognized Jamie, he said, "Well, hold on, now, have I been hit in the head by one too many coconuts, or have I seen you around these parts before?"

Jamie stared at him a beat. "Uh, yeah, I just want to valet."

"Ten dollars, Señor Tequila, gratuities appreciated, pay on your way out, and . . . son?" He leaned in close. "I'd have your ID ready, and don't bother trying to get one past that doorman, he's a stickler!"

Jamie considered explaining, again, that he was just there for a job, not a pineapple filled with . . . anything, ever, that this man had been drinking, but reconsidered and just said, "Thanks."

He walked up the rickety driftwood ramp that led to the building.

The PRETTY MAMA sign was bright pink. Underneath the name it read *Come on why don't we go?*

If he didn't get the lyrical reference, this would have seemed like a bizarre and frantic tagline.

The doorman was no stickler. He nodded him through after a glance. Jamie went in. The place was all palm fronds, sand, parrots, neon beer signs, and day-drunk middle-aged people bonding with drunk college students. The middle-aged men felt flattered by the college girls who took pictures with them for the novelty factor on their Snapchat; the girls accepted one too many free drinks. The middle-aged women told the college boys how cute they were, and how they wished they'd known boys like *them* in college.

The bartenders looked happy and tipsy. One TV screen played *Blue Hawaii* starring Elvis, another showed a 1950s beach party that reminded *him* at least of a *Mystery Science Theater 3000*, and another screen showed an old seventies basketball game—the shorts were a dead giveaway.

"Hi, welcome to Pretty Mama's, how many in your party?"

He turned to see a hostess, younger than him even, her smile as stiff and marionette-like as her voice was. ("Welcome" came out as "walcah," and "party" came out as "pardeee.")

"Uh. Is there a manager around? I'm just looking to fill out an application."

Her eyes lit up. "Oh! Awesome! Okay, yeah, let me just . . ." She looked in her podium. "Here you go, here is an application and a pen, I'll get Steve."

" 'Kay, thanks."

"You can head right to the Cuban Corner, I'll send him over."

The Cuban Corner was a dark black-and-red bar with cigars displayed around bottles of expensive-looking tequila.

He sat as close as he could to a neon Corona bottle so that he could see the application, and started filling it out.

A guy came over fifteen minutes later in khakis and a blue polo, the Pretty Mama logo above his left nipple. Jamie wouldn't have noticed that it was above a nipple ordinarily, but the man had some of the most obvious man boobs he'd ever seen.

"You the one looking for a job?"

Now that he was closer, Jamie could smell a waft of cigarette smoke and fry oil.

"Yes, sir," said Jamie, standing and putting out his hand.

"Whoa-ho-ho!" said Steve, putting his own hands in the air. "*Sir,* huh? More professional than the whole staff I got here combined already."

Jamie picked up his application and started to hand it to Steve. The man shook his head and said, "Nah, don't worry about that old formality."

He was trying to be cool and easygoing, but it just bugged Jamie. *At least pretend to look at it.*

"Ever worked in a restaurant before?"

"No, first time. First job, actually. Except for stuff around the neighborhood at home. Lawn mowing, snow shoveling, dump runs, stuff like that."

The guy nodded, impressed, which Jamie thought was almost exactly the wrong response to that.

"What are you looking to do around here?"

"Whatever you've got. Of course, I want to make as much as I can, I'll work hard, and I'm a fast learner even though I don't have experience yet in this industry."

"Whoo, all right, college boy," said Steve, as though Jamie had just spoken in Latin. "Let's get you a uniform, you got time to start training right now?"

Jamie spent the next hour trailing behind Steve, both of them now matching in blue polos. He showed him the dishwasher, the prep area, the expo line, the surly cooks behind that expo line, where the reeking Dumpsters were, where he could smoke (which he didn't and wouldn't). He showed him the basics on the POS—point of sale—which was the computer, but which he made an easy joke about, calling it the Piece of Shit, and saying it worked seventy percent of the time. He introduced him to everyone working. They all seemed surprised and out of practice at meeting a new employee, as if they had been there a decade and rarely seen a new face—which, perhaps, was the case.

Steve had already let him in on about ten different loopholes, rules that weren't really rules. Jamie knew it was probably because all the other employees broke them anyway, and because Steve liked Jamie well enough. But if Jamie were the manager, he thought he'd start with the rule and let the employee learn to break it, if that's what they chose to do. Seemed like a much better way to manage.

Jamie spent a couple of hours around the kitchen and bar, learning what they'd need from him as an expo. By early evening, he was done and Steve walked him to the front.

The hostess put her hair behind her ear and waved to him.

She reminded him of Roxy. Her irises seemed to slowly swirl like hers.

"Where'd you park?" Steve asked as they left the building.

"I did the valet. It was expensive elsewhere and I just thought it was easier for now."

"From now on park behind the building by the Dumpsters, we've got a lot out there. For today we won't charge you. Would have if you hadn't gotten the job." He laughed.

Jamie tried to imagine exactly what or who would have to walk through the door that Steve wouldn't have hired.

"Who parked for you?"

"That guy." He gestured at him.

"Oh, Ronnie? Dude's a fuckin' whackadoo. All right, cool, so I'll let him know it's on the house, and hey, got a question for you."

"What's up?"

"You got any friends who might be interested in a job?"

"Uh—"

"Girls, especially? You got a girlfriend?"

"Not here. Well, no, I don't."

Steve sighed. "It's a friggin' sausage fest in there, employee-wise. I gotta find some cute girl to start takin' tables or I'm gonna keep runnin' a cougar den. If you think of anyone, let me know. I'll put you on the same shifts and everything if you want." He laughed again, that wheezy smoker laugh.

"I'll think on it."

" 'Ey, Ronnie, this guy's car, it's on us. Fresh meat!" Wheeze.

"Thanks, man," said Jamie, holding out a hand for a shake.

Steve took it, but then released in a slide motion and held out a fist for a bump.

This guy was like an overgrown ten-year-old.

Right before Jamie got in his car, Steve shouted, "Find a girl for me and I'll bump your pay up a dollar an hour!"

He smiled back at Steve and gave him a thumbs-up. "Got it, thanks."

Chapter Twenty-Two

Willa

We put Spotify on the greatest hits of the eighties and went to work, shout-singing along with the music all the way. That, and just having Kristin there, made the time and the work go so much faster.

Plus, after all the dithering I'd spent my time doing over the past few days, it frankly felt good to do the kind of activity that had appreciable results at the end of the day. I loved spackling, always had, I don't know why, and then rolling the paint over on the smooth surface was tremendously satisfying. I wasn't as good at the detail work, which Kristin loved, so she was coming along after me and touching up the parts I wasn't so good at.

At one point, she caught up to me and couldn't go farther without landing on top of me, so she excused herself and went into the other room. I heard her talking for a while and assumed she had gotten ahold of Kelsey and was talking to her.

Truth be told, I wished Kelsey could come. She'd always been good for Jamie when they were kids. He'd never admit it, but I knew she was his favorite of our friends' kids. Whenever we'd have a game night or something, our friends would bring their kids, but Kelsey and Jamie always ended up as the dynamic duo.

We'd all come to the beach that last summer before Ben died. The kids were getting a little older—thirteen, almost fourteen—and I worried that they might be developing crushes on each other. Or, worse, one on the other without reciprocation. It would be such a shame to ruin a nice friendship with romance. Believe me, I'd seen it happen before, and nothing was worse than adolescent romance.

Both the kids had been moody and mopey when it came time for Kristin, Phillip, and Kelsey to leave, and after that they'd gotten squirrely about seeing each other, even though we lived just a few houses apart. By fourteen they didn't need to come with their parents instead of staying home, and after that they had different interests and different friend groups.

As far as I could tell, Kelsey hung out with the good kids, the A-students, the pom-pom girls. Kristin and Phillip didn't seem to have a lot to worry about, apart from the usual worry that came along with having a teenage kid.

Jamie was a bit more of a worry. He was already showing signs of wiliness before Ben died—missing school, claiming he was sick when we both knew he wasn't, and just generally being antisocial. His friends weren't losers, I don't mean to give that impression, but they were more interested in video games (and could rattle off specs and release dates on those like computer scientists) than grades. His friends appeared to do all right in school, better than he was doing, at any rate, but none of them had any great ambitions, and that was a concern to me and B—

To me.

I didn't notice how long Kristin was gone. I was lost in my own thoughts and the ordinary world of Duran Duran. When she came back in the room I was momentary surprised to see her walking in in front of me.

"I've gotten a great idea," she said with a smug smile.

"Good!"

"I'm serious." She went over and sat down on the sofa, then tapped the cushion next to her.

"I'm covered in paint," I explained, and sat on my step stool instead. "What's up, pussycat?"

"You know the Ben thing?"

"Hmmm . . . *Ben thing* . . . what do you mean? Yes, of *course* I know the Ben thing. What about it?"

"Well, I was there painting"—she gestured broadly at the wall—"singing along with Paul Young about every time you go away, and the idea hit me like the proverbial ton of bricks."

"I'm listening."

"Paranormal experts!"

If that was supposed to be some sort of big, obvious revelation, it wasn't. "What does that mean?"

"You know, the show? *Ghost Hunters?* Or the millions of shows like it where people who *are* ghost hunters go to haunted places with a bunch of equipment and find out if there is an actual haunting or some other explanation."

"You mean like a hoax?" Irritation niggled at me. "I can assure you I'm not making stuff up here."

"No, I don't mean that. But sometimes when people say that every time they're on this spot on the steps they *feel a presence*, when the investigators go into the walls they find there's an electrical box there and that accounts for all the peculiar feelings they have there."

"That makes sense! I mean, I *think* it does. If we have iron in our blood, the magnetic pull seems like it would make us feel funny in some way."

"Right."

"But"—I thought about it—"that isn't what's happening here. I'm not just feeling strange and calling it Casper, I've actually *seen* things."

She nodded. "I think they can sort all that out."

She was pandering to me, I knew it. And I didn't blame her. What I was saying sounded insane and there was no way someone who wasn't experiencing it could believe it. She clearly hoped she could get someone in here—and, honestly, who would even be interested in this small-time haunting?—to explain away my visions. Maybe even for her as much as for me.

She wanted it gone.

And that was, maybe, the last thing I wanted.

"Let's ask Jamie what he thinks. Where is he?"

"Hitting the pavement for work."

She looked at her Fitbit. "It's eight forty-five. When will he be home?"

That was later than I'd thought. "Let me just text him." I went to the kitchen counter and punched out, *when will you be home?*

I was starting to walk away, but the phone dinged right away.

On way now.

I smiled with inner relief but, as usual, I was tempted to text back, *why are you texting while you're driving?* But the problem was that he *was* driving and he would read it, possibly even answer, maybe get in an accident, and it would all be my fault. Or I'd feel like it was, forever.

"He's on his way home," I announced, going back into the family room and picking up my roller.

"Texted you that he was on his way, huh?"

"Mm-hm."

"And now you're worried that he's texting and driving."

"The little shit." I laughed. "What does it take for them to learn? Is there anything short of an actual catastrophe?"

"I talk to Kelsey about it all the time. Feels like I get nowhere, but, honestly, a lot of the stuff we said when she was little and we thought it was going in one ear and out the other has actually taken hold. She doesn't smoke, she doesn't do drugs, she's got good grades and good ambitions, so I can't complain." She dipped her paintbrush into the bucket. "Except about that damn texting."

"Amen."

"So tell me," Kristin went on after a moment. "Before he gets here. What really is happening with Jamie? I never see him acting up particularly. Why are you two having so much trouble?"

It was a subject that got me riled immediately because it was subtle and often hidden completely from the rest of the world. "He can be really belligerent," I said. "If I tell him to do something he doesn't want to do, he just won't. It's gotten to the point where he'll even say no right to me." I sighed. "It's exhausting, but what can I do? I'm alone with it."

Kristin nodded. "And you were always the good cop."

"Yeah, now I've got to be both. But more often than not I end up as the bad cop."

"I guess the girlfriend situation isn't helping much."

"Ugh. Perfect example. For a while there he was spending all his time with her—again, regardless of what I said or what I needed him to do—and her manipulations were just *so obvious* to me, but he couldn't see them. He was 'in love' and just had to be with her every minute."

"Unfortunately, I remember being that teenage girl."

"Oh, no, no, no, believe me, you were never *this* teenage girl. This one is different. I'm not being a mom with a prejudice."

Kristin smiled. "Well, maybe a little . . ."

"Okay, maybe a little." I laughed. "But, seriously. No. And I hope he's getting over that, as evidenced by him coming here. But there's another example right there! I had to practically *beg* him to come.

And it took fourteen million phone calls for me to finally get ahold of him."

"Kids." She shook her head. "By the time we know how hard they're going to be, it's too late. We already love them."

I had to laugh. "It's true. But if anyone had told me the magnitude of the worrying I'd be doing *for the rest of my life*, I don't know if I could have faced it."

"Oh, sure you could," she said sagely. "You did. You do every day."

We both proceeded with the painting, with me all nerves and bated breath, until the door opened and Jamie came in. I know it's ridiculous for me to worry so much, particularly during a fifteen-minute drive on roads that also allow bicycles since the speed limit is so low, but my nerves were strung tight and I just couldn't help it.

"Hey," Jamie said, ambling into the family room, neatly dodging the paint supplies and plunking down on the couch. "Hey, Kristin."

"Hey, Jam," she said. "We were just talking about you."

I shot her a warning glance.

"What were you saying?" he asked.

"I was saying how proud I am of you," I said. Even to my own ears, it sounded so patronizing. It was true, but at some point we stop being kids, maybe stop being *ourselves*, and become people in charge of guiding our young, even if we do it in a way that makes them roll their eyes at us.

"Well," he said, clearly feeling awkward. "Thanks. It, uh, it looks like the job at the restaurant is going to work out. I already started training."

"Wow," I said. I wasn't sure what else to say. I was impressed, I was proud, I was sad he wouldn't be here to help me, but maybe that was best since I was going to sell the place. He didn't need to fall in love with it again only to lose it. "That's really cool."

"Think you could get Kelsey a job there when she gets here?" Kristin asked.

We both looked at her.

"Is she coming?" Jamie asked. I knew he'd have been embarrassed by the tinge of hope in his voice if he'd known it was there.

I felt the same sort of tinge myself, hoping she *would* come and add some normality, but I made the mistake of asking, "Do you *want* her to come, Jamie?"

He looked at me. "I don't know. Whatever."

"You *totally* want her to come," I said. "I do too! Kris, what's the deal, is she coming?"

Kristin shrugged. "She's got another day or two of summer school, and then I'm hoping she'll want to come, yeah."

"Oh! And summer school," I said, and gave Jamie a look. "See, it's not that unusual to have to take supplementary classes."

"She's trying to graduate early," he said, and didn't add, *Versus me, who is just trying to graduate at all.* "And I just finished my class. Turned in the last essay."

"Good." I looked at Kristin. She nodded, a little red-faced at the exchange between Jamie and me. "She was always ambitious, that kid of yours."

"I don't know where she gets it."

I hated that she didn't feel like she could reveal the pride she must have been feeling. Hell, I was proud of Jamie for so many things that weren't academic, I tried never to let comparisons get into the mix. "That girl kicks ass, just like her mother," I said.

Kristin smiled, a real, wide, happy smile. "She does kick ass. But so does Jamie." She nodded at him.

Before he could object, I said, "God knows it. I can't wait until he's out of high school and starting on what he *really* wants to do." I'd meant it as encouragement. As a sort of, *I understand you hate it now and in many ways high school is bullshit, so just hold on because you're going to like the rest of your life so much better than that.*

But I hadn't said that. I'd chirped that I couldn't wait until he was out of high school, as if there were some doubt that would ever happen, and that was a shitty thing for me to say, even though it wasn't what I'd meant.

Man, sometimes there is just no getting it right.

A shadow crossed his expression, exactly as I knew it would, and he stood up. "I'm going up to bed," he said. "I told them I'd go in tomorrow at ten."

"Okay." Every nerve in my body was screaming out for me to *fix this*, to somehow make it better, but I couldn't, I had to just let him go. Anything I might have said to clarify my statement would only have seemed like overcompensation. I'd been there before. Enough times that you'd have thought I'd learn.

When he was gone, I turned to Kristin.

Before I could speak, she held up a hand. "They're all moody and constantly ready to take offense."

"I should have been more careful."

She looked at me, straight in the eye, and said, "Actually? He should be getting better grades and giving a shit about his future instead of leaving all of that worry to you."

It was only at that moment that I realized the extent of my self-consciousness about my parenting, that I had been embarrassed, not about my son's level of achievement, but at the level—or lack—of my involvement in it one way or the other. I knew I needed to step up more, but, deep down, I also knew that no amount of my stepping up could give him the motivation that needed to come from within.

"Thank you," I said, heartfelt.

She gave a dry laugh, but her eyes were a little sad. "Remind me of

that myself, okay? Kelsey's doing okay at school, but she's so uncommuni-
cative at home that I can hardly believe she's the same little girl I read to
every night and watched *The Sound of Music* with over and over again."
She sighed. "I know she's not a mean girl at school, but damned if she
isn't one at home sometimes."

"I had no idea!"

"Of course you do. We deal with these little monsters all day long, every
day, a hundred and eighty days a year. We see their nice phases and we see
them go totally retrograde. No reason to imagine ours won't be the same."

I nodded. "I think I imagine everyone's doing a better job than I am
so that I can punish myself for something real, something that might *actually* be my fault—and therefore under my control—rather than the sad
circumstances that took over Jamie's life."

"I've seen you do it a million times," she answered. "I'm actually glad
you brought it up because, as much as you want to control things, and I
don't blame you, *none* of this is your fault. And you're doing a much better job under the circumstances than most people would, myself included.
Sometimes you have to just accept that life can be random."

"Random good I could accept. Random bad just sucks."

She gave a half shrug. "Yeah, but can you deny it? Your life has obviously seen some random bad."

"No denying that."

"And on top of that, you've got this ghost stuff happening now. If
it's your imagination—and I'm sorry, but I do have to mention that
possibility—then I think it's a fairly easy fix with a shrink. Grief, loneliness, all the usual suspects."

I took a deep shuddering breath, then let it out. "I agree," I said honestly, although it was embarrassing. "I've thought of that."

"*But.*" She raised an eyebrow. "If something *real* is happening here,
maybe even someone gaslighting you, well, we need to know that too."

"Gaslighting seems a bit unlikely."

"What else is there?"

I shrugged. "Gaslighting implies an intention on someone's part to drive me crazy. And, yes, I can see how a visitation like that can drive someone crazy, but there's also the possibility that it's just that—a visitation. Innocuous. Unlikely. A tear in the universe that lets two souls who miss each other terribly embrace, if only vaguely, once again."

She watched me talking, and then I noticed her eyes were filled with tears. "That is so beautiful," she said. "I only wish it were true."

"You don't know that it isn't."

There was a very long hesitation then. And I sympathized with her, because her answer couldn't come easily. She hadn't been in my shoes, she hadn't seen what I had, heard what I had, *felt* what I had. She hadn't run the full gamut of thoughts and emotions through this (though admittedly I myself had gone through the skepticism she was clearly feeling now). How could she believe the fantastic story I'd told, having not experienced any of it herself at all?

"I'm sorry," I hastened to add. "I don't mean to put you on the spot. I know you're worried about me and trying to help, it's just that . . ." I didn't know what else to say. "There's a lot I haven't told you yet."

Chapter Twenty-three

Willa

A few days later, the plumber was back, doing the final touches on the new bathroom sink. It looked amazing. If I kept going and changing the place up, it was going to be hard to leave.

But it was impossible not to, so I continued to pack while Kristin continued to paint and Jamie continued to work at the restaurant.

"I've got a surprise for you," Kristin sang as she came into the bedroom where I was packing up years' worth of summer clothes I'd left there. I was giving them to charity and trying not to look at them as I tossed them aside. It was too easy, in this packing process, for me to talk myself into keeping things, and that was dangerous. My house was already full of stuff *and* memories. I didn't need more of either.

"What is it?" I asked, a little excited at the prospect.

"Guess who's coming."

My excitement suspended. "Is it a bunch of nerdy men with ghost-hunting equipment and high hopes? Because I really think that's a bad idea."

She looked puzzled for a split second and then said, "No, no. It's Kelsey."

Then my heart really did warm. Kelsey was coming! For one thing, she was a very pleasant girl and fun to have around. Like her mother, she had the gift of making the maudlin seem okay. That would be particularly good for Jamie. He'd always loved hanging out with her, and maybe that would still be true.

"That's great!" I enthused genuinely. "I haven't seen her for ages!"

"Neither has Jamie," Kristin said, and raised an eyebrow. "And, frankly, I think she'd be good for him."

I tossed a too-small T-shirt that read NAMASTE IN BED into the box. My yoga period had passed a while ago and I wasn't sure it was coming back, but if it did, I didn't need to wear a shirt that had always seemed better suited for Barbie than for me. "I think she would too. In fact, that was my first thought." I sighed. "I'm sorry he's been so grumpy."

She brushed it off. "He's a kid. He's a kid in a place he dreaded coming to."

"That's true. I know this isn't easy for him. It's not easy for any of us, but I worry about it the most for him."

Kristin nodded. "That I understand. I've seen that kid go through so much, he definitely doesn't need a negative influence in his life." She looked at me. "Which reminds me of something I should say more—Willa, you've done an amazing job soldiering on through this. You really have, and I don't think you hear it enough. I know I don't say it enough."

I smiled through tears. "Thank you."

"I mean it."

At that moment, it felt like the kindest thing anyone had ever said to me. Because the truth was, I'd felt weak. I'd felt weepy and needy and whiny and weak at times, to the point where I didn't know how I could go on.

That's the thing, though. If you're not the kind of person who's going to kill themselves—and I'm not—then, when you reach rock bottom, say you can't take it anymore . . . you have no choice. You have to keep on going, if you're not going to stop. Time marches on and even if you take to your bed, Camille-like, you still march on with it. You still think, you still grieve, you still grow if you're lucky. Gain the distance that allows you to go from one day to the next without pacing the floor thinking, *I don't think I can I don't think I can I don't think I can.*

You can because you must.

But I wasn't sure I'd always done it so gracefully.

"I think we should go to the boardwalk," Kristin said abruptly. "And go on the Ferris wheel." She was always like this with sensitive topics. She'd raise something she was not entirely comfortable saying, explore the topic until her point was made, then maneuver out of it so that the other person didn't have to linger on it and start feeling defensive or overly appreciative or whatever else would come.

This was one of those moments where, if she'd said anything else, I probably would have cried my eyes out.

Instead I was suddenly humoring her again, rather than the other way around. "The Ferris wheel?"

She nodded, like the idea was taking hold and she was liking it more and more. "What the hell? We're here, it's summer, there's a Ferris wheel three miles away. Let's take a quick break and ride it!"

My first instinct—as well as my second, third, and fourth—was to say no, that was silly, I had stuff to do and couldn't take the time. So instead I followed my fifth instinct and said, "Let's do it."

We got in the car, opened all the windows, and drove across the bridge over the bay to the inlet. It was a sparkling sunny day and the light danced on the water like shards of gleaming glass. The scene took my breath away, it was so perfect, and for a moment I forgot all the heaviness I'd been carrying around for so long and felt light.

"This was a good idea," I said to Kristin, who was in the driver's seat.

"Good. I thought you were going to say no."

"I was."

"You just need to break up the monotony a little bit now and then. Get those thought paths going in different directions."

I looked at the skyline of hotels and condominiums and thought about how many people came here just for fun and had a great time. If the buildings were mood rings, they'd probably be mostly blue.

We threaded our way through the traffic on the Coastal Highway and got a prime parking spot by the wide end of the boardwalk. "See?" Kristin said. "It was *meant to be*."

I laughed and we got out of the car. The unique smell of the beach hit me: sugar, popcorn, fries, cotton candy, pizza, and salt air. It made me hungry for everything, which I took as progress, since I hadn't had much of an appetite for a while.

"Fisher's?" Kristin asked.

Fisher's meant caramel popcorn, a longtime Ocean City staple. "Absolutely," I agreed.

We got a bucket of caramel corn, then went to the ticket window to buy tickets for the Ferris wheel. The line was long and we were taller than most of the people in it, but we stood and waited, people-watching and munching our caramel corn, until we finally got up to the front and a dubious-looking guy with cigarettes rolled in his sleeve and two dead teeth ushered us on to the seat. I imagined he probably had whiskey on his breath as well.

"Don't worry," Kristin said, as if reading my mind. "It's not like he assembled it."

"But he's in charge of running it," I said, as the wheel jerked back and the next people were loaded on. "What if he forgets to turn it off, or turns it on too fast?"

"Then we'll have a great time!" She tossed a few pieces of caramel corn in the air. "Hey, remember when we used to bring the kids here?"

"Jamie *hated* the Ferris wheel!"

"He did! And Kelsey loved it. She used to tease him about being scared."

The ride moved again. "And then she'd hold his hand during the ride."

Kristin smiled. "That's right. She's a pretty good egg, when it comes down to it. They both are."

And with that the Ferris wheel swooped up and I felt the familiar rush of fear and excitement that always seemed to come with the ride. We rose into the air and the ocean stretched, vast and endless, ahead of us, and I felt a peace I hadn't felt in three years come over me. It was almost as if nothing bad had ever happened, because the moment was so full and complete. Just my best friend and me on a boardwalk ride, it could have been twenty years ago or now, the moment was just timeless. Nothing was missing.

The ride did seem to go on for a long time, soaring and dipping, and eventually stopping to let riders off. We hung, suspended, at the very top for a moment, and the wind gently blew the chair, which creaked like the riggings on a ship.

"This is perfect," I breathed.

"It never gets old."

"We should play hooky today and just do all the rides."

Kristin looked at me, surprised. "For real?" She put a hand to my forehead, pretending to check my temperature. "Is this really you?"

"Yes, it's really me." I laughed. "This is the new me. I'm tired of being neurotic and walking on eggshells and always, always, always trying to figure out how to do things *right*. I can't think of a reason in the world why we shouldn't just pig out on Tony's pizza and go on the roller coaster till we're afraid we're going to throw it all up."

"You know how to tempt a girl!"

"Oh, you know you want to do the same thing."

And so we did. We spent the next two hours riding everything except for the littlest toddler rides. (And we only had to forgo those because we weren't allowed on them.) We ate pizza and drank Love's lemonade, bought too much fudge from the Candy Kitchen, then waddled our sorry selves to a bench that overlooked the shoreline.

"It's going to be hard to say goodbye to all of this," I said, and found myself putting my hand to my chest.

Kristin looked at me. "Have you thought about maybe not doing that?"

"Not what?"

"Not selling. Keeping the place." She shrugged. "I'm not saying you should or you shouldn't, but it's the first time you've been here since, you know . . ."

"Ben died." It came out easier than I expected this time.

"Yes, since that. And I know you dreaded coming all this time, but now that you're here . . . I don't know, you seem to be . . ." She splayed her arms. "I don't know, you seem to be loosening up a little."

I knew what she meant. It wasn't just that I'd agreed to come here today and then made the unusual-for-me decision to blow off work, but I also hadn't obsessively called Jamie to micromanage him, for once. I *knew* that was progress and that if I wanted our relationship to improve and become what it should be (at least as far as I was concerned), I needed to do more of that.

But keep the house?

Maybe you're noticing a change because I'm crazily seeing Ben when I'm there, I wanted to say. But what could she say to that?

And, really, no matter what prompted the change in me, wasn't it good regardless?

But still . . . keep the house?

"It would be crazy for me to just keep it for myself, without Ben. I mean, he was half the heart of the home, you know?"

"I know," she conceded. "But you kept the house in Potomac, as you totally should. You've moved on there. You changed it up, redecorated, made it into something old *and* something new. And, it's hard to say this because I don't know how you're going to take it, but, honey, you're young. The chances of you meeting someone new and making it into a happy old age with him are really good."

I felt a stab in my heart. Someone new? Who was this nameless, faceless person that was trying to change my life and make me into something else? That's what it felt like every time I contemplated moving on, and yet she was right. I didn't want to grow old alone. Die alone. Of course I didn't want that. No one did!

In the distance, the ocean rolled and crashed onto the shore. I could see the telltale section of the waves that indicated a riptide, and it occurred to me that I was trapped in a riptide myself. Trying so hard to resist the pull of reason that I was getting exhausted.

I *had* to move on.

Maybe these visits from Ben indicated just that. A mind that had grown so stuck on what it wanted that it was creating it in a way that was nothing short of nuts.

"Did I say the wrong thing?" Kristin asked, worried.

I shook my head. "No, no. I'm sorry, I was just lost in thought. As hard as it is for me to fathom, I think you're right. Life goes on and I have no choice but to go with it. I'm just not so sure keeping the beach house is the way to do it."

"Understood." She lifted an eyebrow. "Let's just see what we can do with it in the next few weeks, no matter what you want to do with it."

Chapter Twenty-four

The place really came together in the next couple of weeks. It was amazing what a fresh coat of paint and a weeding-out of old furniture could achieve. It felt like a new place, and, with all the windows open and the sea breeze blowing through day and night, I was truly beginning to feel like a new person.

During that time I didn't see or "sense" Ben at all. I'd like to say it was because I reached such a new level of mental health that I didn't need the crutch of an imagined ghost anymore, but the truth is that I was worried that somehow my conversation with Kristin about finding someone new might have pushed him away, despite the fact that he had suggested the same thing. Which, of course, made me feel like I needed to retract it all and vow to go beyond our wedding promises of "till death do us part" and just commit my life to being a widow.

But that was an idea that didn't hold much appeal.

And some small part deep inside of me was *glad* I recognized that. Still, a whole other part of me was still waist-high in memories as I went through his things—and our things—and boxed up everything that gave me even a moment's pause or a hint of negativity.

"Oh, Ben," I found myself saying one day as I was working in the master bedroom. "I can't believe I'm doing this. If you're really around, please come and tell me what I'm supposed to do."

The box of clothes I was working on was full and I sealed it and shoved it aside. This was hard but cathartic. I dragged another box over, this one emblazoned with the Amazon Prime logo, and opened it. I was surprised to see it wasn't empty. At the bottom of the box there was a flat plastic-covered item, almost invisible. I'd overlooked smaller inclusions in Amazon boxes before, so it wasn't surprising that Ben had too. I reached in and took it out.

It was one of those flat magnets, with an old-fashioned picture of a woman on it and the inscription *A CLEAN HOUSE IS A SIGN OF A WASTED LIFE.*

He always did say I broke my back cleaning too much. He helped out, of course, but I was a bit OCD about cleaning. That's annoying for the other people in the house, I know that. It always carries an implication of *Help me out* or *Why aren't you doing more? Do I have to do everything around here?* A person can't just relax while someone else is working their butt off.

So this was just a little joke from him. Typical and kind of adorable, even while it was heart-wrenching.

I held it to my chest for a moment, then set it aside, deciding I'd put it on my fridge as a reminder of him and as a posthumous joke that would always make me smile when I saw it.

Even if it was somewhat through tears.

Then I returned to my work, everything into the box. I barely even looked at the items, just tossed them in.

"Wait, wait," I heard behind me. "I always liked that one."

I was holding a green crop top that I hadn't worn since my bartending days in my twenties. As soon as I heard the voice, I closed my eyes for a minute, fervently praying it wasn't just my imagination, and then turned to see him.

Ben was back, sitting on the bed, watching me. Interestingly, he was dressed differently this time. Whereas before he'd been wearing jeans and a T-shirt that read ATHLETIC DEPARTMENT, which I'd seen him wear a million times (where *was* that T-shirt now?), this time he was in jeans still, but with a different shirt, the short-sleeved white cotton one I'd gotten him from Banana Republic. I didn't always score at that store, but that time I had; the shirt looked great on him.

"This?" I raised the top. "You've got to be kidding." Then it hit me, as it had before. This was Ben. Or this seemed to be Ben. I was talking to Ben.

"It's sexy," he said with a lascivious grin.

Man, I loved that grin.

"It's indecent," I corrected, though my heart was pounding at the sight of him. "Particularly at my age."

"Oh, yes. You're such an old woman."

"Hey, I'm a widow." I couldn't help looking at him accusingly, as if he'd *chosen* to leave me in this position. Quickly I corrected my expression, but not before he'd taken note of it.

"So you are. The Merry Widow."

"Not so merry."

"Oh, hey, that magnet! You found the magnet." He laughed heartily. "I thought about that damn thing so much more than I should have. Don't you just hate how Amazon does that, sticks little tiny things in a big box full of paper towels or whatever and you never even know they're there?"

"Yes, I—"

"I kept meaning to go check that box again, I thought about it right up to the time . . ." He shook his head, still smiling. "I can't believe it. You know, if I weren't here, that's just the kind of thing you'd think was a sign from me, but honestly, I had no idea where the damn thing was."

I had to laugh. That was just so Ben. Losing presents, thinking he should do something but not getting around to it. I can't say literally *dying* was his style—that part was unprecedented—but he was right, I would have wanted to see it as a sign. And it was—it was a sign that people pretty much are who you think they are, and that transcends life and death.

Which was actually a good thing, because I also thought he loved me, and this was pretty good proof of that.

Except I had this niggling question about why it was so seemingly easy for him to come and go, to be with me then to disappear into a world I couldn't join him in until the end. "Why don't you want to stay?"

Confusion crossed his expression, then alit. "You don't think I want to be here with you?"

I shrugged and was embarrassed to feel my lower lip start to tremble with uncontrolled emotion. "You are now," I said. "You were before. Why did you leave?"

He pressed his lips together and thought for a moment. "I don't know. It's not up to me."

"Where did you go when you disappeared?"

"I don't know."

"What do you mean, you *don't know*?" I had raised my voice and immediately thought of Kristin, hearing me yelling to myself. "You're here, then you're gone, now you're back, you're a kid, you're my young husband, now you're . . . you're you. How is all of this happening?"

"I honestly don't know," he said. "You obviously needed me, so I came. I was sent. I was allowed. I'm not sure how to put it, but time and place are different over there. I can't give you the answers you want because there's no way to make you understand."

"Then make me understand this one thing only: If you're here now, why can't you stay?" My voice broke. "At least until it's time for me to join you. Can't you just stay? Didn't you say time is different there? Isn't a lifetime here just the blink of an eye . . . *there*?"

He looked at me sincerely and stood up to move toward me. As before, he grew a little blurrier as he moved close. He must have seen the upset in my eyes and he stepped back as if he understood. "I don't belong here," he said earnestly. "You *do*, but I no longer do. You know that."

"I don't know that."

"Inside, you do. It's time for you to move forward."

"No. I can't." I shook my head. "None of this makes sense. Every other death I've known made some sort of sense—he was out of his misery at last, or she had lived a full life. I can't make sense of yours. You were so young. You left behind such a young son, who misses you so much. And me . . ."

He looked sad, an emotion I had kind of thought he couldn't feel anymore. "I heard what Kristin said to you. About how brave you've been and what a good job you've done with Jamie."

Hearing him say our son's name broke a whole new level of my heart. A place I hadn't really realized existed. "Did you see?" I asked, like a child wondering if there is really a Santa Clause. "Have you been watching us?"

It actually *was* like Santa, I realized. Did he see when we were sleeping? Did he know when we were awake? That's kind of how I'd always thought of God and angels, and I guess I was labeling Ben an angel now because "ghost" seemed so harsh and spooky.

When I was young, I had an old record album of haunted house sounds. It was a Disney production, much older than I was, but I'd found it at a garage sale I'd gone to with my mom and I was captivated by the moody, Halloweeny cover and simply *had* to have it.

And I listened to that thing like I was a teenage girl in the sixties listening to the Beatles. Don't ask me how or why, it was crazy that I did, but I could listen to those creepy creaks and howls and boos from dawn till dusk.

It was pretend then. I loved it. I think we human beings want to *feel* things, but safely. That's why horror movies and thrillers are so popular. We feel scared or tense or on the edge of our seats but we know, even going into it, that everything will be resolved in the end. It's a few hours of safely *feeling*.

So it was with my haunted house record—I'd listen and I'd *feel*, then I'd go upstairs and put on my Carter's pajamas, watch some silly sitcoms or movies with my parents, then go to sleep, carrying with me the *Cheers* episode we'd watched, or *Trading Places*, rather than the ghosts.

Now I couldn't bear to associate Ben with those sad, lonely ghost cries I remembered from my childhood. And there was nothing to suggest he was suffering or would moan through the night like they did, so I was being morbid about this anyway, but I still preferred to look at him as my own private guardian angel now.

"No, I haven't been watching you," he said, and in so doing deflated my guardian-angel hopes. "I don't have that kind of control between worlds."

"But I swear sometimes I have *felt* you around me. Was that my imagination? The crazed thoughts of my grief?"

"No," he said gently. "Of course not. I have sometimes felt the pull of your heart and I've been drawn to it. That's the best I can explain. So, yes, I have been there when you've needed me. I hope. Maybe not every time, because"—he shook his head—"we all know that's not how it works. Unfortunately."

There was comfort in that. Just in knowing I'd been right when I'd felt him. I hadn't been alone at my times of greatest sorrow. "But you can't control it at all? Is it every time I'm really sad?"

"You tell me," he said knowingly. "Have I been here every time you were really sad?"

"No . . ."

"No." He gave a rueful smile.

Now, that was honesty. I was glad he didn't try to dress it up like something prettier than the sow's ear it was. He couldn't be here for me reliably. For all the great things that spirit was, or could be, it failed in the mutual-support department. Mortality had that all over spirit.

"Do you ever need me?" I asked, half afraid of the answer. "Are you ever scared there?"

His smile was so clear and genuine it touched my heart. "I'm at peace, baby, this isn't that hard for me, but it's rough knowing how hard it is for you. If there was any way for me to stay by your side until you were okay, I would. You know I would. But I can't. I don't even know how long I have."

I wanted to say that was cruel, that no one could reasonably withstand this, but how could I say that when I had him at all? Most people didn't get this. I was exceptionally blessed and it was time for me to act like it.

This was the time to ask him all those things I had ever wanted to ask, about him, about his feelings, about how to raise Jamie without him, what to tell him as a message from his father. So much.

But before I could speak, he did. "But I'm here to make you happy. To help you *get* happy. To make sure you're going to be happy for the rest of your life. I promised you that when we got married, and things have taken a little turn, but there's no reason that lets me off the hook now."

I gave a nod. "Right. So what are you going to do?"

"I'm going to make sure you stop mourning and move on with your life."

Chapter Twenty-five

Willa

No sooner had Ben told me he wanted me to just trot along without him—an insult, to my mind, extremely unromantic—than he started to fade away.

"Wait a minute, you can't just say shit like that and disappear!" I cried, not even mindful of being overheard.

He laughed. "Oh, my delicate little blossom. There's such a lilt to your words, you're like Longfellow."

"Oh, shut up! Come back here so you can explain!"

He shrugged, and before I knew it he was gone.

"Sonofabitch!" I spat.

"Whoa." Kristin was at the doorway, holding her hands out in front of her, palms out. "Slow down, sparky. I didn't mean to piss you off."

"It's not you," I muttered.

"Actually, I know that, I just got here. So who the hell *are* you yelling at?" She looked around surreptitiously.

"I was just . . . I was on the phone." I was disconcerted by my interaction with Ben, and part of me wanted to sink into the despair of him leaving, yet I felt certain he'd come back. He'd come back again.

Wouldn't he?

"Your phone is on the counter, charging."

Oh, my god, leave it to her to notice a little detail like that just when I needed her not to. "Landline, obviously," I said absently, then made a show of throwing a pile of unexamined clothes into the box and closing it up. "I've got to take these over to the donation drum," I said, as if the matter had some sort of urgency. "Want to come?"

"Donation drum? Is that what those things are called?"

It took some effort, but I tried to rein my thoughts in to the conversation at hand. "I have no idea, but you knew what I meant!"

"I did, yes. Actually, I do want to come because we, my friend, need to go back to the grocery store. We ran through the fresh stuff fast. You're pretty well stocked on wine and wafers, but I don't think that's such a great diet for Jamie."

"Probably not, no."

She laughed. "And besides that, I'm just dying for some cheese and you've got nothing, not even Whiz."

"Mm, I love Cheez Whiz." Ben used to make fun of me for it. Even a dippy little fact like that kept my heart throbbing.

"Me too. And the kind in the cans that you spray out onto crackers? I love that crap. I never understand how they come up with the flavors, though. *Bacon cheddar* contains neither."

"Yeah, but it's like green apple hard candy. It tastes nothing like green apples, but damned if it doesn't consistently taste like green apple hard candy."

"You know, you're right. Same with watermelon."

I shot a finger gun at her. "Bingo."

We went into the kitchen, where, indeed, my phone was charging.

I turned it on. No messages, no missed calls. I could hardly complain, since I'd actually been *speaking* with Ben, but I did wish Jamie had interest in staying in touch.

Instead I texted him. *Going to store, what do you want to eat? Also, when do you get off?*

I started to head for the front door when my phone dinged right back. It was him. Totally unlike him.

I'm off in fifteen. Can you get Chef Boyardee canned stuff?

No, I typed. *What actual fruits, vegetables, and meat do you want?*

There was a long pause, then, *You know what I like. Also Beefaroni.*

I would cave, of course. Kid wanted Beefaroni, it was probably better than not eating at all, so if he got hungry and I didn't feel like cooking, that would be a perfectly good stopgap. Particularly if I got some good Parmesan to put on it. I made a mental note.

We left in Kristin's car, a sleek Lexus SUV that held my three meager boxes of donations handily in the back compartment.

My mind kept slipping back to my interaction with Ben. Of course. Part of me didn't want to get rid of the things I'd been working on when he showed up, but I knew that was not only silly sentimentalism, it went completely against what he'd been trying to tell me about moving on.

And as much as I didn't want to move on without him—as much as I hadn't wanted to in all the time he'd been gone—when he'd said it, it had resonated as absolutely true and correct.

I guessed that was why I was able to try and push the melancholy aside after seeing him: because I knew that he wasn't here to fulfill some need that couldn't be fulfilled without him, but rather to push me back into life. Because I had no choice, I had to live it.

"I've got to get rid of more stuff," I commented, knowing it was true, as we pulled up to the big trash-can-looking thing that people put their clothing donations in. As usual it was surrounded by broken children's toys and bags that looked as if they probably contained trash. All this de-spite the very clear, very big lettering on the thing that read CLOTHING DONATIONS ONLY. People were so lazy they'd just leave their trash here and let someone else handle it.

"You do," Kristin said. "I agree."

I'd lost track of the conversation. "Huh?"

"Need to get rid of more," she said. "Your house at home is so full already—cozy, homey, but full—you just don't have room to take more stuff back there."

"It's true."

"And you already have more clothes than you could possibly know what to do with. I say not only do you get rid of everything here, but we should go through your closets at home too. You wear the same few things all the time and I would bet my eyeteeth that it's because your closet is so full you stand at the edge and just grab the closest thing so the rest doesn't avalanche down."

She had it exactly right. That was literally what I did and why I did it. Naturally, the things that were most accessible were the things that had just been washed because I'd just worn them, and so I wore them again because they were most accessible. It was a vicious cycle. "You're right," I said. "You're right, you're right, you're right. Clutter is chaos. I'm going to pull myself up by the bootstraps and get it done."

"Good!"

I dropped the boxes off, ignored the pang of regret that tried to tap on my heart, then got back into the car.

"Where to?" she asked.

"Food Lion on Racetrack Road," I said, though I really would have pre-ferred to go to Rehoboth and get some fresh fish and cheese from the markets there. This would do for now. That wasn't what was important. What was important was my latest interaction with Ben.

I wanted so badly to tell Kristin about it, about not just seeing him but *talking* to him, but could she possibly understand? Could anyone? She'd been patient with my tales of seeing him, but I knew that seemed like a pretty normal imagining for someone in my position.

The conversations were not.

Hell, I couldn't even understand and only half believed it myself, yet it was true. In my heart and even in my head I knew it was true. We'd reached a point where it was actually *more* far-fetched to conjure a "logical explanation" than to just admit that there are things in this world, and around it, that we can't explain or even comprehend with our human limitations.

We drove for a few minutes in silence, the radio playing an old Beach Boys tune quietly in the background. "God Only Knows." I loved that song.

"Phillip sang this to me at our wedding," Kristin said, and glanced at me. "Did I ever tell you that?"

"No! How cool! I didn't know Phillip could sing."

"He cannot. He. Cannot." She laughed. "It was a cute, if embarrassing, attempt to make a romantic gesture."

I tried to imagine it. "Does he know he can't sing?"

"If he didn't before he started, he certainly knew by the time he finished."

"Oh, no."

"*Howls* of laughter," she said with a nod. "He's such a joker, everyone thought he was kidding. Honestly, I couldn't blame them."

I chuckled and tried to picture it. "I wish I'd known you then."

"What fun we would have had, huh?"

"We always have."

She nodded thoughtfully. "So, about this Ben thing."

"Which Ben thing?" I knew exactly which Ben thing. I only hoped she wasn't going to mention my talking to him in the bedroom earlier. Or talking "to myself," I guess she'd think of it.

"You thinking you're seeing him." She held up a hand to stop me from objecting. "I'm not sure it's not true."

It was not what I'd been expecting to hear. "You believe me?"

"You, yes, I definitely believe you. The question is how to believe that what you're seeing is real. And, I don't know, it makes no sense, but I don't understand cell phones either, but I know they work. You could strand me on an island for a thousand years, and even though I know all about using one, I wouldn't be able to begin to make one."

"To be fair, an island probably wouldn't have a lot of materials that could be used for a cell phone."

"Oh, you know what I mean. Send me back in time, even just fifty years, and—why am I defending this? You know what I mean?"

I laughed, a good, hard laugh. It was relaxing. It had been a long time since I'd really let go. "I do know what you mean. Even though I'm pretty sure I could build an iPhone. But, yeah, I don't understand this Ben thing either."

"Did it ever happen before you got here?" she asked. "I'm sorry if it did and you didn't think you could talk to me about it. You really can now."

"I know I can." But I didn't know it. I didn't know how much I could say. I'd hesitated even to tell her the part where I saw him interacting with "Jamie" and "me"; I sure didn't know how to tell her I'd been chatting with him like normal. "I never saw him before I was here. At least not beyond the usual face-in-a-crowd sort of thing that happens all the time and you know it isn't real."

She nodded and turned right onto Racetrack Road. "But the thing is, if it's real, maybe it's because you need to let him go in a more real way. Tell him to follow the light or whatever."

I knew what she was saying. She thought I was holding on in an unhealthy way, whether my "visions" were real or not. And I had been for a long time. I had to let him go for him and for me.

"I don't know," she went on. "I'm sure it's a lot more delicate and sensitive than that, but, honey, *if* some vestige of Ben is still in the house, surely you want him freed."

"I don't know," I said, more to myself than to her. I felt wistful and alone, unable to truly get counsel from anyone on this.

She swung the car left into the parking lot. "I don't want to push you on it, but I want you to know I'm here if you want to talk. No matter *what* you want to talk about." She put the car in park and turned the keys in the ignition. "No matter what you want to do."

Chapter Twenty-six

Jamie

The yard had a couple years' worth of nature puke that had piled up in the grass. Right away upon arriving, Jamie had removed the easy armfuls of soggy leaves, but there was far more left.

The grass—what little there was of it—needed to be cut, but he couldn't do that until all the millions of pinecones and pine needles had been dredged out. His mom hadn't even asked him to do it, but it drove him nuts and he couldn't stand to look at it. Even he knew the concept of curb appeal and how lacking that was in this yard.

Maybe it was because of all the shows he heard as ambient noise at home, HGTV blasting while his mom diced garlic and sizzled chicken breasts. Or maybe, hopefully, it was just common sense.

He had in his wireless Bluetooth earbuds, the ones that sank so deeply into his ears that they canceled out any of the tweeting birds or cars zooming by.

All he could hear was "Vicar In a Tutu" by the Smiths. His skin was baking in the sun, slick with the sunscreen he'd sprayed on and the sweat

that fought to roll it off. He was in a pair of his dad's old shorts, which
were a little too big for him. He had been reluctant to put them on. (It
was one thing for his mom to wear a pair to paint, but it started to seem
like they were treating his clothes either as too holy to leave folded or too
unneeded to do anything but ruin.)

In the end, obviously, he'd put them on anyway. He was hot, and all
he'd stupidly brought with him were actual pants. Usually he was fine in
those and a T-shirt, even in summer.

He was leaning over, collecting everything that wasn't grass, tossing it
into a bag. He'd been out for almost two hours, and the yard was finally,
satisfyingly getting to look like the grassy lawn it used to be.

He was about to reach for another fistful of damp pine needles and mud
when he saw a sandaled foot a few feet in front of him. The sandal was
dark tan leather, and the foot was connected to a thin tan curvy leg. Unmistakably a girl, even before you saw the handmade anklet.

Jamie stood up.

He dropped the pile of brown muck.

He wrenched the buds out of his ears and they hung on his bare collarbone.

"Shit," he said when he looked at her.

"That's what I *hope* you're not grabbing with your bare hands."

She smiled.

"No. Already did a round of cleaning that up. This is all just . . . you
know, nature trash."

She laughed, and it sounded just like it used to, even though her voice
was lower now, a little raspier.

"What are you listening to?" She threw down her canvas bag, right
onto the dirt. He noticed this because she didn't go inside and hang it up
neatly in order not to ruin it. Just like always, that wasn't how she was.

She put a bud in her ear for a second, awfully close to his chest. "'Some

Girls Are Bigger Than Others'?" she said. He didn't mean to, he tried to avoid it, but for a brief second his face was in her hair. She smelled like soap and something else. Salt water? Like the beach? Maybe it wasn't that she smelled like the beach, but that the beach had always sort of smelled like her.

"Probably. It was on 'Vicar In a Tutu' when I tore them out in shock."

"I prefer 'Frankly, Mr. Shankly.'" She released the bud.

"Typical," he said with a shake of his head that didn't really mean anything.

More than anything, it was unsurprisingly typical that she knew the album right away.

"This lawn looks terrible. The grass has gone from . . . military buzz cut to mid-nineties Jared Leto."

He narrowed his eyes in question.

"As in, too long to look good. Deflated and flat." She laid a hand on her chest. "But loads of potential."

"It'll get there, Mrs. Leto. I'm working on it."

"Are our moms here?"

He shook his head. "They went to the store."

It was so strange to see Kelsey. He didn't really use social media. He had Facebook but only because you sort of had to. He never posted anything. She didn't much either, which had both impressed him and bugged him. It impressed him because he was glad she hadn't turned into one of those girls who posted every single little thing they ever did or didn't do. She wasn't one of those girls who went on to get attention through hot pictures or through passive-aggressive, potentially tragic comments.

Roxy. Roxy with her misleading, always varied, frequent Facebook *Goodbye world* . . .

It bothered him that Kelsey posted so little, because he didn't feel right "reaching out" to her and having some stupid messenger relationship, but he kind of still just wanted to know what was up with her life. What was she doing, what was she like?

He could almost not believe she was in front of him now, that he could talk to her and that she could become real to him again. He would almost sooner believe she was a mirage.

She broke his eye contact and looked up at the house.

He was afraid she was going to turn back and ask, *Is it tough for you being back here?*

But instead she gave an almost imperceptible shake of the head, and then looked back cheerily and said, "I'll go change and come help you."

A few minutes later she came out in a big white T-shirt and ratty denim shorts, worn-in Nikes and mismatched socks. Her hair was up in an amusingly spiky ponytail now. He actually didn't see her come out, he had begun working again, when he looked up and saw her trying to figure out the speaker on her phone. He watched her until she sorted it out and then pulled out his own music.

It was the rattlesnake start to "Southern Girl," by Incubus. They'd listened to the CD countless times at the beach. They had iPhones, but even as kids, and only at the beach, they liked doing it the old-school way, like their parents.

She put her hands out and let them fall.

"Forgive my nostalgia, but it really just feels right."

"I agree. Bags are over there. You're about to ruin any manicure you might have."

She rolled her eyes at him. "It's like you don't remember me at all." She flapped the trash bag open. "It's Kelsey. Remember me?"

He laughed.

Half an hour later, their moms pulled up. The greeting scene happened. High-pitched, lots of hugs, compliments all around. Kelsey turned down the music from her phone in her back pocket when her mom told her it was way, way too loud. He laughed at Kelsey's cringe. Jamie's mom was looking at him when he laughed. She was looking a little too knowingly.

He acted normal.

The yard, he decided as he surveyed it instead of looking back at his mom, was about ready to be mowed. That big, satisfying moment that he'd been looking forward to, for whatever reason.

The three of them went inside. He mowed the lawn. It was as immensely satisfying as he'd hoped it would be.

Once inside, he saw all three of the girls sitting in the living room chatting. He didn't listen full-on as he washed his hands and dug under his fingernails to get the dirt out. What he gleaned was that Kelsey had broken up with a boyfriend a couple days ago, and finished her summer-school class and was tired of her best friend who was constantly hanging out with her boyfriend and had no concept of the third-wheel effect.

So he kind of listened.

He grabbed a bottle of water and stood in the kitchen drinking it.

"Jamie, come in here!" said Kristin.

He downed the rest of the water, tossed it, and grabbed another one.

Kristin scooted over. "Take a seat. Not, you know, too close."

He sat down directly next to her. "Sorry, am I sweaty?"

She cracked up and pushed at him with her elbow. "Good lord, you're *slick*." He popped up onto the armrest of the couch, and gave Kristin a wink. They always had that give-each-other-as-much-shit-as-possible relationship.

"So how's the job?" she asked.

He shrugged. "It's pretty good. Good in that it's really easy and they give me free wings every day."

They offered him beer too, once so far, which he'd taken them up on. He didn't mention this.

He glanced at Kelsey, who almost seemed to know what he was thinking. He narrowed his eyes at her and she smiled.

"I'm just an expo, so I run the food from the kitchen to the tables. I get tipped out and make hourly. Apparently it's a couple steps up from where I could start at a restaurant. I'm not a dishwasher or a busboy. They said they might want me barbacking."

"Any talk of serving?" asked Kristin.

"Nope."

She shrugged. "I don't know, maybe you can't even serve when you're under eighteen. Can't remember the law; anyway, you may not be able to."

"Not sure."

"So, wait," said Kelsey, "you're staying the rest of the summer?"

He glanced at his mom. Shrugged again. "No reason to go home, really, got the job, so I guess I'll see."

His mom tried not to look glad he was considering staying. She pressed her lips together in a thin line and looked elsewhere in the room.

Kelsey looked angrily at him.

"What?" he asked.

"You're *staying*. I'm jealous. Going home sounds awful." She looked at Kristin. "No offense, Ma, just everyone at home is so . . ." She took a deep breath and lay back.

"You're welcome to stay as long as you want or your mom will let you," said Jamie's mom. "But I'm putting your skinny ass to work, you know that."

She sat up. "Wait, are you serious?"

Jamie wanted to ask the same thing.

Both of them were looking at her now, and Kristin was looking at Jamie and Kelsey.

"Y-yeah? I mean, if you want to stay here while the house is still ours, might as well get some more use out of it. And I could use the help. The company would be nice too, you're always a pleasure, Kelsey."

Kelsey gaped and then said, "I would literally shave my head to stay here with you guys for the whole summer."

Jamie's mom looked at him. They hadn't intended to stay any determined amount of time. But he didn't want this plan to get cut down. It would be awesome to hang out with Kelsey again. She was like a guy. No pressure.

Willa looked away from Jamie and then said, "I get the feeling you'd shave your head for fifty bucks."

Kelsey looked wryly at her. "Don't tempt me unless you've got a buzzer in the house."

"Are you serious?" asked Kristin. Jamie expected the question to be directed at Kelsey, but it wasn't, it was directed at his mom.

She shrugged. "I don't know, I guess—why not?" A look passed between them that Jamie didn't get. "I think I'm not putting a necessary finish date on the house fix-up. Definitely by the end of the summer. But not like this week. Plus Jamie's got this job! It's sort of perfect. One last summer send-off."

"Actually," said Jamie, sort of hoping to hammer in the last nail, "my job asked if I knew any girls who might want a job."

Kelsey raised her eyebrows and then lowered them and looked around the room, putting her hands on her thighs. Gesture of *Well, that settles it.*

Their moms exchanged another look. There was no telling what it meant, but the look itself was unmistakable.

Jamie got the feeling everyone in the room had stronger feelings about this than they were letting on.

Chapter Twenty-seven

Willa

When we'd gotten back to the house, Kristin was delighted to find Kelsey there, and I was even more delighted to see Jamie looking so happy to be talking with her. He hid it, of course, wiping the excitement from his expression the moment I arrived (because he knew I'd see it) but it was still a relief to see. He needed some fun, some normal conversation. Something that wasn't a whiny, moody girlfriend.

Kelsey certainly fit that bill.

We had a pleasant dinner together, and then played a game of hearts, which I am hopelessly bad at. I can never remember what the trump is, or what the last person's move was. So, naturally, I lost three games in a row before Kristin announced she was exhausted and I took the opportunity to grab my laptop and tell everyone I was going to go upstairs and do some work on next year's curriculum before hitting the hay myself.

The kids looked at each other like something suspicious was going on, so I added, "I'll be up for a while, probably in and out of the kitchen, so let me know if you need anything." It sounded like I'd be checking up on them, but the truth was I just wanted some alone time and I was grateful that everyone had each other now so that I could sneak off by myself without leaving anyone alone and lonely.

The truth was, I was hoping to see Ben again.

I followed Kristin to her room and asked, "How's it going in here? You doing all right?"

She looked at me, her expression completely unassuming. "Great, yeah, no problem. It's really nice to wake up in here and see the sea and sky. When I'm in my house I'm glad that the neighbors are close so they could hear me scream if I needed them to, but there is a lot to be said for having some privacy. I could walk straight out buck naked here and no one could see me."

No one except the ghosts, I thought.

An hour later I was in my room when Dolly suddenly lifted her head from her snore spot on the bed and started staring at a spot where I could see nothing. Her hackles went up.

"Ben?" I asked quietly, and moved in front of her to see if there was a cold spot.

There was. I shivered.

"Ben? Are you here?"

A warmth came over me. Not a physical warmth—the spot was still cold—but more a feeling of well-being.

He was here.

And a moment later, he was. I could see him. Relief flooded me. Apparently that spread to Dolly as well, because as suddenly as she'd been on alert, she put her head back down and closed her eyes.

"It's almost time," he said.

"Time for what?" But I knew. Without him even saying it, I knew he was saying he was going to leave for good.

"You know." He gave a nod. "I love you, Willa. You're doing a great job with Jamie. He's a good kid."

"He misses you." Something frantic was building in me, trying to make a case for him to stay.

"But he *has* you. And you are enough for him."

"I haven't been!"

"You have to be." His voice grew firm. "I know it's not what you signed up for, but life is unpredictable." He splayed his arms and gave a wry smile. "Witness."

A lump rose in my throat. "This is too hard. It's not fair." God, I hated the whininess in my voice. More, I hated the whininess in my heart. My inner toddler was stamping her feet and saying, *No! I won't go on! Not until I get my way.*

But my way was impossible.

"It *seems* unfair," he agreed calmly. "But you have a lot more ahead of you. Great things that you can't even see or imagine are right in front of you if you just open yourself up to them." He eyed me. "There are *people* you have yet to meet who will make you so happy."

My heart gave a jump, but I honestly couldn't say whether it was because the words were encouraging or *discouraging* because he wasn't jealous or possessive of me. That he didn't think we were the only people for each other. In short, I guess, that he didn't love me with all the romance of Lord Byron or Shelley in death.

"People aren't meant to be alone," he said. "You in particular are not meant to be alone. You're at your best in a relationship, and I want you to have that again. You've been incredibly strong on your own, and like I said, you've done a great job with Jamie, but no one should have to do all the stuff of life alone."

I put my head in my hands and felt deep sobs coming on. I held my breath and tried to keep them back, but they came anyway.

Dolly raised her head again and looked at me. I put a hand on her and felt myself calm down marginally.

Even in his otherworldly state, Ben seemed confused by what was happening. Another strike against eternal romance. I would have thought he'd understand everything, be able to read my every thought, but instead he was as lost as he'd ever been with me.

"What's wrong?" he asked. "What did I say?"

"Don't you miss me?"

He cocked his head. "Miss you?" I could tell he was playing for time. He always cocked his head like that and repeated my last words back at me when he was trying to stall for an answer.

My heart broke fractionally more. "Yes, miss me. You're gone, you've been gone three years, don't you miss me?"

"I love you," he said, as if that were compensation.

"But—"

He put up a hand. He knew what I was saying and he wasn't going to make me struggle for it. "Do I wish we could be together like before? Yes. In that, I wish I could show you everything I see, feel, hear, experience now. But there's no sadness here. Missing someone implies that there's an uncertainty about ever seeing them or being with them again, and I don't have that because I *know* I'll see you again and that we'll be together again."

My throat tightened. "You *know* it?"

He smiled. "I absolutely know it. Of course I know it." He moved closer to me. "I have a few advantages in this regard that you don't have." He touched my nose, or at least made the gesture. I didn't really feel it except as a swipe of cool air.

I looked at him longingly. I could feel the desperation on my face, in my expression, the pleading in my eyes, but I couldn't control it. "When?" I pleaded. "When will that be?"

"A hundred years for you is the blink of an eye," he said. "Soon enough. And you need to enjoy your life in the meantime. Your purpose is not fulfilled."

"And what is my purpose?"

He shook his finger at me. "No, no, no, I can't tell you that. No one can. You have to figure it out for yourself."

I frowned and ruffled the dog's fur. "Great. So you know the big secret of my life, but you can't tell me because it's my little journey to figure it out."

"Actually, it's a big journey, and no, I don't know." He was as patient as a saint. "I don't know any more about your path than anyone else could tell you, which is primarily that you still have our son to live for, take care of, and set a good example for."

I felt shamed by his words, not because of the way he said them or even the fact that he said them, but because I knew it to be true and I'd been giving myself too much of a pass by indulging in my grief when I should have been setting an example for Jamie by *living*. Not dying along with the dead.

"You're right," I croaked through a tight throat and tears I was trying to withhold. "I should go talk to him right now, tell him how sorry I am for not stepping up to the plate."

"Whoa." Ben put his hands out. "Right now is not a good time. He's hanging out with Kristin's kid. That's good for him."

"You have no idea," I scoffed. "Or do you? Did you ever see his ex-girlfriend?"

"Not really. When I'm around, I can *feel* you guys but not watch you like you're on TV or something."

"I don't get it."

"I know you don't." He chuckled. "And I can't explain it better than that. Most of the time I just don't have a clear view of your day-to-day life so much as what's in your heart."

"Okay."

He looked skeptical. "Okay?"

I nodded. "I mean, I don't really get it, but I'm trying."

Before he could answer, there was a knock at the door.

"Mom?"

I looked to Ben quickly, hoping this glorious moment of overlap would result in Jamie getting the chance to experience him.

But he was gone.

Chapter Twenty-eight

Willa

Instead, he'd probably heard me talking—vehemently, no less—to "my-self" in here and was worried I'd lost my mind. I looked around and my view landed on my cell phone on the bedside table. I picked it up and said, audibly, "Hold on," then, "Come on in, Jamie!"

From somewhere, I swear I could feel Ben's amused gaze on me.

"I heard you talking to someone," Jamie said, coming into the room. Dolly lifted her head and thumped her tail at him.

I held up a finger, stalling for time in my own way, and said into the phone, "I'll have to call you back. Okay. Right. Bye-bye." I pushed the home button and hoped he didn't see the phone illuminate to the home screen and no extinguished call.

"Who was that?" Jamie looked puzzled.

"A friend from work." I thought frantically and could only come up with the scene in *The Brady Bunch* where Jan made up an imaginary boy-friend named George Glass. "Georgina," I said, as a little joke to myself in honor of the Bradys.

"Never heard of her."

"Yeah, we've gotten closer in the last couple of months. She's trying to get me 'out there,' as they say." Might as well use this opportunity to run Ben's ideas past Jamie, particularly here in front of him, since I was pretty sure Jamie would acknowledge that it was too soon for me to feel the pressure to start dating.

"What, you mean like going out with guys?"

"Yeah, isn't that nuts?"

"No." Jamie breathed what sounded like a sigh of relief. "Shit." He looked at me sheepishly and corrected himself, badly. "Hell, I've been thinking the same thing."

I felt like I hadn't gone low enough for the limbo stick and had snagged my neck on it. "What are you talking about?"

"You've been mourning Dad for years now. It's time for you to get a new, maybe not *husband*, but at least a boyfriend."

It's hard to express how much my heart ached at that moment. I had just been "with" Ben, and Jamie was right in front of me, yet I had never felt more alone in my life. Never felt less understood. How could they both think I could just move on and forget?

My grip tightened on the phone I was still holding. "I don't need a boyfriend," I told my son. And my husband, by default, if he could still hear me.

"But I know you're lonely," Jamie said. "You spend so much time alone. Until this . . . this *Georgina* came along, it was like Kristin and I were your only friends."

That was an additional blow I could have done without. Not that he had intended it as one, or as anything other than truth, but basically Jamie was pointing out that I was a lonely loser.

And, worse, that I was slightly less of one now that I had an imaginary friend.

"Jamie," I said calmly. "I'm fine. But I really do appreciate your concern."

He nodded, his brown curls bobbing their need for a cut. "Okay, but I just want you to know that I'm cool with it. If you get a boyfriend, I mean. I know Dad's not coming back."

Emotion caught in my throat. I knew Ben wasn't coming back too, even though he was right here. Jamie couldn't detect him one bit. If I'd had any lingering hopes that now that he'd appeared Ben could stay and wait out my life with me in some approximation of normal, they were gone now. It was a silly notion, even though I was spending time with him now. He was still just an echo of himself.

As he had already said on several occasions, I couldn't understand. I wasn't going to understand and he wasn't going to be able to explain it to me. That much was clear.

It wasn't that I was reluctant to get it. Although I think I kind of was. But it was more that I just plain wasn't capable; my human mind just couldn't wrap itself around these metaphysical concepts. There is just so much more to life than we can ever understand—every religion tells us that, and in much the same way. It's all about faith and trust, two of the hardest things in the world to conjure when you need them most.

They say God is found in foxholes, but I have felt it was the opposite—whenever I was in a foxhole situation, that was when it was hardest for me to maintain faith. I hoped like hell, but I was scared to death there was nothing.

I guess from now on I wouldn't be able to say there was nothing out there—I had seen Ben and interacted with him and I believed that wholeheartedly.

But, damn it, I wasn't sure it was fair. I wasn't sure any of it was fair or that it ever would be.

"I'm not getting a boyfriend anytime soon," I reiterated to Jamie. "But

I sure do appreciate your care and the fact that you thought to tell me that."

He gave a half shrug. "Sure. 'Night."

"Good night, sweetheart. I love you."

The door was already closed before I heard a muffled, "Love you too."

There was something about an *I love you too* that seemed infinitely less sincere than *I love you*, but I sure wasn't going to quibble with that now. I'd take it.

"He's a good kid," Ben's voice came, almost as soft as the wind against the windowpane.

I nodded, unable, suddenly, to speak.

"You've done good, girl."

"No." I shook my head. "Don't give me all the credit. For better or worse, *we* did good."

He looked sad. "I haven't been here, babe."

"You were," I argued.

I heard footsteps on the stairs and picked up my phone, just in case, and lowered my voice.

"You were there for all the important early milestones. You were there for those crucial foundational years. You were there for birthdays and Christmases."

"And funerals?" he added. "I'm sorry, but that was you. You've been there for the hardest part of his life. I can't take credit for that, it's all you, baby."

Are there people out there who would love that acknowledgment? Who would love to be told that they, alone, had climbed the mountain and gotten to the top? Sure. Probably most people would love to hear that and get that pat on the back.

But I had never liked it as much as you'd expect. Even when I was a kid and I got the best grade in the class, I'd be embarrassed to stand out by myself. I didn't like being the center of attention. Especially for something good. I think maybe if I'd been singled out for sucking, it would have been less lonely. After all, when you suck, someone else always comes along—usually sooner rather than later—to suck more.

But his praise for my surviving and not taking my son down in a cloud of smoke just made me feel alone. What was praiseworthy to Ben—and probably to a lot of people—just put a spotlight on how solitary my life was and how—yay me!—I had managed to not wither and die even when that was what I'd wanted more than anything.

"You don't understand," I said to him. "All those things you're saying I don't understand and can't understand? Well, there are a few things *you* don't understand either."

I wanted to tell him to go, to just leave me alone to my self-pity. Once upon a time, I would have pulled that crap. Flounced up to the bedroom alone, maybe slammed the door. Watched some *Real Housewives* on Bravo, or something like it, frowning the whole time and continually chewing on whatever had pissed me off.

But I couldn't do that now. I didn't dare tell him to go away or leave me alone, because I didn't know the rules of this game we were playing. Maybe if I told him to beat it he'd truly disappear once and for all instead of coming back to me tenderly and telling me how sorry he was to have been so insensitive and how much he loved me and how he'd spend the rest of his life doing everything he could to make me happy and let me know how much he appreciated me . . .

So instead I just rolled over and pulled the sheets up to cover my shoulders. I knew he remained there, still looking at me, because I could feel the slightly eerie cold on my back.

But I didn't care about the cold, I only cared that he was still there, that he was able to be there, and that he would, please God, stay there and let me soak in his presence so it could last me as long as possible once he was gone.

"I love you," I said to him softly. *You are the love of my life*, I didn't add out loud. *I adored you the moment I saw you and I knew I would know your face forever. You took my whole heart and soul, and every minute we spent together was a treasure. Our son is a treasure. Our home was a treasure.*

Our life was a treasure.

And if I never see you again, as I fear every day is the truth, then I will never forget you and I will never move on with someone else no matter how much you want me to, because if I let someone else into that space, I'm scared to death they will edge you out of my memory, if only from some self-protective mechanism.

So I love you, Ben, and I won't move on, and I won't forget.

All those things I thought but did not say.

I don't know what he thought.

All I heard was the very softest, most achingly familiar, "I love you too, baby."

And somehow, even with those words, I knew he was gone.

Chapter Twenty-nine

Willa

I think the kids went out last night," Kristin said over a breakfast of crispy bacon, a puffy pancake I got the recipe for online, and strong French roast coffee with real cream.

If I was going to be depressed, I was going to do it with real cream.

And Kristin, god bless her, was the kind of trooper friend who would take a hit for me and join me in indulgent foods. The fact that she never gained an ounce, and frequently lost too much if she wasn't vigilant about eating, was beside the point.

I poured some cane syrup and lemon juice on my pancake. "You're not saying you think they had a . . . *rendezvous*."

"I am." She nodded, lips pressed together, though I could see the smile in her eyes. "I certainly am."

"But . . ." I thought about it. Jamie and Kelsey? Weren't they still, like, six? Of course not. They were teenage kids, hormones jumping. What did I expect? "Well, that would be absolutely adorable."

"Wouldn't it?"

"What would?" Kelsey came in like a play character, right on cue. She went straight to the stove and took a piece of bacon out of the pan. "Ouch ouch ouch, omigod." She blew on it, then popped it into her mouth, leaving part of it hanging out like a cigar. "This is so hot," she said through her teeth.

"You took it out of a hot pan," Kristin pointed out, then cut a piece off her pancake. "That should have indicated it was hot. Speaking of hot, what did you—"

"Want for breakfast?" I hurried, shooting Kristin a withering glance. I didn't want her to make the kids self-conscious. If, by some miracle, they were interested in each other, I didn't want to interrupt that.

I had to fight visions of Roxy melting in a steamy puddle after water was thrown on her.

"I guess I'll just have what you guys are having," Kelsey said. "Except, why just one pancake?"

"Because," I explained, gesturing at the plate, "as you can see, they are enormous."

"I'll have three," she said anyway. She had her mother's metabolism. I took out the mixing bowl and put the makings in for three massive pancakes—six eggs, one and a half cups of flour, and one and a half cups of milk, plus a generous grinding of nutmeg. Bake in a pan for twenty minutes at four twenty-five. I'd done it a million times for Jamie and Ben. The result was like big puffy pan popovers and she was going to hog down the equivalent of something like twelve.

I bet she could do it too, but whatever she couldn't eat, I was sure Jamie would.

Which reminded me. "Where is Jamie?" I asked.

A guilty flush rose in Kelsey's cheeks. "I don't know. I haven't seen him since last night."

"Last night?" Kristin asked, her voice the equivalent of an arched eyebrow.

"When we were all, you know . . . here."

"Of course," I said pointedly. Her flushed face gave her away—she and Jamie *had* snuck out together. How cute. And how funny that they didn't want us to know. "When you were here. He's probably still asleep. He doesn't go to work until the afternoon."

"Yeah, he works at four today," Kelsey said, wrinkling her tanned nose. "I'm going to go with him tomorrow because he's going to try to get me a job there too."

Kristin swallowed and wiped her mouth with her napkin. "That's good, but honey, I don't know how long we're staying."

"Well, actually . . . if you were serious last night . . . I was kind of hoping I could stay on here and work for the rest of the summer," Kelsey said, looking at me hopefully. "If it's all right with you, Willa. I mean, I know Jamie's hoping to stay and do the same, so, even if you wanted to go or whatever, we could take care of the place."

Jamie walked in. "I'm doing what?"

"Staying all summer," Kelsey told him. "I wanted to stay too. If it's at all possible." She looked back at me.

I looked at Kristin, behind her, and she shrugged. *Whatever you think.* "It's fine with me," I said, pretty happy with the idea of having more people guaranteed to stay in the house at least as long as I was here. "By then I'll have a Realtor listing the place, but as long as you guys understand that you'll have to pack up and go back home if there's a sale, I don't see any reason you shouldn't stay here."

"Oh, thank you!" Kelsey wrapped her arms around me and squeezed tight. "Thank you so much."

I made eye contact with Kristin and she was smiling. This was a great opportunity for Kelsey.

And I dearly hoped it would help Jamie to reframe his idea of the house into something fun and warm, rather than just the sad place where his dad had passed. Already he did seem to be enjoying himself, though. I wasn't sure any of us were going to gleefully take over the master bedroom when Kristin went back home, but it would be great if he at least carried happy memories of this place that had meant so much to us.

The kids leaned on the counter and ate. I wasn't surprised Kelsey could not eat everything she'd asked for but, as predicted, Jamie did. They were almost out of here when Jamie stopped at the sink and asked, "So, Kristin, do you know this Georgina person my mom was arguing with last night?"

"Georgina?" Kristin set her coffee cup down and looked at me. "Never heard of her. You were arguing with her?"

I felt the blood drain from my face.

Before I could speak, Jamie continued, "She works at the school. Doesn't she, Mom?"

All eyes were on me. "Um." Brilliant start. No one would ever suspect I was floundering. I fixed a quizzical expression on my face and turned to Jamie. "She doesn't work at the school. And we weren't arguing."

"I've never heard of her," Kristin said, raising a suspicious eyebrow. "Who is she?"

Visions of Monty Python crying, *Nobody expects the Spanish Inquisition*, came to mind.

"You misunderstood," I said to Jamie. "I don't *work* with her, I *work out* with her." Boy, it was lame. Everyone knew I didn't work out. But I did have time off to do things alone, so who was to say I wasn't working out in some way, shape, or form?

Besides my son and my best friend, that is. Both were looking at me as if they'd caught me in a huge blunder.

"What?" I demanded, with more indignation than I could bring myself to feel. "I work out."

"Okay." Kristin shrugged.

"*When?*" Jamie wanted to know. He was with me more than Kristin, so he was predictably the one more skeptical of my claim.

"I go to yoga sometimes at Sol Yoga in Frederick," I said. "What is your problem, do you think I'm making Georgiana up?" As if the very idea were *outrageous*.

He started to back off, then frowned and said, "You said her name was Georg*ina*."

I had. He was right. I rolled my eyes. "Georgina *is* Georgiana. It's just . . . short for it."

"Georgie would be better," Kelsey said, but she was shushed by her mother. "I just mean as a catchall nickname." She looked at me. "Is she Greek? Georgie is a common Greek name."

"I think she is." I nodded thoughtfully. This was ridiculous. "I don't really know her that well, so I'm not sure."

That quieted everyone for a moment.

"We should go, Jam." Kelsey was in full chipper mode, ready to go conquer the boardwalk. I was glad to see it. Jamie was always a bit understated, but she burned a fire under him. As soon as she spoke, his eyes lit up.

"Right," he said. Then he looked at me. "Call me if you need me, okay? It's not too hard for me to get off work if you need something."

"I'm *fine*," I told him. "Don't worry about a thing. I've got Kristin here. We'll be good."

He looked dubious. "Okay."

He and Kelsey clomped out of the house and banged the screen door after them. I loved that sound. Almost no one had an old-fashioned screen door anymore. Even at home I had a sturdy double-paned storm door that had a soft-touch lock, meaning that it slowed itself down when you let go of it and closed with a gentle *snick*.

Kristin was at the sink doing the dishes when I returned my attention to the kitchen, and I went to the table and brought her plate over, scootching Kelsey's over too as I passed.

"Thanks for doing the dishes," I said. "The dishwasher works, so you can just put them in there."

"All right." There was something off about her tone, but I couldn't say what. She opened the dishwasher and loaded everything in, shooing me away every time I tried to help.

Finally she finished, sponged down the countertop and dried it with a dishcloth, and put it all away.

Then she turned to me with a look that was something between concern and accusation and said, "What's the truth about this supposed Georgina person?"

"Oh, nothing," I said. "Honestly, I was talking to myself when Jamie knocked and I was embarrassed to tell him that."

"Ah." She nodded as if that made all the sense in the world. "Then you gave yourself a good talking-to."

"I did."

"About time someone did."

"Like you don't!"

She laughed. "I'm not shy; you have a point."

"What do you think about me dating?" I asked seriously. "You know, *getting out there.*"

She lifted her brows. "Oooh, do you have an actual *date* on the table, or are you talking hypothetically?"

"Hypothetically." A breeze blew the sheer curtains and the scent of sea air touched my face. I frowned. Could I really do it?

As weird as it was, maybe Ben's all-too-brief (and way too ethereal) visits had reminded me what it was like to have a companion. I missed that. I missed *him*, of course, but maybe he was right, or even telling a truth that he knew. Maybe there *was* happiness on the horizon for me if I could just crack myself open a little bit.

"Honestly, I think it's a great idea," Kristin said. "You're so fun. You should be having fun all the time."

Fun. Gosh, I hadn't thought of myself as fun for a long time. "I've been a real drag, haven't I?" I asked her.

"No," she said firmly. "Not at all. You've been amazing. But you haven't been happy, and we all know it." She looked thoughtful. "I know you're determined to sell this house, but I wonder if maybe being here isn't what's contributing to this lift in your mood."

I nodded. There was so much I couldn't tell her about my visits with Ben. Even though *I* believed they were real, I'd be hard-pressed to convince any other sane, logical adult that they were. It was bad enough that she knew I'd been seeing him around.

"Have you seen him again?" she asked, as if reading my mind.

I smiled. "Nope."

Was it my imagination, or did her shoulders relax fractionally? "Maybe he just came through to reassure you that the end isn't really the end and it's safe to go on."

"I'm *sure* of it," I said. She'd summarized it perfectly.

"In that case," she said, "I think it's time for you to put your toes in the water. Literally *and* figuratively. Let's go to the beach!"

"The ocean will be freezing!"

"Aw, come on, you've been in during June before. It's not that bad. It's a perfect analogy for life! Take the little discomforts bit by bit until you get used to them. The cold will warm right up if you let it."

"You should be a life coach, you know that?"

"I am," she said with a laugh. "I'm a teacher. Just like you. We have all the knowledge we need inside of ourselves, we just need to find a way to *act* on it. Sometimes it takes a push."

"Well, you're definitely pushy."

"Lucky for you. Come on, let's go."

Chapter Thirty

Jamie

After breakfast the next day, Jamie went to the store to get khaki shorts for work and when he returned an hour or so later, it was to the sound of noisy conversation in the kitchen and—once he'd listened enough to identify the sound—whipped cream being sprayed out of a can.

Not that he'd exactly forgotten, but he remembered with a crash that Kelsey would be there. Same as it was when he was a kid, he knew that today would be a more interesting version than it would have been without her.

He glanced in the mirror by the door as he came in, then mentally stopped himself. Whose opinion was he concerned about? Kelsey's?

As he headed for the kitchen, he heard Kelsey's voice. She was telling a story. She always had that tone when she told a story. Whatever it had been, it made their moms crack up.

He hadn't heard his mom laugh like that very much lately. When she did laugh it was more rueful, or that "gallows humor" she was always talking about.

When he went into the kitchen, they all greeted him with smiles and a variation on, "You're back! Find some pants?"

"Yeah. I did."

"Coffee?" asked Kristin. "We're all pretty caffeine buzzed at this point."

"Oh, oh, let me make it," Kelsey said. "I worked at Starbucks for like a year, so now I'm sort of a pro. Plus I got a discount on a bunch of stuff and I brought some. Sit!" she said.

He saw a silver canister of whipped cream on the counter. He'd been right, then, that was what he'd heard, and she had probably been—yep, as she turned the stovetop on and filled a small, angular silver pitcher with water, she sprayed whipped cream in her mouth.

"You are such a pig," said Kristin.

"Ohmigod, I know." She nodded back.

She poured milk into a saucepan and then pumped in vanilla syrup.

"It really is about the best latte I've ever had," said his mom. Her eyes were damn near dancing.

Kelsey put a hand on her hip. "Thanks, Willa, I agree." She stirred the milk and looked at Jamie. "So you've got work today?"

"At four."

"Okay, I'm coming with you, then. You really think they'll hire me?"

"I can't see why not. Didn't even hesitate before hiring me, plus he told me specifically he wanted to hire another girl. Not too many there, apparently."

"Got it. Perfect. I'm glad I brought something besides a bikini, then. Although it sounds like this guy might be more likely to hire a girl if she showed up barely clothed."

"It's like you've already met him."

Kristin looked concerned, but Jamie shook his head. "Don't worry about it, he's harmless. Just a dork."

She sipped her coffee with an if-you-say-so look that he recognized to also mean, *If he tries anything, I'll destroy him.*

Kristin was a shark like that. One of the coolest people he knew, but he would never mess with her. And he'd advise anyone else not to either.

"Oh, yeah, I totally interrupted, Mom. So she just called you out of nowhere, first time in ten years, go on." Kelsey popped up on the counter just like she always used to when they talked in the kitchen.

They continued talking about some story, some old best friend with a way-belated apology. He didn't really listen, just ate his lunch and drank his coffee. But he couldn't describe the feeling he got then.

It was like old times. Like how things might have been if they were here simply because it was summer, not because it was time to pack it up. Kelsey was supposed to grow up a bit, and start fitting in more with the women. He was supposed to sit there and listen, but not really. They were supposed to do this every day while they were all here; his hair was supposed to be grainy from sand, and Kelsey was supposed to be tan and getting blonder just like she used to. His dad was supposed to be out at the store getting beer and snacks with Phillip. Dolly was the only one who was behaving as usual, sleeping wherever she decided to lie down.

They were supposed to be watching movies at night, and now Kelsey and he would be allowed to watch anything with the parents.

The porch table was supposed to have two more chairs at it, not one fewer. He and Kelsey were supposed to be included in playing Trivial Pursuit now, and their parents were supposed to be impressed that they knew

as much as they did. Kelsey and he were supposed to introduce them to
new games, like the card game Presidents that he felt sure his parents
didn't know. Or wouldn't. Whatever.

They'd be allowed to have a beer or two. Kelsey would get giggly, he
was willing to bet, probably pink in the cheeks. He'd probably end up flirt-
ing with her, and their parents would tease them—she flirted with everyone, that was just how she met the world, so it would lean on him and
he'd get embarrassed but it'd be funny anyway.

The nights were supposed to happily cap off busy, hot days. They were
supposed to get boardwalk splinters out of their toes while his dad made
those buffalo chicken tenders he used to make and while his mom made
a salad she insisted on including "for nutrition."

Then one day, when he and Kelsey weren't the kids anymore, they'd
have their own kids and start a whole new generation of memories
here.

Not, like, *their* kids, but just the kids each of them had. You know.

He bit his bottom lip hard. He used to do this as a kid when he didn't
want to cry.

He wasn't going to cry now, he was well beyond that, but still he felt
extremely, supremely gypped. None of that could happen now. Nothing
could ever happen like it was supposed to. And if everything happens for
a reason, he couldn't imagine how life being worse than it should be could
ever have a reason.

His dad shouldn't be gone. The fact that he was just made life a solid
level worse.

He glanced up. Kelsey was staring at him. Their moms were chatting
back and forth, his mom lively for once. But Kelsey seemed to see right
through him and into his mind.

Jamie looked back at her. She gave a small nod, her brows just barely
furrowed. Like she was saying, *It sucks, it just does.*

Maybe he was reading too much into it.

He had a feeling that he wasn't.

Jamie was grateful for the seeming understanding from Kelsey, but was just as glad that she hadn't brought it up. He put on his blue polo and khaki shorts, and after Kelsey laughed at him, he pointed out she was undoubtedly going to end up in the same dorky uniform. She stopped laughing.

They got in the car and she took control of the music—Jamie was, as always, impressed by her taste. Or at least glad it was so similar to his.

This wasn't like things had been with Roxy.

They parked in the employee lot and went in the back entrance. They found Steve in his office.

Jamie knocked and pushed open the door as Steve said, "Come in!" and paused the old *SNL* episode he'd been watching on a laptop.

"Hey, there, Jamie, and—"

His puffy face turned hot pink and he stood up, inexplicably wiping his hands before handing her one to shake. God knew what he was wiping off them.

"Kelsey," she said with an easy smile.

"Streve—Steve," he said, and ran the back of his hand across his forehead.

"Hey, Steve," she said, her face growing slightly pink.

Jamie knew it was an effort on her part not to call him *Streve*. He probably would have let her.

"Your girlfriend, Jamie? Lucky guy!"

"No, no, just a family friend," he responded, as Kelsey shook her head, still smiling. "I know you mentioned you needed some more help around here, possibly a girl, and I happened to know one who was looking, so . . ."

He gestured at her.

"Well, when can you start?" Steve laughed heartily, although all three of them knew it was no joke.

"Today! I wore khaki shorts and everything." She gestured, and Steve's eyes followed down to her legs.

Jamie experienced a prickle of irritation with him.

"Have you ever served before?"

"No, I haven't. I was a barista at Starbucks for a long time, but that's it."

"Ah, you have to get experience somewhere, right? Let's get you a V-neck. Jamie, why don't you head down to the expo line, and I'll start training your pal here?"

"All righty," said Jamie, for some reason using a term he never really used. Again he felt a pang, feeling like maybe he should stay with her. Maybe this was a stupid mistake having her work here too.

They started off, and Kelsey turned back to mouth, *V-neck*, and then point at his polo.

He winced at her, and then went down the kitchen stairs to the expo line.

The place was a mess and he ended up playing catch-up for almost an hour, throwing away the stale chips they never kept covered, ridding the fridge of expired Saran-wrapped premade house salads, filling and date-marking plastic containers of ranch, blue cheese, honey mustard, and house sauce (essentially Big Mac sauce). They weren't that busy yet, but if he hadn't scrambled for an hour, he would have felt three minutes behind all shift.

He got everything prepped and ready just in time for the happy hour rush. Two-for-one draft beers and sixty-cent oysters, clams, and peel-and-eat shrimp—it was a huge draw. It was almost impossible to rack up a bill higher than fifty bucks, so it brought in all the cheapskates—or so the whining servers had told him when they came into the kitchen to eat spare fries and complain about their tables.

Kelsey had been put right to work, not even shadowing another server—Steve had, nobly, taken on the responsibility of training her first-hand. This was *total bullshit* according to the one and only other female server, who said that when she got hired, she had to shadow another server for two whole weeks, basically doing everything and never making any tips, even though she'd worked at Blue J's down the road for almost a year.

Kelsey did seem to learn fast. She was flying through the swing door and happily checking on her food orders or sweetly apologizing for a mistake she'd made when sending the order through. The kitchen forgave her instantly, the fry cook especially, saying, "It's no problem, Mami, it's no problem," every time.

You could argue that they were being kind since she had just started, but he doubted that was why. And considering the commiserating look she tossed Jamie after talking to him, he thought she had enough sense to see through it too.

They both worked through happy hour and the first dinner rush, when orders went from appetizers to more serious orders of blackened grouper and fettuccine Alfredo with seared shrimp.

Things always calmed down after that, and the late-night crew came in, the better bartenders stepped behind the bar, along with the lazier cooks who were decent enough only to make fried late-night food, and the DJ set up on the dance floor. Jamie and Kelsey were too young to work the late-night shift, and Jamie was privately glad that Kelsey wouldn't have to deal with late-night drunk customers who would undoubtedly harass her.

He paused in his thoughts. Was he jealous? Who was he all of a sudden?

She came in, taking off the short little black apron she'd had tied around her waist, and said, "So, apparently I tip you out for running my food. That means it's up to *me* how much you make." She leaned on the silver island, grinning devilishly at him.

"I do make hourly, you know. More than you do."

"Yeah, you make more in hourly, but I made *a hundred freakin' bucks*." Her face was alight.

His heart did a stupid trippy thing. "Are you serious?"

"Damn right. And so here's what I'm thinking. As a celebration of us being reunited, and of us being employed together, I tip you out half what I made, and we go blow it all at the boardwalk. Hm?"

He tossed his rag in the bin. "You don't have to tip me half."

"Um, you got me the job, and they gave me a better position than you, all because I have boobs, so I think it sort of helps make up for the total unfairness of that. Plus you're way smarter than all those dopey dudes out there, you should really be serving."

He suddenly had a vision of her standing out there at the server station, surrounded by dopey dudes.

"I'm giving you half, so deal with it." She threw down a pile of cash and looked up at him. "Apparently we get a discount at most of the places over there too. Thrasher's fries, anyone?"

"What? He didn't tell me about any discount."

She laughed, and they exited the kitchen, passing the smoking cooks, going off shift. "Thank you, guys, see you tomorrow!"

They said their goodbyes, and talked in Spanish to each other after Jamie and Kelsey were a few feet away.

He was going to have to start learning a few phrases.

Kelsey kicked her sneakers off and put on the flip-flops she'd brought in her bag and made him close his eyes once they parked, so she could throw on a tank top instead of her work shirt. He grabbed a shirt from the back too, refusing to be the dweeb in the polo next to the hot girl in the spaghetti straps.

Hot girl, huh? asked a voice in his head.

He texted his mom and Kristin in the group text with Kelsey that she had started, and said where they were.

Sounds fun! answered Kristin.

Back by ten please! answered his mom.

Eleven*, corrected Kristin.

Kelsey and he laughed and started their journey of junk food along the boardwalk.

First stop was fries. Second was a hot dog smothered with everything from Boog Powell's BBQ. Next stop after that was talking Kelsey out of an impulsive belly-button piercing. After that they went to Kohr Brothers for frozen custards.

"No, no, wait, let me order for you," said Kelsey. "He'll have, um . . . he'll have the chocolate peanut-butter twist with extra chocolate sprinkles. Oh! In a chocolate-dipped wafer cone!"

"Nice," he said. She remembered his order. He remembered hers too. "And she'll have the vanilla custard swirl with orange sherbet, with a completely disgusting amount of rainbow sprinkles, in a cake cone."

She laughed hard. "Oh, my god, how have we gone this long without this?"

She meant the custard, or maybe she didn't. But he didn't know how he'd gone so long without laughing with her, much less doing it over sticky custard.

Once they got their frozen custard, she grabbed him and said, "Oh, my god, they still have the crappy old photo booth. Come on, let's commemorate this moment!"

"Holy shit," he said as they came up to it. "We have so many of these strips."

"I know. I'm so glad they haven't replaced it with those new photo booths—you know, the ones that print in color and just are like worse than an ancient-digital-camera's quality? This is old-school, black-and-white, always a little damaged, and they never take it at the right time, but they're so much better."

"I totally agree. Now get your butt in there, my custard's starting to melt."

She paused before entering. "Never has a more masculine sentence been uttered."

"Shut up," he said, but again his heart dinged in a way it hadn't for quite some time.

They got in. The quarters felt quite a bit more cramped than when they were kids and used to sit there.

"Here." He took her by the waist and planted her on his leg. No time for deciding whether it was awkward or not. It didn't have to be.

She giggled and then squealed as a drip of sprinkle-ridden vanilla ran down on her hand. "Oh, crap!"

Flash.

"Oh, that ought to be really flattering of you," he said, looking up at her. She glared at him.

Flash.

"You're the worst!" she said in a singsongy voice.

They both smiled at the camera just in time.

Flash.

"Nope," he said, then smoothed the frozen custard into her face, "now I'm the worst!"

She yelped and then smashed hers into his face, and, of course, then . . .

Flash!

They both collapsed into laughter and tried to clean themselves off, though the cramped box was making that hard, which only made them laugh harder.

They got out and grabbed napkins from a nearby table and cleaned themselves off.

The pictures printed and renewed the hilarity.

"Oh, my god," she said. "They're just perfect."

"Here, I'll hold on to them, I've got deeper pockets."

"Don't you dare lose them," she said, with that fire in her eyes she always got when she bossed him around.

"I promise I won't."

There was no way he was going to lose them, or, maybe, her.

Chapter Thirty-one

Willa

In the week following our discussion about my new life, Kristin and I pulled the house together in a way that was so beautiful that even I was tempted to buy it. And, indeed, I wondered how I could possibly *sell* it with Ben there. I thought about all those articles I'd read about people selling ghosts on eBay and whatnot, but I didn't want to get rid of mine. Somehow my grief had been slowly and subtly replaced by a hum of anticipation, never knowing when or where he'd show up.

For example: "Nice job," he said behind me, as I finished carefully painting along a corner in the front room late one afternoon. "You've gotten better at painting."

"I've always been good at painting. I just *pretended* I wasn't, so you'd do it."

"Ah." He tapped his temple with his index finger. "I'm glad to see you've got everything under control. Makes it easier with what I have to say."

"What's that?"

"That it's time for me to go. More to the point, it's time for you to really go on without me."

I stopped painting and turned to him. "What?"

"It's time."

The bottom dropped out of my stomach. "But . . . I *need* you."

He gestured toward the painting job I was doing. "Clearly you don't, you're doing great on your own."

I looked at the wall. Should I have acted less happy to see him? Should I not have slipped back into our easy rapport? Then would he stay here with me instead of abandoning me again? "Yeah, well, I wasn't expecting you to help with this under any circumstances."

"Good." He lifted his hands. "I'm not equipped."

I tried to think of something else to say, some way to move the conversation away from what he'd come to tell me, and yet it resonated so deeply that I knew it was true no matter what I said.

"Who are you talking to?" Kristin came into the room, paint splattered on her face and clothes.

I glanced from her to Ben, wondering if she could see or sense him even a little bit.

"You've been caught." Ben moved behind Kristin, looking amused.

"No one," I told her.

She frowned and unconsciously rubbed her hands on her arms. Behind her, Dolly started into the room after her, but stopped abruptly, turned, and went back into the kitchen. "Are you okay?"

"Of course."

"We haven't talked about him in a while. Did you . . . did something happen?"

Man, I couldn't fool her for anything.

"She's a good friend," Ben said.

I gave a slight nod in response to him, but she took it as an answer to her question. "I'm sorry," she said. "I figured I should just follow your lead, but I don't want you to think I'm tired of hearing about him by any means."

"I appreciate that, but . . ." I shook my head. "It's all too crazy."

"What is?"

"Come on," Ben urged. "Tell her I'm here. What have you got to lose?"

I gritted my teeth for a minute, then said to Kristin, "You know what? My phone is just ringing like crazy. The buzzing is just—" I took my silent phone out of my pocket and pretended to answer. "Hello? Oh, yes, this is Willa." I held up an index finger to Kristin and went into the kitchen, whispering, *"Come!"* to Ben as I passed him.

He did. "I can't talk about it," I said to him, only into the phone. I could see Kristin in the front room, halfheartedly messing around with a paint brush to kill time until I came back in and she could grill me. She had her eye on me, could probably see every move I made.

"Why not?"

"Because everyone would think I was crazy and she'd be worried about me forever."

"To the contrary," he said. "I think she'd understand what you're going through a lot better and it would help you power on."

"Why can't you just show yourself?" I was careful to keep my voice down so all Kristin could hear, hopefully, was my voice instead of my words.

He shrugged. "I can't, I don't have any control over that." I could see how that would be a pretty unique frustration.

"How can I be the only one?"

"I guess you are the most important one."

My face flushed with reluctant pleasure. "Okay, but still. I think you need to help me out here."

Kristin came to the door. "Are you all right?" she asked.

I put my hand over the receiver. "Fine, fine. It's just . . . a . . . plumbing thing?"

She raised an eyebrow. Nothing got by her. "Are you asking me or telling me?"

"Telling." I shook my head and returned to the phone as if it were Dave Macmillan. "So you can't show up, say, now? Right now?" My eyes were fastened on Ben.

"Nope. I'm as here as I can get."

Kristin was still looking at me, so I gestured toward Ben with my free hand. "Do you see anything unusual?" I asked her.

"*What?* No. Where?"

"Right here?" I made a vague motion toward him.

She frowned. "*What* are you *talking* about?"

"This is impossible," I said, then tightened my grip on the phone. "I'll hold, yes."

"You're a terrible actress, you know that?" Ben pointed out unnecessarily. That had always been the case. I could barely convince someone of the truth. "If I'd known you were such a bad actress I never would have been jealous over you."

That melted me a little. *Finally* a tiny nugget of romance. Unhealthy romance, perhaps, but still—better than the let-me-find-you-a-new-husband variety. "Oh, you were jealous?" I asked automatically.

"Who are you *talking* to?" Kristin demanded.

I pointed at the phone and mouthed, *Plumber.*

"He's jealous?" She looked very skeptical. "Of what, other plumbers? Did you cheat on him with an electrician?"

Ben laughed. "Good one. Don't let the lawn guy find out or he might tell the contractor."

"Oh, *very* funny," I said to him/the phone.

"That is *not* the plumber," she went on. "There is no way that is the plumber."

"It *is*! Shh!" I felt Kristin's eyes on me and turned my attention as if to the phone. "Yes, I can be here in the—"

I was interrupted by the phone ringing. Right in my ear. Right while I was talking, or pretending to talk, to my plumber.

The jig was up.

Kristin crossed her arms.

"Bad luck," I heard Ben say. "I have to say, I thought it was really smart of you to pretend to be on the phone, but you should have turned the ringer off."

"I *know*," I rasped, then looked back at Kristin.

"You weren't talking to the plumber," she said. She'd always had a very keen sense of the obvious.

I shook my head.

"You weren't talking to anyone. On the phone, anyway."

"No."

She raised an eyebrow, but then she looked again where I had asked her to. "Is someone here?"

"Not exactly." I winced.

"I have to be honest, you're kind of scaring me." She looked at me, then next to me, and back into my eyes. "Do you need some sort of help? Counseling? Maybe"—she paused—"a restful stay somewhere?"

I took a deep breath, then went to the couch and sat down, dropping my head in my hands. What on earth was I supposed to do now?

She sat down next to me. "I know I should probably be walking on eggshells right now and trying, carefully, to figure out what the hell is wrong with you, but you'd save us both a lot of time and sanity if you just told me. What is going on?"

"Ben is here."

A tense silence settled between us and stretched.

"Ben."

I nodded, then clapped my hands together and stood up. "Feel better? Does that answer all your questions?" I laughed lightly. "Is the conversation over now?"

She bit her thumbnail for a moment and stood up too, pacing in front of me. "Wait a minute, just a minute, this is okay. I mean, it's kind of normal. You're talking to Ben. Okay, is he answering?"

"I'm answering."

"He's answering."

"He's answering," she echoed both of us. "Okay."

"He has been for a few weeks."

"So he's . . ." Kristin nervously gestured toward the space next to me. "Ben's there right now? And he can hear us?"

"Yes. Well, not *there*." I indicated. "He's there." Then to him I said, "Can't you do *something* to show her you're here?"

"Like what?"

"I don't know, maybe you can move a pillow?"

"I don't know how to react," Kristin said.

"I know." I shrugged. "I don't either. But it's true. It's one hundred percent true."

"And there's nothing else going on?" She reached over and felt my forehead.

I had to laugh. "Insanity doesn't give you a fever," I said. "If that's what you're wondering."

"A fever can give you insanity," she countered.

"I'm not insane!"

"I want to believe you!"

"Don't fight," Ben said. "That is the least productive thing right now."

"Then *do* something," I said, no longer worried that she'd hear me, obviously. The cat was out of the bag, now I just needed for her to see it. Or at least believe me.

"Let me think," he said.

"He's thinking," I told her.

"Good." She nodded. "Okay." She was clearly trying to stay calm and was barely keeping her grip on it. "Shit fuck damn it, I don't know what to do in this situation."

The way she looked at me was as if we weren't friends but I was a lost child she suddenly had responsibility for. Frankly, I could imagine how she felt; earlier she'd been joking around with her friend, equals, comrades, and now she thought I—a grown adult with my own ideas—had lost my grip and she alone had to figure out what to do.

"Kristin, you've got to believe me," I said, emotion strangling my voice.

"Maybe I should call Phillip."

"Please don't get everyone worked up about this." I wanted to cry, to scream, to throw things. This wasn't fair. Hadn't I been through enough? I'd gone out on a limb telling her the whole truth. What if she continued to not believe me? What would she do? Would she stay anyway? Leave Jamie? Take both kids and leave?

This was a mess.

"Phillip," Ben said.

"Her husband, you know, Phillip."

"Of course I know Phillip." His voice remained calm and easy. "I might know Phillip a little too well."

"What do you mean?" I asked him.

"What's going on?" Kristin asked, her voice tight, her body still in its fight-or-flight stance.

"He's saying he knows Phillip," I told her.

"That proves he's here, then," she said. "What was I worried about?" I was glad to see her sarcasm coming back.

Ben held up his hand. "There's something I know that you don't."

"About Phillip?"

"What about Phillip?" Kristin wanted to know. Now she sounded curious. Alarmed still, but also curious. That was progress.

"I don't know," I said.

"Well, *ask* him?"

"Oh, now you believe he's here?" I raised an eyebrow at her. "A minute ago you were ready to have me committed."

"I'm still ready to have you committed," she said. "But what is he, or you, saying about Phillip?"

"He says he knows something I don't know." I looked at Ben. "But Kristin does? So it would prove you're here? Is that it?"

He nodded. "I don't know that we want to go there, though."

"Honey, we're already halfway there. If you don't take me all the way, I'm going to have to cash in frequent flyer miles that I don't have, so *please* just say it."

"Phillip has a child with another woman," Ben said. "Someone he knew when he first started dating Kristin."

"*What?*"

"What?" Kristin echoed. "What? What did he say?"

"Are you *sure?*" I focused on Ben. This wasn't possible. Kristin and I were best friends. Why wouldn't she have told me about this before?

"Kyle. I think his name is Kyle."

"Kyle," I repeated.

I heard Kristin gasp.

I looked at her, the enormity of this information settling over me. "Phillip has a son named Kyle?"

She raised shaking hands to her face. "How do you know that?"

It was proof. Proof to her and proof to me, if I'd needed it. I couldn't have conjured this apparently accurate information by myself. "Ben just told me. Why didn't *you* tell me?"

I felt Ben come closer, his presence soothing and exciting simultaneously.

"Phillip doesn't talk about it," she said, her voice quavering. "He doesn't want anyone to know because the woman took the child away and wouldn't let him see him. She even denied in court that Phillip was the father, and that was before DNA was routinely used."

"So where is Kyle?" It felt weird to suddenly be talking about this person who, moments before, hadn't existed to me but who was apparently the grown son of my best friend's husband.

"His mother took him out of the country. Phillip lost track a long time ago." She shrugged. "It's not that he's ashamed of having fathered Kyle, but he feels like he let him down by losing him."

"He just doesn't like to talk about it," Ben added softly. "He only told me because he'd had a lot of bourbon and it was heavy on his mind."

"I didn't know he'd told Ben," Kristin said.

"Me neither." I glanced at Ben, feeling a selfish little pang of betrayal because he had known something so monumental and never told me. Of course he hadn't—he was a good friend who could keep a secret, and for whatever reason Phillip had not wanted me or anyone else to know. That was his right.

It's just that I'd thought Ben and I had no secrets between us and suddenly I was learning that we did.

What else might I find out?

"I'm sorry I never told you," Kristin said, articulating a thought that hadn't even occurred to me. "It was Phillip's truth and not mine to give out."

"I understand." And I did. Both her and Ben. This wasn't about me, but it was a good reminder to me that people have levels that go on and on.

"So," Kristin said, slapping her hands down on her thighs and taking a deep breath. "Where is he?"

Kyle? Phillip? "Who?"

She gave a little smile and said, "Ben."

Chapter Thirty-two

Willa

I glanced at Ben. "Okay?"

He gave a bow.

I rolled my eyes at him, then took a steadying breath. This wasn't going to be an easy admission, even to my best friend. It was so outrageous, and so lacking in proof (besides the Kyle thing, which wasn't necessarily that solidly posthumous) that it risked making me look legitimately crazy. "He's right here. Next to me."

"Here?" She reached out and ran her hand right through him. The minute she did, she drew it back. "No way."

"Yup."

She looked alarmed. "It's cold."

"Oh." I nodded, glancing a little apologetically at Ben. He'd been such a warm person; it must suck to constantly have people recoiling at his coldness now. "Yeah. That seems to go with the program."

He shrugged, but he looked uncomfortable. I knew he understood this to be kind of creepy. "I don't get it," he said, in answer to my unasked question.

Kristin took a short breath, held it for a second, then let it out. "Willa, I don't know. I can't really . . . I mean, how can I believe this? It's not possible."

I shrugged. "I know. That's how I felt."

"This must have been so hard for you." Realization came into her eyes. "Oooh, is this what was going on when you made up that story about the workout partner with Jamie the last week?"

I nodded.

"Man." She gave a low whistle. "I had no idea. Okay, so if he's here . . ." she said. "*Since* he's here, what is he doing here? Is he . . . stuck?"

"No, I don't think so." I looked at him for clarification and he shook his head. "No."

"Then, what?" she asked, her frown deepening. "Most of the time when people die they just move on, whatever that means. We don't constantly see the ghosts of our lost loved ones or we'd go crazy. Or we'd be so used to it that there would be nothing strange or surprising about it. In other words, it would be really different than *this*." She wiped at her eyes. "I'm sorry, I just don't get it."

"I came to help you. You were too sad. Too stuck. But now . . . now you're going to be all right."

"He knew I was sad," I said to her. "Too sad."

"Well, you haven't really been *happy* . . ."

"No, definitely not," I agreed. I turned to face him. "I needed you. I *need* you. And"—tears came upon me suddenly—"and you're *gone*."

Just like that, I realized it. He *was* gone. I mean, I'd realized it for three years, but I had lived as if in limbo, day-to-day, waiting for the days to pass until . . . what? Until I was old and beyond the place where anyone would suggest I should move on? Maybe.

Certainly the days had turned to weeks, had turned to months, had turned to years, and it had all passed in the blink of an eye without me ever stopping to think about how to do anything but eventually die.

I never thought about how to live.

But he'd come to tell me it was okay to be happy without him. Suddenly it all made sense.

"You're going to be all right," he said softly.

"I'm going to be all right," I repeated, then looked at Kristin. "I *am* going to be all right."

Confusion was still evident in her expression, but she still managed a smile. "Well, yeah, you're going to be all right. You're going to be better than all right, you're going to be *great!*"

"There it is," Ben said. "Believe it." Once again, he began to fade. There was no rhyme or reason to it, he just disappeared arbitrarily.

"Don't." I reached for him, as if that could do anything. It couldn't and it didn't. He disappeared into the ether once again. I looked after him, feeling bereft.

"Don't what?" Kristin asked, pressing her hands together, ready to spring forward. "What did he do?"

"He's gone," I said to her. "He disappeared."

"What, he just . . ." She snapped her fingers. "Like that?"

I nodded. "That's how it goes. We don't have any control over it."

I heard my own words and felt irritated at the adoptation of *we* that I'd taken on. *We don't have any control . . .* While the statement was true, it implied a togetherness that we no longer had or could have. *We can't join you for dinner that night. We will try to get a babysitter for Jamie. We just bought a beach house, come visit . . .*

Whatever *we* once did we would never do again, so that one small word had become something kind of sad and silly both at the same time.

If she noticed my use of the word and thought it was strange, she didn't show it. "Well, now that he's gone, start over at the beginning. Tell me everything."

Chapter Thirty-three

Willa

Weeks passed without me seeing Ben. Ever since I'd told Kristin the truth, it was like the winds had shifted. There was something different in the quality of the air. It was somehow lighter. And even though I still missed Ben terribly, an unexpected peace had settled deep inside of me. I couldn't even say what it was, whether it was because of the fact that I knew now—I truly believed—that there was more to everything than met the eye, or if it was simply a matter of having "exorcised" my sadness with him, I don't know.

I still looked for him, of course. I watched Dolly for sudden alertness or interest in something I couldn't see, but she was back to her normal old self, begging in the kitchen, sleeping on the sofa, snoring on my bed at night. Yes, she'd leap up and bark when the mailman pushed mail through the door slot, but it was a different bark. Threatening, but not curious.

Kristin and I talked about it a lot at first. She was constantly asking if I saw him recently. And also what it was like to hear his voice. Did he sound the same? Was it like he was literally standing in the room as real as she was? Could I touch him or feel his form?

And it was funny because, until she started asking those questions, it hadn't occurred to me how much of a veil there had been when he showed up, even when he was talking to me or teasing me. I never had the sense that I could touch him or in any way *be with* him.

"But that would have been enough for you?" Kristin asked, as we were sitting on the beach one evening, having wine from water bottles. We'd gotten a ride to the boardwalk with the kids on their way to work and had decided to relax on the beach until we wanted to amble over to a restaurant, drink our fill of wine, and then take an Uber home.

The sun was setting slowly over the bay to the west and the entire shoreline was cast in an amber golden light. The breeze lifted my hair and the light felt healing on my face. "I thought it would be enough," I told her. "Some Ben is better than no Ben. But he made it clear from the beginning that he couldn't stay." I took a sip of wine. "Actually, his death made it pretty clear he couldn't stay."

"Pretty clear," she agreed, taking a sip herself.

A family several yards away started closing up their striped umbrella and collecting their towels and children. I watched them for a few moments, then said, "I miss those days."

Kristin followed my gaze, then nodded. "They really grew up fast, didn't they? I mean, they'll be out on their own so soon. It makes me melancholy too."

I remembered Jamie running on the beach, dashing toward the waves and jumping the white line of phosphorescent foam like it was a rope, then standing there while the wave drew back, burying his little feet in the sand. I could remember him kneeling in the surf, digging for sand crabs, always begging to bring them home as pets, and never understanding when

I said we couldn't own them because they needed to be where nature had put them.

There was obviously a lesson in there for me as well. One I'd have to learn over and over again in life, apparently.

Easy enough to say, *If you love something, set it free,* but hard to truly set something free if you really love it.

"You could still have another one, you know," Kristin said.

I turned my attention back to her. The sun was gleaming off her hair, making it shine like a new copper penny. "Hmm? Another what?"

"Another kid!"

A wave crashed on the shore as if to punctuate what she'd said. Another baby. With Jamie almost out of high school. "I can't even imagine it," I said.

"Maybe you should start. Thinking about it, that is. You were so young when you had Jamie, you're still well within your childbearing years—"

"I don't know about *well within.*"

She flattened her hand and tipped it side to side. "Okay, maybe you're not where you were at twenty, but, yeah, I'd say you're still *well within* your childbearing years. Didn't you and Ben ever talk about having another one?"

"Early on." I thought about it. "But it just never happened. We decided to be philosophical about it and take it that Jamie was all we needed."

"There's something to be said for that," she agreed. "But, honestly, look at where you are. Your life is truly beginning again now. It's not what you expected, it's not what *any* of us expected, but that's the fact. There are a whole lot of possibilities you probably never thought about before that are now available to you."

I turned my gaze to the ocean and to the horizon that stretched out far beyond. It wasn't endless, but it looked like it was. That was true of my life too. From where I sat, there was a long way to go. No one knew what was coming up. But, as Ben had said, there were some glorious possibilities. "Sometimes it's hard to let go of the known, even when it's not so great," I said.

She nodded. "We've all been there. But that is a stuck place. Fear never keeps someone in a wonderful situation, it just puts everything on hold."

It had for three years now. The sharp shock of finding out about Ben when it had happened had worn down to a soft pain that was constant. It was always there, it never let me down. And even while I hated it, when the waves of sadness came over me, they were familiar, and there was a certain comfort in that.

The comfort I should have taken, of course, was in my family and friends. Everything that remained. Because a *lot* did remain. It felt like I'd lost everything, but I hadn't. Yet in that mire of grief, I'd let too much important stuff go.

"Part of me feels like I'd be betraying Jamie if I moved on in a new relationship, even though he *says* he thinks I should," I confessed.

"Jamie! He'd probably be the happiest one!"

I looked at her. The sun, behind her, was hovering just over the low buildings along the boardwalk, cutting straight shadows down the sand. "Do you really think so?"

"He's about to spread his wings and fly into his future. Of *course* he wants you to be happy and not be some sad sack at home that he has to worry about." She smiled at me. "Not that you're a sad sack."

I smiled. "Thanks."

"And you know, frankly, he's not too old to develop a good relationship with a man if you find someone you like that much. The guy wouldn't be his father, obviously, but all boys could use a good male influence."

I agreed with that. One of my biggest regrets was that Jamie didn't have anyone to show him how to be a good man. He'd remember Ben, of course, he hadn't been that young when he'd died, but don't we all have role models of some sort throughout our lives?

We sat in relative silence for a while after that, listening to the waves hitting the sand, watching the tide come in closer and closer to where we'd propped our Tommy Bahama chairs in the sand.

After a while, we finished our drinks, met each others' eyes, and nodded in unison, then laughed. Our stomachs were on the same exact time table. It was time for dinner.

We shook the sand out of our towels and chairs and started walking on the still-hot sand.

What is it about summer at the beach that makes you feel like it should stretch on forever? These hot, sun-soaked days felt permanent; I couldn't even picture snow and cold winds right now.

If I were home in Potomac, would I feel the same? Probably not. With no sea breeze to cross through the house, I'd have the air-conditioning on, and that was always too cold, no matter where I set it. And the artificial hum drove me crazy, made me want to scream every time it kicked on. Admittedly, I loved the sound of a lawn mower and the smell of fresh-cut grass, but that was nothing compared to the unique mix of sugar and salt on the wind of the shore.

It was going to be damn hard to get rid of the beach house. A big profit, to be sure. The kind of profit that made the future a lot less scary. But I made a good salary and both houses were nearly paid off, since Ben had been determined to take the shortest mortgage we could reasonably afford. If I kept the place, I might have to live on a tight budget for a few years, but then things would get a lot easier.

I thought about it while we walked to Phillips Crab House for dinner. Thought about continuing to come here without Ben versus starting anew at home without all the memories that tied me down.

I honestly wasn't sure which would be harder.

"So the Realtor is coming tomorrow?" Kristin asked, reeling me back in. We'd finished pretty much everything on the list and were ready for a new assessment of the house.

"Yes," I said.

"How do you feel about the way the place looks now?"

I sighed. "Kind of like I want to buy it all over again." We checked in at the hostess's station and sat on hard wooden benches to wait for our name to be called. "There's really something to that whole business of removing clutter."

"I read a book about it. It's supposed to make a huge difference in your mind-set." She shrugged. "Then again, talking to the ghost of your late husband can do that too."

I looked at her. "So you really don't think I'm crazy?"

She shook her head. "I wish I did. Then I wouldn't be so scared that *I* am. But, no. I don't think you're crazy. No one else could have known about Kyle. To say nothing of the fact that I've never really known you to be crazy. Not certifiably, at least. You're a little nuts under the best of circumstances."

"All the best people are."

She laughed outright. "Ain't it the truth?"

I put my arm around her and gave her a squeeze. "I've thought so for years."

"All right, all right, I get it." She let out a sigh. "Okay, if all goes well, the house goes on the market this week."

"We should bury Saint Joseph in the front garden."

She looked at me sideways. "Did you kill him?"

"No, I mean we should get a little statuette of Saint Joseph and bury him there for good luck. There's all sorts of rules about which way he needs to face and so on, but I've heard people swear it works."

"You're continuing the crazy thing, you know that, right?" she asked, lifting a brow at me. "Is this a test to see how far you can go?"

I laughed heartily. "No! I'm serious! That's what I've heard!" Though, given everything else I'd already thrown at her over the past few weeks, I couldn't blame her for asking.

"Okay." She shook her head. "We've come this far this summer, let's go to a religious icon store and get Saint Joseph after dinner."

Chapter Thirty-four

Willa

Sue Branford declared the house "magnificent" and her eyes glowed as she looked around the place. I imagined I could see dollar signs in them like on one of those old cartoons.

"The repair work is remarkable," she said, examining the place where there had been a leak. "I can't even tell there was an incident."

Incident. When I'd first arrived, broken and ill-prepared for anything ahead of me, that *incident* had damn near made me give up on everything. It had been the perfect example to my then-stressed mind of how hard it all was to do this alone.

But I had done it. I mean, I'd hired Dave and *he'd* done it, but I'd managed to address it. It was fixed now. Likewise the painting and moving things. Yes, I'd needed help, Kristin had been a godsend, but somewhere along the way I'd stopped feeling like life was impossible without Ben and I'd started to just . . . I don't know, I'd started to just *live* it.

Sue had just finished her tour of the house when the kids came running in, laughing unselfconsciously at some joke between them.

"Oh, hi!" Kelsey beamed when she saw us. "Sorry, didn't know you had company. We're about to go to work."

"Hey, Mom," Jamie said, and gave the most genuine smile I'd seen on him in a long, long time. "What's up?"

I introduced them and finished with, "This is Ms. Branford, the Realtor who's listing the house."

Both kids' expressions fell.

"Oh." Jamie extended a hand. "Nice to meet you." He tried to brighten when he looked at me. "Is it looking good?"

Sue answered for me. "It's looking very good! I think there are going to be a lot of excited clients clambering to bid!"

"Great," Jamie said, utterly without sincerity. It hadn't been that long since he'd declared he never wanted to come back here. Now, after a few weeks of sun, gainful employment, and—it could not be denied—the company of Kelsey, he looked as if I'd just told him I was going to sell Dolly to the highest bidder.

"Oh, indeed it is," Sue confirmed, apparently thinking she was enhancing the mood with her good news. "I bet it won't last a week on the market. Don't quote me on that, we never do know what's going to happen, but I have a hunch this one's going to go fast."

"How soon will it go up for sale?" Kelsey wanted to know. She exchanged a glance with Jamie.

"I'm not sure," I said, before Sue chirped up with the news that if we got it on the market quickly enough, it might just be sold yesterday.

"Well, there are a few things we have to do first," I said, wanting to slow her down before she had a new family moved in on top of us.

I felt Kristin looking at me curiously.

"Oh, I don't know," Sue said, continuing in oblivion. "I think you've done a fab job of getting it ready. I can't think of anything major that needs to be done at this point besides getting the signs out and setting up some viewings."

"Well . . ." I didn't have anything to say. Well, nothing.

"Come on," Jamie said to Kelsey. "We've got to get ready to go to work."

Kelsey's gaze lingered on me for a moment, her blond hair lighter by the day, framing her lovely tawny face. "Willa, let me know if you need anything done. I'm glad to help however I can. I'm just so grateful to be here, you know?"

I could see that. "Thanks, sweetie."

I watched them, feeling a pang. Their youth, their fun, their carefree days at the beach.

Lord, I didn't want to take that away from them.

"I don't think you want to sell," a voice said in my ear. It was Ben, of course. Except I didn't see him this time and I wasn't sure it was really him and not my own imagination, knowing what he'd say because he'd know what was truly in my heart. I closed my eyes hard for a minute to stave off tears. *Look at the kids*, I imagined him saying. *They look so happy here. Like us. Once upon a time.*

I glanced to my side and *thought* I caught a glimpse of him, but he was so close he was blurry to the eye. Or maybe those were my own tears, obscuring my view of the new curtains that were rippling in the wind.

It really didn't matter which it was. I knew how he'd feel and he knew how I'd feel and so the reality of the conversation didn't even matter. It was already *my* reality.

And then I knew that, although love could transcend anything, including death, romantic love had nothing on the love a parent feels for a child. If anything could make him feel the emptiness that the afterlife had apparently filled, it would be Jamie.

I reached my hand subtly into the cold next to me. I could imagine his hand reaching for mine, but, as always, I could feel little more than the imagined touch.

"Well. Thanks so much for coming, Sue. I'll be in touch soon and let you know what I want to do."

Sue, still apparently confident in her commission, extended a hand to me. "So nice to see you again, Willa. All right, so I'll be in touch. You just let me know what you want to do, but I honestly think we can turn this place around within weeks."

My stomach hurt at the prospect.

Sue put her paperwork into her messenger bag and tucked it under her suited arm.

It was hard to break the habitual feeling that Ben should be acknowledged too, but of course he shouldn't. It was all me now.

I was on my own, whether he was close in spirit or not.

I realized that shouldn't have been a revelation, but it was. I'd been going through life after his death barely breathing, just trying to get from one moment to the next, but I had. I had done it for years.

I was going to be all right, I knew it.

Because I already was.

Chapter Thirty-five

Jamie

Jamie and Kelsey pulled up to the house, both laughing unstoppably. Their inside jokes were such journeys that no one in the world but they could laugh at them. One dumb impression would turn into an entire tongue-in-cheek conversation that bred its very own jokes. It was happening now. Suddenly she was talking in an extremely terrible Dutch accent, and all because of the initial joke they'd had that began from the injury she'd incurred at the dump. They were taking out this cheap old bookshelf and throwing it in, but when she insisted on helping, her hand slid whip-fast over a sharp edge and was cut.

Jamie shoved the shelf over the ledge upon seeing the instant blood, and then flew to the back of the car and tore an old Metallica T-shirt. When he came back with it, she was cracking up. He ignored her and wrapped her hand, and she finally calmed enough to say, "Oh, my god, you flew into action like Superman! That was amazing. Suddenly didn't *need* help with the bookshelf . . ."

"To be fair," he'd said, "I never needed any help with the bookshelf."

"Bull!"

He made her elevate her hand and let him toss the rest of the junk on his own. She made noise about being *fine*, but he didn't budge on this. Once they were in the car and saw that her hand wasn't as bad as it seemed, they had found their way to the stupid joke.

There was another car in the driveway when they got home, so Jamie had to park on the street.

"Who is that?" asked Kelsey.

"No clue. The plumber has a truck. Probably an electrician or something."

"In a Prius?" She opened her door. "That either makes no sense or perfect sense, I'm not sure."

They went in, and a brassy woman's voice bounced off the walls and floors of the mostly empty rooms.

"Right, right, oh, sure, I agree completely, I agree completely. Yeah. Well, my sister's husband is a contractor, it would be no problem to get him out here if you think you want to go that route, but I think it's already magnificent the way it is."

"I don't know . . . probably not, though."

"You don't need to, honestly, this place will sell like that." He heard the snap of fingers and they walked in to see a woman standing in their kitchen with Kristin and his mom.

The woman was shaped almost frighteningly like a pigeon from the side, and had one of those haircuts that made you wonder how she had come upon it in this day and age—didn't she know it was, like . . . a joke to have something so mulletlike?

He was being nasty, and he didn't mean to be. But he was really irritated by her presence.

Kelsey said, "Umm . . ." but he was pretty sure he was the only one to hear her.

His mom introduced the woman as the Realtor who was going to be listing the house for sale. Sue Branford. She was probably a great salesperson, because she talked right over everything anyone else said. Heaven help anyone who tried to say no to her.

After a moment of polite chitchat, they all said goodbye, and, after offering his mom any help she could give, Kelsey excused herself to go get ready for work. He knew she'd go into the room she was staying in and take that small purple makeup bag into the bathroom and come out looking pretty, though he liked her before she put the makeup on and after she took it off. The Kelsey he knew didn't have candy-apple-red lips and all that black eyeliner. But he could see that she was doing it right.

Then he'd start the car and let the air-conditioning cool it down a little, and then they'd go out and get in. She'd bring him a water and one for herself, and about one song in, she'd say, "Can I play something?" and then choose the music for the rest of the drive.

It was strange that their routine, new as it was, would be cut short soon. He couldn't envision that they'd ever have another opportunity like this again.

In fact, he might not see her. He hadn't seen her in the past three years, except in passing now and then on the street. They'd make an effort more now, probably, but he knew how those things played out. They'd talk about seeing each other, and maybe they would sometime or sometimes, but it wouldn't be the same as this. This was an era defined part by circumstance and part by each other.

Meeting halfway between their houses to have coffee in some busy Starbucks wouldn't cut it. Neither would bringing her around at home. Not that he wouldn't want to, he'd love that, actually . . . but it wouldn't have that same . . . he didn't know what. It would feel so pointed, like a *date*. He didn't want that. Did he?

Shit, he thought.

He wanted to stay here. He wanted to stay the whole summer, soaking in this atmosphere with Kelsey. He wanted to kiss her on the boardwalk, if he could ever work up the nerve, and he wanted to share funnel cakes and fries and enjoy this time in their lives that he already knew was unlike any other time would ever be again.

That was how it had been for his parents when they met here all those years ago. Maybe it was a lucky house, or a lucky beach, or maybe it was just fate, but he just knew—without a doubt—that he was supposed to be here with Kelsey this summer.

And maybe other summers too.

"Jamie?" His mom had clearly been trying to get his attention for some time.

He was embarrassed to be caught in such slushy romantic thoughts. "Sorry, what?"

"Thanks for going to the dump. Tomorrow I guess we'll have to start taking pictures of some of the good stuff here and posting it on Craigslist. Do you think you and Kelsey could do that? I'm just realizing how much is left. It's like this is how we *should* have had it when we were here."

But they *were* here. Right now. "Uh, yeah. Sure. We're actually off tomorrow."

"So that guy really put you on all the same shifts, just because you brought in a chick, huh?" Kristin leaned on the counter drinking a coffee he was willing to bet she wished had been made by Kelsey.

Man, he really could not get his mind off that girl.

"Yep. He was pretty desperate. That works for me. Us. I guess it makes the drive over there easy."

"She's been making such good money! It's unbelievable."

"It's a good job. Easy. She barely works." He added this last part as she ran in, half her face done and a mascara wand in hand, to get a bottle of Coke from the fridge.

"Shut up!" she yelled behind her as she ran back to the bathroom. "I know you're talking about me. I *totally* work!"

He laughed and watched her go. When he turned to see both women looking at him, he left the room quickly, lest they should read his mind.

He was quiet on the way in, though Kelsey was too distracted singing along with her music to notice. She was on one of her rare diversions from their shared musical taste, and had on the soundtrack from—as she explained to him—"the original cast recording of *Evita* with Patti LuPone and Mandy Patinkin, literally so much better than the Madonna one, which was so bleh. But seriously, it's good music even if you're not a musicals person, which clearly you're not into musicals, but anyway, just indulge me for the day while I listen to it."

This soundtrack involved her doing a lot of different accents and voices, which was amusing even though he wasn't really into the music itself. It was worth it to see her doing an uber-serious face, brow furrowed, hands gesticulating wildly, singing along in what she clearly thought was a convincing male voice.

Work was crazy. Everyone made so much that even he made a lot, and he spent the entire night running food all over the restaurant. It seemed like it was every server's personal mission to mess up one thing on every table, which inevitably led to *him* having to apologize to the customer and find the manager and then go work on remedying the situation, since the servers were usually hanging out with their cool tables or visiting friends, or sneaking a cigarette outside while they thought their tables were handled.

Kelsey was the only one who took all her own food to her tables without an expo to help, or as much as she could. She also was the only one to remain cheerful even when she was exhausted. She would shake her head, smiling, amazed at how everything was going to shit, rather than getting pissy and treating anyone like crap.

At one point she grabbed him by the arm as they passed each other on the floor and said, "I need extra-crispy fries for table six on the fly because the ones I dropped off tasted *too potatoey*"—she took the time to draw this out—"and also can we go to the beach after work?"

"Pile of burnt sticks and twigs coming right up, table six, on the fly. And yes, sure."

"Thank god. Though I didn't bring a bathing suit." Pause. "Hi! Yes?" A customer flagged her down with some menu clarification needed, and she clearly didn't realize she was interrupting a possibly important private moment.

Mind whirling, Jamie went back to the kitchen and almost forgot to get the rush order of fries.

They ended up working an hour later than usual, the restaurant emptying out as fast as it had filled up. She did her checkout, and he did his side work and did hers too, just so they could leave sooner.

She came up around ten-thirty saying, "Oh, my god, I'm so sorry, my checkout took forever, I was missing the signed receipt for this *huge* check, but it turned out they room-charged it to the hotel next door, which is fine except they took the slip with them and then they ended up calling, so—it was just a whole thing."

"No problem, don't worry about it."

"But I, *thank you*, but I still have two crates of roll-ups to do." She cringed.

"Already did it."

"What?"

"Already did it."

"You did . . . my roll-ups?"

"Yeah."

"What about your own side work?"

"Dude, you took, like, literally forever," he said, imitating the voice she did when she spoke like a Valley girl.

She did the voice back. "Shut up! You did not!"

He nodded. "Yeah, it's all done, so let's blow this Popsicle stand." What the hell was that from, and why was he saying it? The girl made him lose his mind.

She smiled at him and walked over to clock out. She turned back again to him and narrowed her eyes. "Hm."

He smacked her with the rag he had been finishing the cleaning with and then threw it in the bin.

The night was incredibly hot and muggy. No wonder so many people had been driven in to the restaurant. There was no cool breeze to serve as relief. Usually, here on the shore, a breeze was a given. But the air was unmoving. Even the sand was still hot, its grains holding on tight to the rays of sunshine they'd been beaten with all day.

They parked down one of the residential streets, far from the boardwalk, though they could see it. They both left their shoes in the car and Jamie left his keys on the driver's seat.

They went out with nothing but themselves.

The light from the surrounding hotels and motels stretched far enough to cast their shadows into the hungry waves. They walked into the surf.

"Yeah, the water is barely any colder than the air," Kelsey said. "It'll really only make a difference if we go in."

"Thought you didn't bring a bathing suit."

"I didn't."

They looked at each other.

"Oh, come on," she said, and he could see even in the dim light that she was blushing. He probably was too, though he didn't know if he blushed. He hoped not. "Bikini, bra and underwear, it's exactly the same thing."

"Almost."

"Boxers." She gestured at him. "Almost the same."

"I promise not to look."

"Okay." She made a swirl motion with her finger.

He turned around.

He stared out into the distance, gnawing on the inside of his cheek, waiting for her to say it was okay to turn back even while knowing she was undressing behind him.

"Okay, you promised not to look," she said, and he saw her clothes fly through the air onto the sand to his left. Suddenly she was behind him as she said, "I don't promise."

She pushed him and then ran into the waves.

He pulled his polo over his head and tossed it onto her clothes. He kicked off his shorts and was glad he was wearing dark blue, slightly longer boxers than some of the ones he owned. Some of them had Peanuts characters on them or the day of the week. He even had one embarrassing pair that said, . . . BUTT WHY? on the ass.

Though he thought Kelsey might actually think that was funny.

He ran into the water after her, waves crashing at his ankles, knees, then thighs, until he could dive under and catch up with her. They were at a shallow portion of the beach; it dropped off for a few feet, but then there was a jetty that kept the height of the water at a little under five and a half feet. She was tall enough that she could keep her head above water while wading, and he could keep his neck and collarbone out. They knew to come here because this was where their parents had let them play safely when they were younger.

"Jamie?" said Kelsey once they were out there and had both survived their first small wave.

"Kelsey," he said, leaning back and floating in the water.

"I don't want your mom to sell the house."

He rarely could rightly anticipate anything out of Kelsey's mouth, but this really surprised him.

He hadn't even really thought those words yet.

"You don't think she should?"

"I don't know what she *should* do. I don't know if she needs the money, I don't know if the place is . . . like, unsound, or not a good investment, or—I just hate that it's going away. I hate that your dad died there, that's so awful. I can't believe he's fucking gone. I really, really . . ." Her voice had been strong, but melted on, "can't."

"I can't either."

"But . . . but I also wish we could go back. Or re-create it. Life goes on and maybe it still can, there. I hate the idea that all those years we had there are just over, spent, done. *Kaput*."

She drifted a little closer to him and he nodded.

"I just . . ." she went on. "I always thought one day *we'd* be grown-ups there too. Yeah, I pictured your dad there, I pictured Ben there. Of course, I never—but I at least thought we'd be there one day, maybe even come up ourselves, on our own."

They caught eyes.

"With friends or whatever," he said, giving her an out, when she looked embarrassed. Though she really shouldn't be.

"Right. Right. It's probably bratty, but I always considered it part mine in a way too. Like we all had some right to it and we'd all have our stories there."

He nodded. It really was like she'd read his thoughts. "Me too."

"And . . ." She put her hands up out of the water and splashed them back down. "I don't want the summer to end whenever the house sells. Not just because I broke up with Jason or anything like that . . ."

Of course his name was Jason. All at once Jamie got a full-color picture in his mind of a preppy jock with a lot of money who never had to work in a restaurant one day in his life.

"I just feel at home here," Kelsey went on. "It feels right, us all coming back here. I wish our dads were here—not that—I mean—"

"I know." He smiled at her and nodded to let her know he understood. And he did. He wished their dads were there too. Sometimes he could swear he felt his there, but he knew that was just wishful thinking.

Strong wishful thinking.

"It just really makes me sad."

He looked at her now, the distant lights from the boardwalk and the hotels and motels lighting up her face and her eyes enough that he could see tears glistening there.

They looked at each other for a long moment. He bit his lip.

"Since when are you such a girl?" he asked.

Her eyes widened, and then she cracked up, tears spilling over anyhow, and then splashed him hard. "You're such a jerk."

He splashed her back and then grabbed her underwater by the waist. She stopped squirming after a second and turned back to look at him. Their faces were the closest they'd ever been.

"Seriously," he said, turning her and lifting her off her feet. "When did you become such a *girl?*"

He kissed her, hoping it was the right moment. Hoping the line worked. Hoping she'd kiss him back. Hoping it wouldn't make things weird.

It was good. It was really good. She kissed him back. The waves crashed on them, pushing them toward shore and pulling them back again, his feet planted in the watery sand beneath them, keeping them upright. They were there forever. There was no getting enough of it, this new thing between them that seemed simultaneously bizarre and inevitable. It took the flashing of red and blue lights and a flashlight on the water to get them to stop.

"Oh, shit," he said, while she said something similar, and they ran out of the water, laughing again, collecting their clothes, and running up to the cop standing next to his car.

Jamie got there first, glancing back to make sure she was on her way. She held up her shirt to indicate she'd gone back for it, and then gestured to go, go!

"This your vehicle, son?" asked one of the cops when he got to it.

"Yes, sir."

"You don't have a permit for this area."

"Oh—sorry, do we need one?" Obviously they did, if he was saying they didn't have one. "I didn't know anything about that."

"Yes, it's a square sticker, goes right there in the bottom left of the windshield."

"I'm sorry, we haven't been back since we were thirteen." Kelsey came up beside him. "Usually our parents parked; I didn't realize they'd had a permit."

"Thankfully, we don't depend on adolescent wherewithal, we put a nice big sign, right here for you." The cop tapped the air and pointed at an almost sarcastically big sign that read NO PARKING WITHOUT PERMIT.

"Yeah, that's pretty obvious, now that you point it out," said Jamie.

The cop looked from one of them to the other. "You been drinking tonight?"

"No, sir, absolutely not. We got off work at Pretty Mama's and came over here to cool off. No drinking at all."

He glanced at Kelsey, who was quiet for once. She was full-on pink, though she still hadn't lost her grin.

This made him laugh, and he covered it up.

Not well enough.

"All right, look, I got a pretty good idea of the score here. Don't park here again without a permit. You get it at the admin building."

He let them go, said good night, and Jamie and Kelsey held in their laughter until they were in the car.

She blasted Incubus and shimmied back into her clothes, and then they drove to a Valero gas station, where she went in while he waited in the car. She wouldn't take his money because "obviously one of us is worth considerably more at Pretty Mama's and can afford it."

He had given her his order for junk food—a Three Musketeers bar, Sprite, and Smartfood popcorn. He knew that for herself she would be getting a four-pound bag of the sourest candy she could find in there, or an assortment. They had big plans to watch as much *Arrested Development* as possible once they got home.

Home.

The second she was inside, he called his mom.

"Hey, everything okay?" his mom asked on the first ring. Her voice was tense.

"Yeah, yeah. Look." He ran a hand through his hair, and sand fell out like magic dust. "I don't think you should sell the house."

There was a pause. "You—what?"

"I made it seem like I hated it and I guess I kind of did for a while, but I don't hate it. I was afraid of it. I'm not anymore."

"Jamie, what are you saying?"

"Just that Dad died there, and that sucks, but he died there because . . . because it was so part of you guys. Of us. It makes sense almost. We should have more life there. We still have this house if we want it, right? I think we should keep it. If we can. I don't know if we can. But, I just wanted to tell you that's where I stand."

Chapter Thirty-six

Willa

When Jamie called me in the night to say he wanted to keep the house, I had a lot of time to think. Nevertheless, it was hard to be objective, since my heart and my head were at odds. Letting go was hard, but was that because I was being sentimental or because I was right?

I've never understood how to follow my gut instincts because I could believe my gut was telling me just about anything.

But here's the thing. Although I could make whatever decision I wanted by myself, there *was* another person to consider. Something had compelled Jamie to make that call to me and I wanted to know what was really on his mind. More than that, I wanted to know what was really in his heart.

So the next day, we went to the South End Deli, picked up our favorite sandwiches (these things never seemed to change for us), then went to the beach, just the two of us.

It was a crowded mess, filled with people and screaming kids and various balls and toys flying around in the air, but this was where I'd brought him as a child and this was where I wanted to be with him now. To find out what was really at the bottom of the well for him.

We ate in relative silence, then put our trash away.

"Want to go in the water?" I asked him.

"It hasn't been half an hour since we ate," he said, barely keeping his smile in check.

I laughed. "Did I ask if you wanted to swim laps or did I ask if you wanted to simply put a toe in the water?"

He splayed his arms and shrugged, just like his father used to do. *Whatever you say*, the gesture implied. It used to drive me crazy when Ben would do that, but on Jamie it just touched my heart. "Let's do it," he said, and stood up, holding out a hand to help me up.

For a moment, I wanted to hold on. To hold his hand all the way down to the shore like when he was little. To protect him from the big, scary waves.

But I let go and we walked down to the shoreline side by side, our arms bumping now and then as we traversed the hot sand. I noticed he stepped over the end of the first wave when we got there, just as he used to jump it as a child. Then we stood together, feeling the pull of the water rushing over our feet and burying our heels deep among the sand crabs.

"So you want to keep the house, huh?" I asked. We were both looking straight ahead, out over the water, directly toward Spain, thousands of miles away.

"Yeah. I do. I didn't think we should at first, but now I can't even imagine what I was thinking."

I glanced at him, but he was looking straight ahead, his jaw tight. "I think I know what you mean."

That's when he looked at me, and I could see tears in his eyes. "I miss him," he said, and his voice broke a little.

I put my arm around his waist, skinny and bony and still so boyish even as he careened toward manhood. "I do too," I said, and the tears rolled right down my cheeks, there was no stopping them.

We stood in silence for a few minutes, with all the chaos and laughter ringing around us.

Then Jamie turned to me and said, "I'm really sorry I didn't do more to help."

"Oh, honey, that's okay. I'm just so glad you came and that you've been having a good time. I knew it wouldn't be a lot of fun for you to come paint and vacuum and watch Cranky Dave fix the pipes, but I sure do appreciate your coming."

"I don't mean that," he said. "Well, not *just* that. I should have helped more with the house and I shouldn't have been such a brat about not wanting to come, but what I mean is that I'm sorry I didn't help more when Dad died."

I looked at him and shaded my eyes from the sun. "What do you mean? You were just a kid."

He gave a half shrug. "Maybe, but I knew you were sad. I could hear you crying at night."

I'd tried so hard to keep that from him. Not that he shouldn't have known I was sad, but I'd never wanted him to have any idea just how *broken* I felt. I was supposed to be the grown-up. I was supposed to be the strong one, the protector, all of that. It felt horrible to know that this poor child had been lying in his room, alone and scared himself, hearing his one remaining parent absolutely losing her shit.

It was years late, but I decided to address this with absolute honesty. "I'm the one who should be apologizing to you."

He looked genuinely surprised. "Why?"

"Because I let you down that way. I wasn't nearly as strong as I should have been. As I wanted to be. I never wanted you to hear that or to worry about me. You were a child, you needed a guidepost, and I was all over the place. And ever since then I haven't been able to get back on track with you. I'm embarrassed for not being more parental."

"Mom—"

"No, I mean it. I should have made better dinners, had more tolerance for the noise you and your friends made, taken you more places, maybe taken you to Disney World."

"We did go to Disney World."

"I should have taken you again." I sighed. "I feel like I fell really short right when you needed me most. And even while I felt that way, even while I was struggling with my own demons and failing you, I couldn't get myself together enough to do what I knew I should be doing. *Parenting*. Being a good parent, especially since I was the only one you had."

He shook his head. "That's crazy, you've been a great mom."

A moment passed. "I don't know about that, but I promise you this: I have done the absolute best I could with what I had at the time. And I promise to always do my best by you."

He put his arm around me this time and hugged, hard. "You've been a great mom."

I hugged him back, swallowing the sobs that threatened. "I love you, baby."

"I love you too."

At that moment, my heart felt more full than I could ever, in my life, remember it feeling. Everything was as it was supposed to be, and I knew, for once, without a doubt, that I was exactly where I was supposed to be, doing what I was supposed to be doing.

"So," I said, trying to lighten the mood, since I sensed that Jamie didn't know where to go with it either. "What's going on with you and Kelsey?"

His face colored immediately. "What? Nothing. We're just friends."

"Interesting, I didn't ask if there was something more than friendship there. I just asked what was going on. I could have been talking about work, for all you know."

"You weren't talking about work."

"I was!"

Somehow his face grew an even deeper shade of red. "Work is great. Well, maybe not *great*, it's work, but work is work. You know. Like, we both like it okay, I guess."

It was a lot of words for one simple denial.

I smiled privately. "Almost no one loves their first job."

"But it's cool, you know. I like having money."

I nodded. "That's one of the big bonuses. You're making money and you don't have to spend it on rent or mortgage or utilities or anything. You can just stuff your face and buy video games and *go on dates* . . ."

He shifted his gaze toward me. "I know what you're doing."

"Me?" I asked innocently.

"Yes, I know what you're implying. Were you and Kristin in on this together, trying to hook us up or something?"

"There you go again, talking about you and Kelsey when I'm talking to you about regular life stuff." I shook my head. "It's almost as if you have Kelsey on the brain."

He rolled his eyes, then said, "I kind of do."

I had to hold in a shout of laughter. I *knew* it! I knew he had a thing for her. They were such a cute couple. "Yeah, well, I've got a secret for you," I told him.

"What's that?" he asked with exaggerated patience.

"I think she has a thing for you too."

He couldn't help it, his face lit up. "Do you really?"

I nodded. "I really do."

We turned and walked back to our chairs together.

"Don't say anything to her," he said. "I mean it."

"I won't." I made the sign of locking my lips and throwing away the key.

"So do you think we can stay at the house?" he asked, clearly trying to hide the eagerness from his voice. "At least for this summer, if not forever?"

I thought about that and gave a nod. "I think we can at least stay for this summer," I said. "If not forever."

As we came back onto the dry sand, a little boy ran by with a kite. A little boy who looked like a young Jamie, or maybe a young Ben.

I froze in my spot. Was this Ben? Was this the child I'd seen when I first arrived?

"Oh, man, I used to love doing that," Jamie said, smiling.

"Doing what?"

He gestured. "Flying a kite on the beach. The wind is so strong it just, *whoop*, pulls it right up into the air."

"So you can see him?"

He looked at me like he didn't understand. "See who?"

"That child with the kite."

"Yeah? What the heck, Mom? Of course I can see him."

Right. *What the heck, Mom?* I sounded like a crazy person.

"It's not me," a voice said in my ear. The wind? Maybe. But I didn't think so.

"Let's get back to the house," Jamie said, patting my shoulder. "I think the heat is getting to you."

Chapter Thirty-seven

Willa

I'd seen it coming and yet I hadn't. Jamie's desire to keep the house.

I think I had come here looking to find my own peace with the place and, in so doing, my peace with the past, and at first I had believed his protestations about not wanting to come. So I'd come to reconcile things myself.

And that was what had happened. Because no matter what road it took now, no matter what happened, now that I'd seen Ben again I knew that time would never spin backward and give me back what it had taken.

Even in seeing Ben, as I undoubtedly had, something had been lacking. The completeness of touch. His eyes had looked at me, his voice had been the same, but there was a certain warmth missing. The shared experience was gone, because, of course, *he* was gone, and even if he could "come back" for moments at a time, he wasn't back.

And if he were able to spend the rest of my lifetime doing that, skirting the edges of my existence with a quip here and there, it would do nothing but keep me only half alive, which was the problem when he showed up.

So was it a waste?

Certainly not. Because the fact was, I *was* leading a half life in his absence, and in so doing, I was being half a parent to Jamie. (If you're keeping track of the math, that left him down one and a half parents.) That was not fair to him. He had never asked for that deal and he definitely never deserved it.

I wasn't sure what to do with the house in the cocoon of having decided not to sell it. I couldn't just hold on to it for our convenience. I'd have to keep it from being the money pit it had become, in our absence, over the past three years.

Weekly rentals in summer were profitable. Year-round tenants would pay the mortgage. Either way, I'd be covered. These thoughts made me relax. I'd be covered. And the property would increase in value.

But this year? This summer?

This summer was for Jamie and Kelsey to enjoy. They could stay here, almost the age that Ben and I had been once upon a time, and they could springboard their futures from here, just as we had.

The house had a different temperature when I was in it alone. I was here alone at first, of course, when I arrived to start all this. I was here with Dolly and the empty house. But I felt more haunted then than I did when Ben had appeared.

I had come into this old house with a bag full of chips slung onto my shoulder. My fear followed me like a thick cloud. Self-doubt niggled in my sternum, threatening to take me down the second I believed in it. Memories clashed silently and noisily in every room, and I insisted on seeing through them, ignoring them, because I couldn't watch them.

I came in here with a dry mouth tasting of blood and bile and dread, looking through tear-braced eyes at an old abandoned set of my life, smell-

ing the death that didn't actually hang in the mildewed air, hearing a silence that seemed to beat down the remembered songs that used to bounce
out of speakers and through the halls, feeling my own hand empty without Ben's hand in it, with him beside me.

And now I was free. Free from that. Ben was gone, but he was here.
The house was just a house, lit warmly by the lights strung by my best
friend on the potted palm tree in the corner. It smelled like the coffee my
best friend's daughter had happily made earlier. I knew my son's shoes were
in the front hall, sandy and untied.

Ben was gone, but he was here.

He was in the nails hammered into the walls, in the furniture moved
once and only once through these doors. In the stool that had a broken
rung from a moment that had been positively slapstick at the time, but
which made my cheeks sting now. He was here in the way this house felt
lived in, felt laughed in, felt loved in, felt slept in. He had died here.
Jamie was right. It was terrible that he'd died here. But it made a little bit
of sense. If he'd died at our home in Potomac, how would I have dealt
with that?

He died here, where we came to do things once or rarely. Life was never
like the rest of life here. Life stopped here.

And it had.

It had for Ben. But it didn't have to for us.

It didn't have to for Jamie, for me, for Kristin, Kelsey, and Phillip, for
anyone else who wanted to come here and make the air buzz again like it
was supposed to. This house was supposed to live in settled dust, and then
erupt like a spike of laughter in the summer. I wasn't supposed to give it
up to someone else, abandon it like it scared me.

Would I give up a dog who had been there when my husband died,
just because he'd been the last to see him? Or would I grab him, scratch
his ears, and let him know how glad I was he'd been here?

I would give him a bath and throw a damn bandanna on him. That's what I'd do.

I was frozen in the center of the house. It might very well have been the dead center of the house. My hip leaned against the table. The washer and dryer sprayed and tumbled in the laundry room off to my left, sounding like domestic life. The house was clean and empty enough.

With a lurch of my heart, I imagined how frantic I would feel to get it back if I saw it empty of everything. How too-late it would feel.

My flesh buzzed, not quite cold, just somewhat electrified, as I looked around me.

I stared at the center of the living room, and then, as though we'd been in the middle of a conversation and I'd looked away, I shifted my eyes directly to his own, where he stood now by the sink.

"Willa."

He sounded louder, more resonant, than he ever had before. Like he was really in the room. I would have said he sounded "here," but now I knew that I would have been wrong.

His voice had a different weight. It was like it was real.

I started to say his name and then couldn't. I was bent over suddenly in a sob. One that took me over like a punch in the gut. The kind that felt like someone was reaching in with pliers and yanking out my deepest, molten hot emotions and making me feel them as they left me.

I heard his footsteps, felt them on the wood floor as he came over to me. I gasped for breath as his hand reached the small of my back and then didn't consider before turning and falling into him. I didn't stop to wonder if he was solid enough to hold me, or real enough, I just believed in him and fell hard, so hard I would have fallen on my face if he wasn't there.

He was there.

I breathed in his scent, which had been more missing than I'd realized before. I grabbed the fabric of his shirt with both hands like I used to when I was mad at him, but wrong, and half apologizing, half angry. I sobbed so hard into his chest that I couldn't breathe. His shirt went damp with my tears. My face was warped, all my veins surely popping, every wrinkle being put into use, my teeth bared as if I were a vicious animal instead of a weak, grieving woman. The second my knees started to turn to boiling mercury, he held me up. Actually held me up.

So I spun. I fell. I fell so hard into my misery that I stopped thinking about the kids coming home in a few hours. I stopped thinking about the house and the plumber and how ugly I'd be when I saw my reflection again. I stopped thinking about even stopping my tears. I lived in an infinite moment then. And I believe that when I fell into that, that's what caused whatever broke.

He stepped me back from the kitchen. Piano music started from the speakers built into the shelves by the TV.

"Endless Time" by Roberto Cacciapaglia. He'd heard it somewhere, the year before he died, and we'd listened to it and danced to it in this very kitchen. Everyone had gone to bed, and we were the only ones left awake on the last night of our summer vacation. I'd loaded the last dishwasher load. He had just come in from cleaning the grill. Dolly had run up to sleep in Jamie's room. Phillip and Kristin had gone for a walk and had since returned and retired. We'd been up late that night. I'd showered, my hair was brushed back, and I was warm and clean in my nightgown. He'd come in and showered with me, putting a hand to my lips and telling me they'd gone on a walk, but the kids were still upstairs.

We'd made out like characters in the rain under that showerhead. The shower smelled like Irish Spring, which we only used at the beach house. His eyelashes stuck together and got spiky from the water. He put a hand on the side of my face, and because of the way he looked at me, I felt like a supermodel in a music video.

I had told him this, and he had laughed and said with a shrug, "They were never as hot as you."

This all came rushing back to me so fast that my tears choked me. I breathed in deeply once I caught my breath and looked up at him. He was there, still there. He looked at me like he knew what moment I was reliving.

That night, we had danced in the living room, all the lights out except the warm glow of the night-lights.

He kissed me on the cheek, that sort of kiss that almost feels deeper than one on the lips, and brought me in close, changed our position, moved my arms from his chest to his neck. I leaned on him and felt his hands once again, blissfully on my waist.

In that moment, just like I never did with him, really, I didn't worry about my waist, about anything about me. It was only ever about us, about then, about something deeper and more entwined.

He spun me around and I remembered something else.

I kept my eyes shut but suddenly so vividly remembered a night at Pretty Mama's, out on the sandy patio. The DJ outside had been playing "God Only Knows" by the Beach Boys, and Kristin and Phillip had teased us for dancing like we were at prom. But we were in a moment.

A moment that was apparently being stored for now.

He had twisted me around so slowly in the sand, my feet bare—I could *feel* my bare feet on the sand, the fabric of my skirt around my ankles, even the sunburn on my shoulders—and I had breathed him in, tequila-drunk and happy-drunk.

We revolved again and my stomach felt wrought and sore and . . . *relieved*. Jamie. When Jamie was born. When Jamie was born and we first brought him home, to the other house, and we stood in his room listening to his lullaby CD in the corner, lit by the pale lavender light that stood near the speaker, and our son—our tiny, fragile son who was so quickly about to grow into a young man—slept in the crib, unaware of his parents standing there watching him. I had had my cheek on Ben's chest, and we'd just stood there, holding each other, my stomach still swollen, annoyingly flabby, my back aching, my thighs like quivering Jell-O, and watched him, just watched him breathe.

We spun once more.

Again, and we were here, right here again, to the night we spent here right after we had bought it. It was empty and smelled like cobwebs and dust and it was ours. So mutually and heavenly ours.

The moment of now, of Jamie and Kelsey at work, Kristin out, and me alone, that moment came back now like waking from a dream.

I pulled away from his chest, reluctantly, so I could look at him.

His cheeks tightened in that way that would indicate a smile if you can go through with it. For the first time since he'd visited me, he looked truly sad.

I knew I was the one who looked like the ghost.

He moved a warm, warm, real hand to my left cheek under my freckle where he always did.

"Willa," he said.

"I miss you so much it makes me ache like a nausea I know will never go away."

He nodded. But it was as if he knew. I wasn't any less sad he was gone, I wouldn't waffle over bringing him back, but somehow when I'd wept and felt him here, something had finally, finally been bled out.

We both knew this would be the last time. I knew, somehow, that that was why he was so solidly here.

"It's just hard," I said. "When you're young and you envision your life, you picture your wedding, your marriage, your kid, your other kids maybe . . . I never stopped to wonder what the next chapter would look like. The quiet chapter. The chapter without the busyness of checking off bucket-list items. But if I did, I thought we'd be quiet together."

I shook my head, and didn't realize how much I'd deflated until he lifted me up a little.

"I thought I'd have you to be bored with. I thought I'd have you . . . I thought I'd have you. Ben, I thought I'd *have you.*"

"I thought I'd have you, Willa. I thought I'd have that. I never will. And . . . you know how I told you it's different here? You accept that things are different and that you'll see your loved ones again. . . . Well, maybe it isn't really because it's mystical and all that . . ." He shook his head and shrugged. "I don't know all that woo-woo."

I laughed. Truly laughed. "Ben, good lord."

He smiled. "If you accept that things are different now, that they aren't over, and that we will meet again . . . maybe that'll get you by. Because, I tell you, baby." He made me look at him. "It's not a magic spell they cast here that makes it so I can live without you. I just understand that it's different. It's different and I'm without you. But not forever. It's the same for you."

I stared at him. Just like the house had seemed to settle finally, something, a little, released in the back of my neck and started to spread down my shoulders.

"I love you and . . . and that's all well and good, but the problem is that I *miss* you." The words balled in my throat. "I want to laugh over things with you and share things with you."

He nodded. Then gave a small shake of his head and a bite of his lip. He always bit his lip when emotions threatened to take over. "Baby, I think we'll have a lot to talk about. You just gotta live it first."

The visions of a few minutes before swirled in my head, then cycled down to my stomach, where they translated to sick, vertigo-like nausea.

"I can't believe this is the last time I'll ever speak to you."

He looked miserable then, but gave me that suggestion again of a smile. "You've already talked to me for the last time, honey. And don't forget,

I've talked with you for the last time. You and I share that. But only for the last time in life. And now only the last time like this."

He nodded when I shook my head.

I knew he was right. It sounded so ugly, so unimaginable, but suddenly he felt so long ago. God, I hated to even think that, but it was true. He felt . . . passed.

His solidity started to fade from beneath my fingers.

He looked at me hard and grabbed me by the shoulders, that smile showing his beautiful teeth, brightening his beautiful eyes. "I love you so much. I love you so much."

I nodded, unable to unclench my teeth and respond until he was almost gone.

"I love you too," I said, just in time before he faded.

I fell then, this time—no Ben to fall into. Only air. Only the floor. Only myself.

I sobbed so much I retched. I couldn't breathe, couldn't think, I wanted to time-travel to a moment ago, a day ago, a year ago, a decade ago, and yet I knew I couldn't and never would. It made me feel empty. Cleaned out.

But then, as if he'd left some sort of solid-gold strength in the pit of my heart, something that kept it from evaporating completely, I heard a voice tell me that it was okay. It was okay.

It was okay.

It was okay.

It was Ben, somewhere, in no particular voice, in no particular form, telling me it was okay.

And for probably the first time, and the worst time in my life, I believed him.

Chandler Schwede

Beth Harbison is the *New York Times* bestselling author of *A Shoe Addict's Christmas; One Less Problem Without You; If I Could Turn Back Time; Driving with the Top Down; Chose the Wrong Guy, Gave Him the Wrong Finger; When in Doubt, Add Butter; Always Something There to Remind Me; Thin, Rich, Pretty; Hope in a Jar; Secrets of a Shoe Addict;* and *Shoe Addicts Anonymous.* She grew up in Potomac, Maryland, outside Washington, D.C., and now shares her time between that suburb, New York City, and a quiet home on the Eastern Shore.